James Devereaux, Duke of Langley, looked at the woman in front of him. She was finely built, smaller than his sister Georgiana. "My intentions are not to distress you," he said quietly, "but there is the possibility that your husband may no longer be alive."

There were no tears in her eyes, only a look of pure anguish, much like a cornered fox at the end of a hunt when he knows his time is at hand. Devereaux's impersonal facade was no match for that look. With no thought other than to offer comfort, his arms closed around her.

With a strangled cry, she pulled away violently. The chair she stumbled against fell to its side, rocked for a brief moment and then lay still.

"Don't touch me," she whispered. "Please, don't touch me."

The moment stretched out between them, like the span of a lifetime.

"I'm not your enemy, Tess," he said at last, using the familiar address instead of the more formal Mrs. Bradford. She was Tess in his mind, and had been since the first moment he saw her.

In the startled silence that followed, he watched the desperate fear fade from her eyes only to be replaced by a cold, merciless anger.

"You're an Englishman," she said. "Your ships, even now, sweep across the oceans forcing those of lesser strength to your will. With your government's permission, they sail into American harbors, blockade our ports, invade our cities, and enslave our citizens." Her voice cracked. "Because of them, I might be a widow before I was truly a wife. Do you wonder that I despise all you stand for?"

. . . and she was the one woman in all the world he could never have.

TUESDAY'S CHILD

Jenevy Michaels

Pinnacle Books
Kensington Publishing Corp.
http://www.pinnacle.books.com

PINNACLE BOOKS are published by

Kensington Publishing Corp.
850 Third Avenue
New York, NY 10022

Pinnacle and the P logo Reg. U.S. Pat. & TM Off.

First Printing: November, 1996

Printed in the United States of America
10 9 8 7 6 5 4 3 2 1

Many thanks to Ron Medve, for his help, his great knowledge of history, and his willingness to share it with me.

Tuesday's child is full of grace.

—Anonymous

Author's Note

Never in the history of the world has a people with the same language, the same customs, the same heroes and ancestry, evolved with two such different ideologies as the Englishman and the American in 1812. Nowhere was the difference more obvious than in their attitudes toward marriage, fidelity, and class distinctions.

In England, where unemployment was high and the division between master and servant rigid, less than five hundred families had the means to employ a multitude of servants. Employment was generational and jealously guarded. The same servants had served the same families for hundreds of years. In a country where there was a Lord Steward to lay the fire and a Lord Chamberlain to light the fire, the crossing of class lines was nearly impossible. Marriages were dynastic bonds, entered into for the purpose of breeding children, to promote the lineage in the upper class, to work on the family farms and businesses in the working class. Men born to enormous wealth had little to do to assuage the boredom of their daily lives except gamble, visit their clubs and indulge in affairs. It was not unusual for women as well as men to satisfy their desires outside of marriage after first presenting their lords with the necessary heir. To dirty one's hands with trade was unacceptable for a gentleman.

America was different. In a desperate desire to carve out a country from the wilderness, keep Indians at bay, and expand the frontier, the American worked from dawn till dusk on the business of survival. Because the land was thinly populated, even wealthy ladies and gentlemen worked side by side with servants who knew that if the job didn't suit, another position was available down the road. An indentured servant could come to America, serve his time, amass a fortune in the virgin wilderness and run for political office with no hint of scandal attached to his name. To take pride in one's work was the American motto and the only unforgivable sin was laziness. Morality was rooted in Puritan England and the early sermons of John Knox. Marriage was based on respect, if not love, and it lasted until death. Children were a necessary and desirable addition to the pursuit of one's happiness and both male and female children were highly valued.

On the political scene, Britain was engaged in a costly and devastating war with Napoleon. They needed every available man. When numbers in the British Navy ran short, they impressed Americans from seaport towns. This, and the refusal of the British to negotiate trade agreements, their encouragement of Indian uprisings, their disregard for America's sovereign right to the open seas, were the powder kegs that led to the War of 1812.

Tess and James are fictional characters, but they are typical of their time. Tess is an American, intensely patriotic, despising the smugness of the English aristocracy, and appreciative of France's help in the American War for Independence. James is a British lord, weary of England's incessant fighting with her former colonies, and politically astute enough to know that Bonaparte is more of a threat than James Madison.

Langley and Harrington House are not real. Neither are Nathanial Harrington and Leonie Devereaux. But Lord Castlereagh, his wife Emily, Lord Liverpool, Lady Jersey, Lady Bridgewater and Lady Sefton are familiar names in the Regency Period, as are the famous military leaders Wellington, Ross, and Cockburn.

Beginning in the fifth grade, every schoolchild in America learns the story of the burning of the capital and Dolly Madison's brave refusal to evacuate the city unless George Washington's portrait came with her. Francis Scott Key is famous in American history as the author of our national anthem, but he was first and foremost, as introduced in my story, an attorney-at-law.

The cast, for the most part is fictional, but the events, the attitudes, customs, and prejudices are typical of the period.

One

For the first time in his twenty-nine years, James Devereaux, Duke of Langley, was rendered speechless. Nothing in Georgiana's letters or the Home Secretary's report had prepared him for Teresa Bradford. He remembered wondering what she looked like. Now, he knew.

The slender girl staring back at him from across the room was like no one he had ever seen before. She was young, much younger than he expected, with a regal poise unusual in an American. Everything about her reminded him of moonlight, the silver-blond hair pulled back in a coil at the nape of her neck, the pale gold of her skin, the clear light-struck grey of her eyes. Her face was thin and finely made, with the hauntingly beautiful bone structure of a Renaissance painting. His eyes lingered on her mouth. It was a passionate mouth, slightly chapped, full and pouting, made for the taste of a man's lips.

She was incredibly lovely, acknowledged Devereaux. By far the loveliest woman he had ever seen. But it wasn't her perfection of face or form that tugged at his heart and caused the blood to flow swift and hot, melting the ice in his veins. It was the expression in her eyes. Large and brilliant, her entire soul was revealed in those fathomless depths. Pain and rage, both tightly controlled, were reflected for all the world to see.

This slender woman with her proudly tilted head and straight back was no shallow, simpering miss. Those eyes were incapable of deception. Teresa Bradford harbored passion in its most primitive form and it threatened to consume her.

Devereaux wondered what it would be like to unleash those passions, here and now, in the American minister's fussy sitting room. Immediately, he was ashamed of himself. Teresa, or Tess, as Georgiana called her, was a guest in his country. She was also, he reminded himself, with mocking self-derision, newly married to a man in full possession of all his body parts.

Conscious of those incredible grey eyes judging him, watching his every move, he forced himself, at great personal expense, to cross the room with only the slightest hint of a limp. He was surprised at how small she was when he stood beside her. From a distance, she appeared much taller.

"Welcome to England, Mrs. Bradford," he said, his voice not entirely steady. "I trust your voyage went smoothly?"

"Yes, thank you." She hesitated. "Your Grace."

He grinned. "Please call me James. We are bound to see a great deal of one another and it might be more comfortable for you if we dispensed with my title."

She laughed, a low musical sound, that shattered the rest of his carefully reconstructed composure.

"We aren't accustomed to titles in America," she acknowledged. "It will be a relief not to worry about yours." The grey eyes searched his face. "I appreciate the invitation to stay with your family. It will be much easier living with friends than here at the ambassador's residence."

"Georgiana is looking forward to your visit," Devereaux replied smoothly. "She has great plans to show you the sights of London."

He neglected to mention his own reservations concerning Tess's visit. He hadn't wanted her to come. An American in London, on the eve of a declaration of war, was a responsibility he preferred to do without.

Tess walked to the window and looked out on the busy square where the business of English government took place. The sun reflected off her hair and bathed her face in a merciless glare that only young poreless skin could tolerate. Her hands were clasped tightly in front of her.

"I didn't come to see the sights of London," she said, her voice very low. "I came to find my husband."

"I'm well aware of that." His voice cut like the crack of a whip. "Believe me, Mrs. Bradford, I shall do everything in my power to restore your husband to you. No one regrets the circumstances of his disappearance more than I."

She turned to look at him. Grey eyes met blue in an unblinking stare. Her skin was so clear he could see the delicate blue veins pulsing in her temples.

"I doubt that, m'lord," Tess replied coldly. "My husband's father is an old man suffering from poor health. Daniel is his only child." She lowered her head. "As for myself, we were married less than one week."

James gritted his teeth. He refused to take responsibility for the mistakes of the British Navy. After years of fighting in the peninsula with Wellington, he knew the value of strict adherence to discipline and military law. He had no patience for the bumbling disregard for foreign policy shown by certain captains of the British Navy.

His lips thinned as he recalled his recent conversation with the Secretary of the Naval Forces. Without actually condoning impressment of American citizens, the man refused to admit that it was even occurring, giving his captains free rein to proceed according to their own consciences. This time someone had gone too far. James had been recruited, however unwillingly, to find out who that someone was. Daniel Bradford was the son of a wealthy and influential senator from the state of Maryland. If he wasn't found immediately and returned unharmed, it could mean war.

Balling his fists in the pockets of his breeches, he struggled to control his anger. England was in trouble. Wellington, in the throes of a death grip with Napoleon, needed every available man. Another war with America could mean the end of the British Empire.

"Damn their self-righteous souls," he cursed under his breath.

"I beg your pardon?" Tess stared at him, a puzzled expression on her face.

Recovering quickly, James moved to her side. Taking her hand in his own he smiled. "Never mind. I'm no longer in the military. I sold out several months ago, but I give you my word that whatever power and influence I have will be spent securing the release of your husband."

Tess searched his face. Instinctively she knew that the man standing before her was a presence. That dark inscrutable expression, with its hard mouth and veiled blue eyes, exuded a confidence of the kind she'd never known before. Georgiana hadn't mentioned that her brother was devastatingly handsome. He was very tall and lean, with the high cheekbones, jutting nose and firm chin of one born to command. Well-muscled legs, clad in fawn buckskins, were tucked inside top boots considerably higher than the ones most men wore. The glossy perfection of the soft black leather was evidence of their sophistication and expense. The exquisitely tailored coat of blue superfine, stretching without a wrinkle across those broad shoulders, would keep an American farmer supplied with beef for well over a year.

Color rose in her cheeks. Tess was suddenly ashamed of her thoughts. What did it matter what he spent for a coat? The Devereauxs were fabulously wealthy. A hundred coats wouldn't make a dent in their incredible fortune. She needed help. The more powerful and wealthy the Duke of Langley, the better were her chances of rescuing Daniel.

James smiled a warm intimate smile, leaving her wide-eyed and breathless. The very charm of that smile sent alarm bells ringing through her brain. No wonder the man had the reputation for being a brilliant statesman. Did he know that flash of white in his dark face was his most powerful weapon? She hoped not. There was fire and something else, something deeper than she cared to admit in the blue eyes that stared back at her.

"Shall we call a truce, Mrs. Bradford?" the low voice teased her.

"Can we, my lord?"

"Yes," he replied firmly.

She laughed shakily and pulled her hand away. "A truce it is then."

"Very well, shall we begin?"

"Begin?" she looked puzzled.

He walked to the fireplace and leaned back against the mantel. Tess noticed that he favored his left leg.

Motioning to a high-backed chair directly in front of him he said, "Please, sit down. I'd like to find out everything you know about your husband's activities before he disappeared. That way I can begin making inquiries before I take you home."

Seating herself in the chair she looked up at him, her eyes enormous in her small face. James found it difficult to concentrate. His leg ached abominably and the woman before him looked absurdly young sitting there like an expectant child, her hands folded primly in her lap. Much too young for marriage, he thought, or for the improper fantasies taking root in his mind.

"What did you wish to know, m'lord?" Her voice was clear and cultured, the accent only slightly colonial.

James cleared his mind for the matter at hand. "How did you come to find out Mr. Bradford had been impressed?"

The knuckles on the clasped hands were very white. Tess wet her lips before answering. "He was on his way home from Washington when he stopped to eat at a tavern owned by a friend. Mr. Hawthorne, the owner, closed up early." She stopped for a moment and twisted the gold band on her finger.

James held his breath, hoping she would not succumb to tears. Relieved to see that her eyes were dry, he relaxed and waited for her to gather herself.

Taking a deep breath she continued. "Four British seamen demanded entrance. Mr. Hawthorne had no choice but to obey. No one else was there, you see." She looked up, anxious for him to know she held the tavern proprietor blameless. James nodded and she smiled faintly.

"They demanded that Daniel come with them. He refused and they beat him senseless." Her voice took on a husky quality but her words did not falter. "I fear he was badly hurt. Mr. Hawthorne was almost dead when his wife found him."

The white line around Devereaux's mouth deepened. For a long moment he said nothing. Finally he spoke.

"Why did they leave Mr. Hawthorne?"

"He's an older man. Perhaps they thought someone his age would serve them no purpose."

More likely they left him for dead, James thought grimly. Pushing himself away from the mantel he reached out to pull her to a standing position. She was so close he could smell the faint lilac scent that clung to her hair. His searching gaze rested on her mouth.

"How long did you say you were married?" he asked gently.

"Less than a week."

"How is it that a bridegroom of less than a week leaves his new bride to visit Washington?" The blue eyes looked directly at her, missing nothing.

"We received a message that his father wouldn't last the night," she explained. "Daniel left immediately after the wedding to go to him."

Devereaux's eyes narrowed thoughtfully. Adam Bradford's ill health was common knowledge. It was her other piece of information that intrigued him. How soon after the wedding had his son left Annapolis for Washington?

He looked down at the exquisite face barely reaching his shoulder. He would give a great deal to learn the answer to that question, but it was hardly something a gentleman could ask a lady and still remain a gentleman.

His hands slid up her arms to rest on her shoulders. She was smaller-boned than Georgiana, almost as small as Lizzie. "My intentions are not to distress you," he said quietly, "but there is the possibility that your husband may no longer be alive."

There were no tears this time either. Only a look of pure anguish, much like a cornered fox at the end of a hunt when he knows his time is at hand. Devereaux's impersonal facade was no match for that look. With no thought other than to offer comfort, his arms closed around her.

With a strangled cry, she pulled away violently. The chair she stumbled against fell to its side, rocked for a brief moment, and then lay still.

"Don't touch me," she whispered. "Please, don't touch me."

The moment stretched out between them, like the span of a lifetime.

"I'm not your enemy, Tess," he said at last, using the familiar address. She was Tess in his mind and had been since the first moment he saw her.

In the startled silence that followed, he watched the desperate fear fade from her eyes only to be replaced by a cold merciless anger.

"You're an Englishman," she said, as if no more damning evidence was needed. "Your ships, even now, sweep across the oceans forcing those of lesser strength to your will. With your government's permission, they sail into American harbors, blockade our ports, invade our cities and impress our citizens." Her voice cracked. "Perhaps, even now, I am a widow before I was truly a wife. Do you wonder that I despise all you stand for?"

His dark face was expressionless and his eyes, veiling his thoughts, met hers without a hint of anger in their icy depths.

"I am not responsible for the decisions of the British Navy," he said quietly.

Again there was silence. Finally, her shoulders slumped and she shook her head. "No," she replied unsteadily, rubbing her hands over throbbing temples. "Forgive me for appearing ungrateful. You cannot have known any of this." The words were conciliatory but the eyes were not.

"Apologies are unnecessary," he said, bowing slightly. "If you'll allow me a few hours, I'll return and we shall begin our journey. Georgiana and my mother are waiting to receive you at Langley." He smiled and left the room.

Once again Tess felt that unfamiliar weakness in her knees.

He might have impeccable manners and expensive clothing, but the man had the soul of a rogue. No one else could hide his emotions so completely. One moment, his face carved and remote, was shuttered against her. The next, his eyes glinted with amusement and his mouth curved in a shockingly intimate smile that made her wish she was Miss Harrington again and free to smile back.

Devereaux's mood deteriorated with every step he took on his way to the prime minister's offices. His leg was throbbing painfully but it was nothing compared to the bitterness in his heart. He had been correct in his first assessment of Teresa Bradford's character. She was a woman who loved completely and hated passionately. And it appeared that he was to be the recipient of her hatred.

James Devereaux, Duke of Langley, rising star of British aristocracy and formidable political opponent, had finally met a woman whose candid gaze touched his heart. Unfortunately she considered him the enemy. One of that same arrogant breed who hovered menacingly in the mists along the Chesapeake dragging unwilling victims to serve their stint in His Majesty's Navy.

His mouth turned down in a mocking grimace. She also happened to be another man's wife. By some cruel twist of fate he had been selected to find the elusive Mr. Bradford and return him to her loving arms.

What he really wanted was to be a whole man again, to consign Daniel Bradford to the devil, carry Tess to the most remote corner of England, pull the pins from her hair until it fell past her shoulders in primitive splendor, and bury himself in the promise of that passionate mouth until the hatred died forever.

Two

Lord Liverpool, prime minister of Great Britain, sat in his office at Westminster drumming his fingers. Where was Devereaux, he fumed silently? The Prince Regent expected an answer to the colonial problem and he expected it immediately. Perspiration beaded his upper lip. He pulled out a handkerchief and mopped his brow. It would be a welcome relief to turn over the whole mess into the capable hands of the duke of Langley.

He looked up as the door opened.

"James." Exasperation was evident in every shining pore of his face. "Where have you been? I've just come from Prinny. The worst has happened!"

James, his face inscrutable, sat down in the only comfortable chair in the room. Almost immediately the pain in his leg receded.

"Enlighten me, please."

"The colonies have declared war. That damned Madison listened to the War Hawks after all."

"How long ago?" The clipped voice demanded.

"The eighteenth of June."

James whistled. "My compliments to Liston. The news is barely warm."

"I hardly know what to think." Liverpool laced his shaking fingers across his chest. "How long do you think the militia along the Canadian border can hold out without reinforcements?"

"There are no reinforcements to send them, m'lord,"

Devereaux stated calmly. "They'll have to hold out for as long as it takes."

"Damn it, James," the prime minister's fist slammed down on his desk. "Are you suggesting we simply desert them?"

James's face darkened with anger. "Wellington is in Spain fighting for England's right to exist. May I remind you that Napoleon intends to reign supreme in Europe. If we continue to rob the general of any more men, the British Empire may very well be brought to her knees."

Liverpool quailed under the contempt in the scathing words. Langley was something of an enigma in Parliament. He wasn't a comfortable man to be around nor did he have the heart of a politician. He was too principled, too straightforward and utterly uncompromising. He was also incredibly wealthy. His lands stretched across the length of England and Scotland.

For generations, a Devereaux had taken his seat in the House of Lords. When the late duke died ten years before, it was expected that James would follow the tradition of his ancestors. This he had done with enormous success. Blessed from birth with the Devereaux looks and more charm than one human being should decently have, he had surprised his colleagues with the finest mind to be found in government circles.

The prime minister depended on that mind more than anyone knew. He decided to change his tactics.

"Have you seen Bradford's wife?"

The blue eyes glinted. "Yes," he replied guardedly, "I've seen her."

Liverpool sighed. "It doesn't matter. She may have served our purposes when there was still a chance of averting war. Now, she is useless to us. Send her home, James. You can't wish to house an American when our countries are at war."

"Have you forgotten that Adam Bradford is a staunch Federalist, and the Federalists are overwhelmingly opposed to war with England?" James measured his words carefully. "The senator from Maryland is a powerful statesman. Unless you want the entire United States of America allied against us, I suggest we make every attempt to find his son."

Liverpool stroked his chin with blunt fingers. "What of Teresa Bradford? Can we expect her to cooperate?"

James thought of the straight back and moon-bleached hair, the clear perfection of skin drawn tightly across delicate bones and the low soft drawl of the Chesapeake in her speech. He knew as surely as he drew breath that Teresa Bradford would never cooperate with an Englishman. The bitter hatred for everything British was as much a part of her heritage as those eyes that revealed the secrets of her soul.

"It depends what you mean by cooperate." Devereaux's hooded lids fell over his eyes.

Liverpool exploded. "Don't play games with me. Can you guarantee she won't make a scene or stir up the liberals against us? Lord knows there are enough of those."

"Can you guarantee that American citizens won't be impressed into the British Navy?" James quickly retaliated.

"You know as well as I that half the seamen on American merchant ships are British deserters. We won't win a war that way."

James leaned back in his chair. "We will never win a war with America. The best we can hope to do is hold Canada."

"Explain yourself, man," the prime minister demanded. "You're an intelligence officer. How can a miserably underdeveloped nation with an enormous coastline possibly win a war against the greatest navy on the seas?"

Stretching his good leg, James surveyed the immaculate design of his right topboot. "Have you seen a Baltimore clipper, m'lord?"

"What on earth does that have to do with anything?"

"The shipwrights of Baltimore have managed to turn out a vessel that is capable of outsailing any craft afloat."

The authoritative words succeeded in silencing Liverpool. He listened intently as James continued.

"They have larger blocks, thinner ropes and an immense

spread of sail designed to tack and then dart away under the very guns of our frigates. We've nothing of their like in all of Britain."

"We can build them," Liverpool protested, "or better yet capture them."

Amusement darkened the blue of Devereaux's eyes to a deep sapphire. "Are you familiar with the American privateer, m'lord?"

Liverpool sighed. "No, I'm not but I'm sure I will be shortly."

James threw back his head and laughed. After a moment the older man joined in reluctantly. It was hardly the time for merriment but that contagious mirth could not be denied.

"Tell me if I'm becoming obnoxious, sir," Devereaux said at last, the grin still present on his face. "I've no desire to become another Lord Castlereagh."

Liverpool laughed once more. "I agree, the foreign minister has much to learn about diplomacy. When you see your colleagues disappear as soon as you arrive, then you'll know. You're not there yet, James." He was all business once again. "Tell me more about the American privateer."

"Very well." Devereaux leaned forward again emphasizing every word. "Even if we could build or capture American ships we couldn't sail them. We've neither the knowledge nor the inclination to sail beneath the very noses of the enemy only to turn and run before a single shot is fired." There was reluctant admiration in his voice. "They've bested us this way before. Honor isn't as important to an American privateer as results." He looked toward the window, repressing the urge to walk across the room and look outside. He was long past taking for granted the effortless movements he had enjoyed only a brief year ago. Dancing, sparring, hunting, that life was over for him. A simple walk to the stables from the back door of Langley took enormous concentration, accompanied, as it always was, by white-lipped, shirt-drenching pain.

Through the long window he could barely see the American minister's residence with the stars and stripes of the United States waving proudly in an English breeze. He wondered if it was possible for a woman raised on the warm banks of the Chesapeake to come to terms with life in England? The white line deepened around his mouth. She had no choice. James Madison had declared war and in so doing had consigned Daniel Bradford to the devil. Like it or not, Tess would not be allowed to return to America. She was a prisoner of the Crown.

"How's the leg, lad?" The prime minister's voice broke through his thoughts.

James looked up to find the older man eyeing him anxiously. "It's fine, sir."

"It was a nasty wound. Perhaps you should have stayed at Langley another month to recover." He shivered, remembering the icy fear that consumed him when he'd heard that Devereaux had taken roundshot in the leg during the siege of Badajos.

Through pouring rain, Wellington had written, the duke had been carted senseless, in a rude wagon over rugged mountains for three days, unable to keep down food or water. While awaiting transport to England, his fever had been dangerously high and even Wellington, who refused to admit that the young man he had grown to depend on was seriously injured, knew he would never be back.

It had been left to the prime minister to inform Langley's mother, the infamous Leonie Devereaux, that the fourth Duke of Langley, her beloved child and only son, scion of an unbroken hereditary line over four hundred years old, was mortally wounded and would probably die before his ship reached English shores. Below the knee, his leg had atrophied. Given the crude conditions of the peninsula, there was little the surgeon could do except amputate.

Liverpool would never forget that interview. He had never done anything harder in his life. The duchess had received him in her blue-and-gold sitting room, graciously offering tea. Not once did she weep or cry out. Indeed, he would have felt more comfortable if she had. It was the icy composure in the long, thin hands resting in her lap, and the rigidly controlled expression on the flawless features that unnerved him. Even her eyes were shuttered against him.

It was almost inhuman, reflected Liverpool, for a woman to be capable of such steel.

Thankfully, Langley had recovered. Watching the remote, carved features of the younger man, Liverpool wondered, once again, what manner of childhood the Devereaux offspring must have had with a mother like Leonie.

"You needn't be concerned, my friend," Devereaux interrupted his thoughts. "I'll be at Langley soon enough, with an extremely charming rebel to keep me company."

Liverpool frowned. "What do you mean?"

"Wait until you see Teresa Bradford." James was enjoying himself. "One look at her will push American sympathies to new heights."

The prime minister groaned. "Dear God, what next?" He sighed helplessly. "Do me one favor, James. Keep her at home. We've trouble enough without a beautiful exiled patriot turning the tide against us."

"I'm afraid I can't help you," answered James. "Georgiana has been promised a London season and nothing short of a death in the family will stop her." He moved stiffly toward the door. "I can hardly imprison her friend inside the walls of the Langley town house."

"Wait!" Liverpool's command stopped him from turning the knob. "I know how you feel about this conflict with America, and I'm sorry for it. But," he hesitated, "as a favor I ask you to not speak against it. I could use an ally in Parliament." It was as close to pleading as Lord Liverpool had ever come.

James turned slowly toward the prime minister, noting the lines of strain in the blunt features that hadn't been there before.

"My apologies, m'lord," he said gently. "But, I am pledged to Wellington. Support for the American conflict would be to sell him out."

"Are you sure it isn't the beauteous Mrs. Bradford that has your loyalties so divided?"

From across the room Liverpool could see the blue eyes darken. He was suddenly very grateful he would never meet Lord Langley on the field of battle.

Devereaux's voice was dangerously soft. "It would be a great mistake to repeat such a suggestion." He bowed. "Good day, sir."

James was almost at the door of the office assigned to him when a voice called out from down the hall.

"Devereaux, what the devil are you doing here?"

He turned to find a very tall, fair young man with a thatch of shocking white-blond hair, merry brown eyes and a nose that had never recovered from a childhood break, bearing down upon him.

"Charles." A warm smile lit the duke's harsh features. "You've saved me the trouble of finding you."

"Good Lord, James, you look wonderful!" Charles Mottsinger, Honorable Captain of His Majesty's frigate, *The Macedonian,* clasped his friend's shoulder affectionately. He wore a blue coat with gold trim, an intricately tied silk cravat, and breeches of pristine white.

"You've completely recovered. No one, seeing you four months ago, would have believed it possible."

"You aren't the only one who thought to see the last of me," replied James dryly. "I've never been so deluged with invitations in my entire life. If I attended every dinner party and ball where my presence was requested, I should have no time for anything else."

"There might be another reason for that, my friend." The captain's grin broadened. "You're the duke of Langley, recently sold out of the army and unmarried." He looked at the splendid elegance of the tall man beside him. "You're not entirely unattractive, you know. I'm sure the matchmaking mamas are planning your downfall this very moment."

"Don't be absurd." A tinge of red shone faintly under James's dark skin. "Under the circumstances, I'm hardly in a position to offer marriage to anyone."

"What on earth are you talking about?"

"My limitations should be obvious, Charles. It would take a most unusual woman to look beyond them." Unbidden, a fair-haired image with wide, thickly lashed grey eyes flickered through his mind. He squashed it immediately.

A tide of scarlet surged across Mottsinger's fair cheekbones. "That's the most absurd, self-pitying notion I've ever heard you express," he blustered. "You've sixty thousand pounds a year, a title that goes back to the Conqueror and a way with women that is the envy of every man in London, including myself."

Langley held up his hand. "I've changed," he said briefly. "Now, if you don't mind I'd like to discuss something else." He held his friend's gaze with a level stare.

"Very well," replied Charles stiffly. "I beg your pardon."

James brushed aside his apology. "Never mind that. I've news, and a few questions of my own. Shall we go into my office?" He held the door open for the captain to precede him.

Easing himself into the wing chair behind the desk, James stretched out his aching leg and gritted his teeth. The stump throbbed painfully. What he wouldn't give for the comfort of his own room at Langley. If he could make it through the next hour or so he would soon be on his way home.

Motioning Mottsinger to the chair in front of him, he began his investigation.

"What do you know of Teresa Bradford?"

Charles blinked in surprise. "Only that she was a passenger on my ship bound for a visit to your sister. Why do you ask?"

"You may as well know. Soon it will be all over England," James replied bitterly. "Madison has declared war."

"Good God!" Clearly shaken, Charles slumped in his chair. "I can't believe it."

"Come now, Charles." Devereaux's eyes were steady on his face. "Did you really think the Americans would sit by and watch us blockade their ports, restrict all trade, and impress their citizens without retaliation? You of all people should know they aren't cowards."

"Napoleon is twice the culprit Admiral Cockburn is," Charles protested.

"Perhaps so," agreed James. "But tell that to an American."

"Boston is full of Federalists," argued the captain. "You can be assured they'll not stand for it if trade is interrupted for long."

"Tell me about Mrs. Bradford," James repeated.

"I know nothing." Charles was bewildered. "She was very lovely, intelligent and gracious, but unfortunately, newly married." He frowned. "I didn't think to ask where her husband was."

"Her husband was impressed by a British man-of-war and she's come to England to find him." No hint of emotion revealed itself on Devereaux's implacable face but his eyes were light and hard as steel. "I've given my word that I'll help her."

"I see." Charles looked thoughtful. "Does she know we're at war?"

"Not at the moment."

Charles whistled. "I don't envy you, my friend. What do you want from me?"

Relaxing, James grinned. "I knew you wouldn't let me down. I want you to find out which naval vessels were prowling the Chesapeake on April the seventh of this year. The sooner we find Adam Bradford's son, the better."

"There may be another problem," Charles said slowly. "Mrs. Bradford is the daughter of Nathanial Harrington. The man is as rich as Croesus and one of the most powerful shipping magnates in America. Good God, James, he's the man that designed the Baltimore clipper, damn his unholy soul. He's not a war hawk, but he hates everything British." He ran his finger nervously through the folds of his cravat. "If he finds you're keeping his daughter against her wishes, he may be able to increase production of his vessels to a degree that could threaten English naval superiority on the seas."

"In that case we must be sure to make Mrs. Bradford's stay a pleasant one," replied James smoothly. "She will not be kept against her will."

"You're a sly one, Devereaux." Charles Mottsinger looked at

his friend in admiration. "Take care that you don't overdo it. The lady is charming, although over young. I've been at sea for a long time but if I remember correctly you had a preference for redheaded widows with ripe figures. Have you changed your mind since then?"

James could picture Tess in his mind as clearly as if she stood before him, the clear, speaking eyes, the proudly tilted chin, the lovely curves of her breasts. He would wager his last crown that a woman with eyes like hers harbored smoldering passion beneath her veneer of calm. The redheaded widow was quickly becoming a vague memory. He lowered his eyelids, shuttering his thoughts.

"My feelings for Mrs. Bradford are not a topic for discussion, Charles," he said quietly.

Good God, thought Charles Mottsinger in dismay. In the space of time between his last remark and Devereaux's suddenly guarded expression, he thought he recognized something quite shocking in the level blue eyes fixed on his face. James Devereaux was as close to being a legend as a man could be. England needed him. This was not the time to lose his head over a woman, no matter how lovely. Especially an American with a husband and a father who together had it in their power to challenge the right of the British Navy to control the seas.

Three

Tess was ill at ease. The horses were fresh and the elegant Langley coach sinfully comfortable. The duke, sitting across from her, had been meticulously polite since the beginning of their journey. But whenever she raised her eyes, his own were on her face.

Once again, he was splendidly dressed. The snow-white cravat was tied to perfection and the elegant coat subtly defined the lean muscles of his upper body. Pale yellow buckskins covered the powerful legs and his boots, brown this time and again higher over the calf than normal, were so shiny she could see her reflection in the expensive leather.

Although he was attentive and replied cordially to her questions, Tess knew his thoughts were elsewhere. There was something secretive and frightening in the dark features closed against her. She shivered. Somehow she knew that whatever was bothering him had everything to do with her.

"Are you cold?" he asked.

She stared at him. "In this weather?" She shook her head. "Hardly. It's as warm as Annapolis in summer. I thought England was always cold."

"Something is making you uncomfortable," he persisted. "Perhaps I can help if you tell me what it is."

How could he have known? Tess wondered. Wetting her lips she looked at him gravely. "I'm terrified of meeting your family," she confessed.

"Good Lord, why?" It was the last thing he expected.

She glanced out the chaise window at the glorious countryside. Cattle and sheep grazed in pastures of green farmland. Well-stocked farms boasted fields of golden grain. The people looked healthy and prosperous. Children, pink-cheeked and curious, were followed by flocks of clamoring geese and ducks. Small, quaintly thatched cottages dotted the tree-covered hills, and country manors with wide lawns and weathered trees were set amidst fields of colorful flowers.

"It's so very different from home," she said at last.

"How different?" the smooth voice probed.

Her eyes narrowed to assess his intentions. Was he trying to divert her or was he genuinely interested? Satisfied at what she saw reflected in the eyes gazing back at her, Tess began to speak, hesitantly at first, and then gaining confidence as she went along.

"The smells are different, and so are the trees." She took a deep breath, longing for the salty brackish smell of the Chesapeake. "We've magnolia and boxwood and mimosa, all blooming at once so the air smells like perfume and honey. We use the bay instead of the roads, or at least we did," she amended, "before British ships blockaded our ports."

"It sounds lovely." Mesmerized by the low melodic cadence of her voice, James willed her to continue. He had seen Washington, years ago, when his sister, Caroline, married an American. But he had never traveled as far south as the Chesapeake.

"Yes," answered Tess, her mood broken. "It is lovely."

"Have you no desire to see the world, Mrs. Bradford?"

"It isn't the usual thing for a woman to have such an ambition is it, m'lord?" she hedged.

"That isn't what I asked you."

Her fingernails bit into the soft flesh of her hands. "I had hoped to see the world with my husband," she said bitterly.

"A regrettable occurrence," the capable voice dismissed her pain, "but one that you have little control over at the moment. Why not make the best of the situation and leave the rest to me?"

Tess chewed the inside of her lip. She had no choice but to trust him. This man, this English lord, held Daniel's life in his hands. She looked at the remote guarded face, the hard mouth and jutting chin, and was suddenly afraid. If Admiral Cockburn's men were anything like James Devereaux, the United States of America was in desperate straits.

"I know it can't be easy for you," he said gently.

"No," she replied, her voice cold. "It isn't, but I'm sure Daniel is finding it much harder, wherever he is. How can you condone the policies of your navy?"

"I don't," he said. "But as long as Bonaparte controls France, the British Navy must maintain its strength. Sometimes unsavory means are necessary to obtain crews for their ships."

"That's an outrageous excuse. Even you must see that."

"England is fighting for her very existence. The alternative forces us to behave outrageously."

Tess stared out the window at the peaceful English countryside. Her thoughts were not at all peaceful and her voice, when she spoke, was tight with anger. "Consider how you would feel if circumstances were reversed and you were impressed into the American Navy and forced to risk your life for a fight that wasn't yours."

Devereaux's lips twitched. "The very idea terrifies me."

She glanced at him thoughtfully. Was that laughter she heard in his voice? There was nothing but a warm glint of approval in the piercing blue gaze. She changed the subject.

"I hope my visit doesn't inconvenience your family."

"Not at all," he answered. "They are eagerly awaiting your arrival."

"I wonder if Georgiana has changed since I saw her last?"

James grinned. "Georgiana will never change. She's the same as always, constantly getting into scrapes and expecting others to rescue her. I can hardly believe you two are friends."

"What do you mean?"

James hesitated before answering. "You appear to be older than my sister," he said at last, knowing the words weren't the ones he was looking for.

"My goodness!" Her voice shook with laughter. "And they told me you were a diplomat."

"I did handle that one rather badly, didn't I," he said, a smile curving his lips. "What I meant was that Georgiana's liveliness makes me feel as if I were her father, instead of a sorely tried older brother."

"How odd. You don't strike me as being the paternal type."

His eyes twinkled. "Thank you," he said formally.

Feeling more in charity with him than she had since the journey began, she leaned over to lay her hand on his arm.

"I don't want you to think of me as another obligation, m'lord. Nathanial Harrington is my father. I don't need another."

She was the one woman in England who knew nothing about his injury and she was flirting with him. He couldn't help himself. Reaching for her hand, his fingers closed around hers.

Tess could feel the heat of his skin through her gloves. The warmth traveled up the entire length of her arm and spread across her chest, until she felt as if her very bones would melt.

His eyes rested on her hair, her nose, her cheeks, settling at last on her mouth.

Her throat went dry. She concentrated on the pulse beating steadily along the taut line of his cheek. Inhaling the clean soapy scent of him, she looked up. His eyes were a deep blue and no longer remote. Somehow the physical nearness of him filled the closed air of the coach and a kind of stillness, like a hovering presence, radiated from him.

Tess closed her eyes, powerless to resist, as the back of his hand grazed her throat. Then, gently, he released her and leaned back against the velvet cushions.

She opened her eyes, surprise registering in their smoky depths. His expression was guarded once again.

"I do consider you an obligation," he said softly, "but you would do well to understand that whatever my feelings, they aren't in the least bit fatherly."

A terrifying sensation threatened to consume her. It was as if her skin were peeled back and every nerve exposed. Without answering, she closed her eyes, attempting to recover her poise in the pretense of sleep. The gentle rocking of the carriage wove its spell and her head fell back against the cushions.

Devereaux woke her in time to see an unobstructed view of his home. They had turned eastward and were traveling down a long, well-kept road when he touched her arm.

"We're almost there," he said.

The road turned into a wide drive, lined with trees, bordering a secluded lake. Passing over a stone bridge they came to a park. There, large and sprawling, made of grey stone brightened by a thousand diamond-paned windows, was Langley.

Tess held her breath. From the little she had seen in London, the homes of the English aristocracy weren't particularly impressive. Her own home, on the Chesapeake, built and designed by Nathanial Harrington, was imposing enough, but she had never seen anything like this.

A medieval horror, architecturally hideous to Tess's American eyes, the castle had two towers and the remnants of a moat, making it look more like a fortress than a home. A multitude of additions over the years, with no thought at all to design, had softened it somewhat, giving it a haphazard irregular appearance.

Accustomed to the wide porches and stately grace of the American South, Tess could only stare in amazement at this monstrosity the Devereauxs called home.

James chuckled. "It's dreadful isn't it? The original house was built during the reign of Henry the seventh. Since that time every owner has added something. Fortunately, it has been completely remodeled within. The chimneys don't smoke and the walls no longer drip. Unless you're afraid of ghosts you'll be completely comfortable."

"Ghosts?" Tess eyed him warily.

"From the dungeon," he answered, his expression neutral. "One of my ancestors had an interesting penchant for torture."

"Indeed." She looked up, suppressing a smile. "Is there a rack in your dungeon, m'lord?"

"Of course." His eyes glinted with laughter. "We've kept it in good condition to be sure difficult houseguests behave themselves."

"I'll keep that in mind," she assured him and was rewarded by an answering grin.

Tess was taken aback at the number of liveried footmen waiting to greet the carriage. She watched the butler's dignified face break into a smile as he took his master's coat.

"Welcome home, Your Grace." He beamed. "We are exceedingly pleased to have you back."

"Thank you, Litton. How is my mother?"

"Quite well, sir."

A shriek echoed from inside the hall. "James! We've been waiting an age. Have you brought her?"

A slim young woman with elegantly coiffed black hair and a gown of embroidered cambric flew down the stairs. With a cry of delight she threw herself into Tess's arms.

"Tess, my love, is it really you?" Georgiana Devereaux pulled away to look at her friend. "I can't believe it. You're really here." Slipping her arm around Tess's shoulders she guided her up the stairs and into the center of a vast marbled hall.

"Mama," Georgiana called, "Tess is here at last."

There was a babble of voices and the sound of slippered footsteps on wooden floors. Two younger girls rushed down the staircase and tumbled into their brother's embrace. James was completely enveloped in two pairs of feminine arms.

A calm voice broke through the confusion. "Girls, remember your manners." A tall, dark-haired lady came down the stairs and smiled as Devereaux kissed her on the cheek.

"James," she said, "you're safely home and looking none the worse for your journey."

She turned, and for the briefest of intervals, assessed the American with veiled blue eyes. Her cool lips brushed the girl's cheek and she placed her arm around Tess's shoulders.

"My dear, we are so looking forward to your visit. Georgiana has told us all about you. These are her sisters, Judith and Lizzie. But you must be tired and not in the mood for introductions. I'll take you to your room. Our housekeeper will bring you a tray of tea and hot food. We'll get acquainted in the morning."

Tess, too stunned to protest that she wasn't tired at all, allowed herself to be led up the stairs to her bedchamber.

The duchess of Langley wasn't what she had expected. Leonie Devereaux was slim and tall and amazingly young. Dressed in a gown of pale rose crepe that brought out the glow in her olive skin, she looked more like an older sister than the mother of four grown daughters and a son. Her hair, thick and shining, without a hint of grey, was pulled back and twisted into a coil on the top of her head. Wispy loose curls framed a face that was enchantingly lovely when she smiled. It was a serious face, thin and finely featured, with sharp clear bones. There was a look in her eyes, when they rested on her son, that reminded Tess of a lioness readying to do battle for her cub.

Footmen moved swiftly toward the luggage. A maid scurried past and vanished into the kitchen. Devereaux grinned and disappeared with his sisters into a room at the end of the hall.

"We've so been looking forward to your visit," repeated the duchess. "Georgiana won't forgive me for taking you away, but I know how exhausting the journey from London can be, especially coming the entire distance in one day." She smiled warmly. "Of course, James could hardly do otherwise as you've not brought your maid." She looked inquiringly at Tess. "You do have a maid don't you, my dear?"

"No," answered Tess. "I brought no one."

"We'll see about that tomorrow." Leonie Devereaux patted her arm. "Now that you're here we intend to take very good care of you."

Leaning against the door of her bedchamber after the duchess departed, Tess breathed a sigh of relief. Her fear of meeting the Devereauxs had come to nothing after all. Who would have thought this proud English family would be as welcoming as any of her Maryland neighbors?

She looked around at the opulent splendor of the room that would be hers while she waited for news of Daniel. It was done in pale blue and cream with satinwood furniture and delicate moldings. The friezes on the ceiling reminded Tess of Dolly Madison's sitting room in the White House.

There was a knock at the door and a maid entered bringing hot water and towels. After lighting a fire in the grate, she announced that dinner would be brought up shortly.

Nodding her thanks, Tess closed the door behind her and sank gratefully into the blue satin chair to sip a cup of scalding tea.

Downstairs the duchess of Langley made her way to the library in search of her son. He was seated by the fire in a leather chair surrounded by his sisters. Leonie paused briefly to admire the attractive picture her children made. Blessed with a vitality that glowed from within, the Devereaux offspring were recognized as exceptionally good-looking, the image of their mother.

In the privacy of closed circles it was said that the late duke, a quiet scholarly gentleman, had passed nothing at all down to his children except his impeccable lineage and enormous fortune. The blue eyes and black hair, the quick intelligence, that hint of steely arrogance they all shared without exception, came through the thin blue blood of Leonie St. Clair.

The picture would have been perfect, thought Leonie, except that Caroline, her oldest daughter, was absent. James was first and, after Caroline came nineteen-year-old Georgiana. Judith was a sophisticated young lady of seventeen and Lizzie, at twelve, was not yet out of the schoolroom.

"Girls," Leonie's voice interrupted them. "Please excuse us. I would like a word with James. Georgiana, go up and see if your guest is comfortable. The two of you," she nodded at her two younger daughters, "are free until dinner."

With good-natured grumbling the girls did as they were told, leaving the duchess with her son. Her sharp glance took in the dark circles under his eyes and the white line of strain around the pinched lips. James was in pain. She could feel it as if it were her own healthy flesh and bone that had been severed.

"How are you feeling, love?" she asked gently.

"Well enough." He recognized that hovering look and knew what was coming next.

"James," she said, clasping her hands tightly and working to eliminate the concern from her voice. "You aren't well enough to go junketing across the country on this errand. I'm terribly sorry for Teresa Bradford, but why can't someone else help her?"

"Because Georgiana is her friend and I gave her my word," he explained impatiently.

"Surely she would understand if you explained that you are recovering from a severe wound."

"The situation is much more serious now, Mother. America has declared war on England. This visit is no longer what it started out to be. Mrs. Bradford is not free to leave the country. There is nowhere else for her to go."

"Dear God," Leonie whispered. "Does she know?"

"Not yet." Devereaux's mouth hardened.

"She'll have to be told."

"I'll not have her know until she's more comfortable here. In case you haven't noticed, Georgiana's friend is very much an American. It goes against her grain to be under obligation to an Englishman."

Leonie straightened her shoulders. "I'll not allow it, James. The girl will only hate us more if we deceive her, not to mention the immorality of such a deception. Think how uncomfortable that would be, having a hostile houseguest living under our roof. I'm surprised you would even consider such a thing."

James smiled grimly. "There are a great many things about me that would surprise you, Mama. As much as it distresses you to hear it, my life is my own. I gave up short coats long ago."

Leonie frowned as she stared at the handsome face of her only son. Why did it always come to this between them? With an exasperated sigh she moved to the stool near his feet and sat down.

The firelight brought out the hidden blue lights in her black hair. She placed her hand on his knee.

"Was Miss Davenport in London?" she asked casually.

James's lips twitched. His mother was rarely so transparent. "Yes, I believe she was."

Leonie's blue eyes narrowed. "Did you give her my message?"

"No, Mother, I did not give her your message." His patience was at an end. "I see no purpose in raising the hopes of a woman I'm not remotely interested in."

"James!" his mother protested. "you're nearly thirty years old. It's time you were married."

The blue eyes were very cold. "Do you really believe I would allow you to choose my wife for me?"

"You're not doing very well on your own," she snapped angrily, pulling her hand away. "I'll not see Langley pass on to some stranger because you're too particular to appreciate the qualities of some of the loveliest ladies ever to pass through the doors of Almack's."

James smiled charmingly and drew his mother's hand back to his knee. "Perhaps the lady I'm looking for hasn't passed through the hallowed doors of that establishment."

Leonie felt the cold fingers of dread clutch at her heart. Unwillingly her mind formed a picture of silvery hair, fine delicate bones and grey eyes shining with passionate intensity. She wet her lips to quiet the erratic beating of her heart.

"What kind of lady are you looking for?" she asked quietly.

Ignoring the ache in the nonexistent part of his leg, James stood up quickly and limped to the grate. Pulling out the poker, he stabbed at the wood, inciting the dying flames to a healthier glow.

"I'd rather not discuss it," he said, his voice very low.

The pain in that beloved voice touched her heart. Tears gathered in the corners of her eyes and she brushed them away, angry with herself for her weakness. Taking a deep breath she decided to have it out between them.

"Mrs. Bradford is very lovely." She emphasized the *Mrs.* only slightly, but her point was taken.

James turned around swiftly, a surprised look on his face.

"Am I that obvious?"

"Only to me," Leonie assured him. "There isn't a great deal you can hide from me, my love." She hesitated. "Mr. Bradford may be very much alive."

"And he also may not," said James softly.

"James," his mother pleaded. "The woman is an American citizen. Even if she were free, she isn't for you. The obligation a man of your stature has to his country cannot be taken lightly." She lifted a hand to her throbbing temples. "To use your own words, you are honor-bound to find her husband."

The dark implacable face was so still it could have been carved from granite. "Have I ever given you reason to believe I would not do my duty?"

They stared at one another, identical blue eyes blazing with emotion. Leonie gave way first. Sighing in defeat, she answered. "No, dear. Never once in your entire life have you disappointed me. I pray you don't start now."

With a graceful, fluid movement she stood and walked to the door. "Dinner is at eight. The girls and I will understand if you don't feel well enough to join us." She smiled as if nothing of importance had passed between them, and left the room, leaving her son to stare after her retreating figure, a look of resignation on his face.

Four

"I'm terribly sorry about Daniel." Georgiana's animated face warmed with pity. "It must have been dreadful for you so soon after the wedding."

"It would have been dreadful at any time," Tess replied. "I've known Daniel all my life. We were friends long before we were married."

They were sitting cozily near the fire in Tess's bedchamber drinking tea, Georgiana in the satin-covered chair, Tess curled up on the Aubusson carpet, her feet tucked under her body. A fever of questions burned in the American girl's mind, but a natural reticence and the two-year separation from her friend held her back.

Georgiana had no such scruples. "Tell me everything," she demanded. "How is Caroline? We hardly hear from her now that American ports are closed to us." She frowned. "It seems so odd that I'm an aunt and I've never even seen my nephews."

Tess smiled and pushed her unbound hair away from her face. "Caroline is well, although very busy with the boys. She thought of coming home to England for a visit until the conflict is settled, but her husband is against it. He's very much a patriot, you know."

Georgiana lifted her head and looked down her nose. "Caroline is a Devereaux," she said haughtily. "The man can't be such a monster as to forbid his wife to see her family. My brother will have something to say about that, I'm sure."

Losing the struggle to control herself, Tess leaned her head back against the chair and broke into peals of laughter.

"If you could only hear yourself, Georgy." She wiped her eyes and laughed again. "You sound like such a dreadful snob."

Reluctantly Georgiana smiled. "I do, don't I? Mama says I'm getting worse every day."

"Never mind," Tess assured her. I'm here to make sure you don't become too high and mighty." Her smile faded. "Your brother has been very accommodating. I only hope he can find Daniel."

"Don't worry, love. If James isn't able to find Daniel, no one can."

"That's what I'm afraid of," replied Tess.

Georgiana bit her lip and decided to explain. "James was Wellington's chief intelligence officer until he sold out several months ago. I know he can be terribly fussy and overbearing, but as far as getting things done, there is no one better." She lowered her voice.

"Remember, my brother was only twenty when our father died. Since then, he's done a wonderful job of taking care of us. James is a very special person and we all depend on him. If he treats you more like a helpless child, than a married woman, you'll understand why."

The grey eyes widened as she stared at her friend. Could Georgiana be speaking of the same man Tess had met the day before? Was James Devereaux, of the hawkish nose and hard mouth, Georgy's fussy older brother?

Color rose in her cheeks as she recalled that moment in the chaise when his eyes blazed liked blue sapphires and her very bones dissolved under the heat of his touch.

Georgiana stared at her oddly. "Tess? Are you listening to me?"

"Why does he limp?" she asked suddenly.

"He was wounded in Spain. We thought he would die. I've never seen Mother in such a state." Georgiana's brow cleared and she smiled, showing even white teeth. "Ever since then, she's been trying to marry him off."

"Why is that?" Tess asked curiously.

"James is her only son. She had three stillbirths before he was born. Devereauxs have lived here at Langley for four hundred years and the estate is entailed. Without a male heir the lands and title are inherited by the closest relative. When you come to know Mama better, you'll see that she can't bear to fail at anything." She laughed. "James was the answer to her prayers."

"But she has four healthy daughters," protested Tess.

Georgiana smiled. "This isn't America, love. A woman cannot inherit an estate. By giving my father a son, Mama assured all of us a home for as long as we like."

"You can't be serious!" Tess was truly shocked. Accustomed to a world where men and women shared an easy camaraderie, and Nathanial Harrington welcomed each new daughter as lovingly as he would a son, she found it difficult to understand how a proud woman like Georgiana Devereaux could find her way of life tolerable.

"It isn't as bad as all that," Georgiana reassured her. "Most of the time everything works out quite well." She grinned wickedly. "If James would only cooperate and find himself a wife, Mama would be like a cat at the cream pot."

"Why isn't he cooperating?" Tess asked casually.

The tip of Georgiana's pink tongue rested at the corner of her mouth, a habit she reverted to when thinking seriously.

"I imagine," she said at last, "that James doesn't like being told what to do by anyone, least of all, a woman." Her voice sank to a conspiratorial whisper. "And of course, he's not without the company of females, so why does he need a wife."

"You mean your mother and sisters?"

"No." Georgiana's blue eyes twinkled. "I'm talking about the outrageously expensive opera dancer he keeps in London."

Tess's mouth dropped open. "You mean he keeps a mistress?" she stammered.

"Of course. You can't expect a man to wait until marriage to satisfy his," she floundered for a word that would not appear too indelicate, "instincts," she pronounced at last. Georgiana leaned forward until her dark head was level with the blond one. "Even married men have mistresses," she confided. "I'm sure my father had several."

Tess was horrified! Although not a Catholic, she was a true daughter of Maryland. Lord Baltimore had intended his colony to be a refuge for those who found themselves in a moral dilemma, caught somewhere between the Church of England and the harsh solemnity of Puritan New England. He had succeeded admirably. The hardships of the New World had created a different mentality among the people who lived their lives on the Chesapeake. Men and women worked together from dawn until dusk, carving a civilization from the flat marshlands that was as warm and gracious as it was strictly principled. The result was a binding of souls, of hearts and futures, that went far beyond the sharing of a bed and a family name. Tess had no sympathy for infidelity. Even now, nine years after her mother's death, she remembered the warm affection between her parents. Nathanial Harrington had been inconsolable for months after his wife's untimely death. Only the demands of the six motherless daughters she left behind, forced him out of his desolation.

Tess had been brought up to believe that marriage was forever, a bond closer even than that of parent and child. How could Georgy speak of her father's defection so easily?

She thought of her own marriage. Tess's engagement to Daniel had the hearty approval of both the Harringtons and the Bradfords. The two families shared a border on opposite sides of the bay. Their children had grown up together. It seemed the most natural thing in the world for Nathanial Harrington's daughter to marry Daniel Bradford. Now he was gone, snatched away with the arrogant approval of an enemy nation who believed its personal motives justified the beating and kidnapping of a man for no other reason than that he was alone and the odds against him.

"I'll leave you now, Tess." Georgiana's voice interrupted her thoughts. "You look tired. Ring the bell if you need anything."

She brushed a soft kiss on her friend's pale cheek. "Mother will send a maid to help you in the morning." She closed the door behind her with a soft click.

Tess shivered despite the proximity of the grate. She felt troubled and very alone. To win her husband's freedom she must depend upon a man whose heavy-lidded eyes read the secrets of her soul, a dangerous man whose very charm weakened her resolve and stirred the slumbering blood in her veins to fevered heights.

Bright sun pouring through the window woke Tess from a deep sleep. Stretching lazily she realized that someone was in the room with her.

"I have your morning tea here, ma'am," a voice said. "My lady thought you would like it in your room."

Tess nodded her head. "Thank you." She looked at the serving girl. "What is your name?"

"Rosie, m'lady," stammered the girl. "I hope I haven't offended you, but Miss Georgiana told me you preferred to be awakened early."

"Of course you haven't offended me," Tess assured her in surprise. She couldn't imagine what she had done to bring that look of terror to the girl's face. "I do prefer to wake early. You did exactly the right thing."

"Oh," the girl breathed gratefully. "I'm so glad. You see, ma'am, I'm not usually an upstairs maid, but there was no one else to send."

"I'm sure we'll suit each other very well." Tess smiled and Rosie sucked in her breath. She had never seen an American before. This one was lovelier than an angel and kind as well.

"May I help you dress, m'lady?"

"I suppose so," said Tess thoughtfully. "I've never had a lady's maid before. What exactly does one do?"

"The duchess said I should do your hair, help you dress and keep your clothes in order."

"I see."

"The duchess is very thorough," said Rosie.

Tess frowned. "I suppose since she is the duchess, she knows best." She looked at the maid and smiled apologetically. "I don't want to hurt your feelings, Rosie, but I won't need much help. I'm the fifth in a family of six daughters. There isn't anything I can't do for myself. In fact," she confided, "the first time I ever wore a dress made especially for me was after my marriage. Even my wedding dress belonged to Katherine, my older sister."

Rosie's eyes grew very round. Members of the Quality were usually not so forthright as Miss Georgiana's American friend.

"I don't mind, ma'am, if you don't," she said loyally.

"Very well," replied Tess, holding out her hand. "You may call me Tess."

"Oh, I dare not, Mrs. Bradford." Rosie lifted scandalized eyes to her new mistress's face. "The duchess wouldn't approve."

"I see." Tess smiled and swung her legs over the side of the bed. "Mrs. Bradford will do just as well."

"Thank you, ma'am, I mean Mrs. Bradford. I'll remember that." Rosie sighed with relief. She pointed to the dressing room. "I saw a lovely white dress hanging in the wardrobe. Would you like to wear that today?"

"Yes, please. Then, you can help me find my way downstairs."

Twenty minutes later, Tess entered the breakfast room. The duke, already seated, was reading the morning *Post*. He stood up the moment he saw her.

"Good morning, Mrs. Bradford," he said politely.

"Please," she protested, "call me Tess."

"Very well." He smiled and lifted the steaming silver lids from the serving dishes. "What do you prefer for breakfast, Tess? Bacon, grilled kidneys, toast?"

"Toast, please, and black coffee." Seating herself at the table she took the plate he held out to her.

"Why didn't you tell me you were with Wellington?" she asked, startling him with her frankness.

He grinned. "You were breathing fire and brimstone. It was most entertaining to have you think me cowardly."

"I never thought that," Tess protested.

"Didn't you?" Tiny lights flickered in his eyes. He had the most incredible eyelashes for a man.

"No," she said hastily, ashamed of the direction of her thoughts. "May I have part of the paper?"

James folded it, quickly hiding the boldly printed headlines announcing Madison's declaration of war. He tucked it underneath his chair.

"Why don't we talk instead?" he suggested. "I know very little about you."

"What would you like to know?" The grey eyes looked at him warily.

"Tell me about your family."

Tess relaxed. "My family is enormous," she said, biting into her buttered toast. "There are Harringtons all over Virginia and Maryland." She smiled at him from across the table. "We have something in common, you know."

"What might that be?"

"An abundance of women in our families." She buttered another piece of toast. "I have five sisters."

"Good Lord!" he groaned. "Your father has my sympathies."

Laughter, clear and rich as Waterford crystal, escaped her lips. "Papa says when everyone is home, it's worse than a field of chattering magpies." She wiped her mouth with a linen napkin. "To be fair, he's never complained about not having a son."

"A remarkable man. I understand his business is building ships."

"Yes." replied Tess. "Are you interested in ships, m'lord?"

"Actually, I am." He watched a hint of suspicion creep back into her eyes. "You needn't worry," he reassured her. "I have no intention of pilfering the family secrets. Ships are a hobby of mine, nothing more."

"That was hardly my concern," she said quietly.

"What was it then?"

The clear-eyed gaze held his without wavering. "Our countries are on the verge of war. I imagine a description of the kind of vessel my father manufactures, as well as the numbers he plans to turn out, might be of some use to your navy."

Amusement softened the lean planes of his face. "My dear child," he laughed, "you underestimate me. If I wanted to know about the projections of the American shipping industry, you would be the last person I would ask."

Tess's eyes narrowed. "Now, you underestimate me, m'lord."

"How is that?" James was enjoying himself. He couldn't remember when he'd enjoyed a breakfast conversation more. Usually he preferred silence and the morning paper to the prattling of his sisters. Tess Bradford was a welcome diversion, beauty, conviction, and a sense of humor, all at half past seven in the morning.

"I know enough about mathematics and construction to tell you that the scaffolding holding up your south tower won't last another week unless you reinforce it at the base," she explained calmly.

"Indeed." James's expression was carefully neutral. "Would you mind telling me how you arrived at your conclusion?"

"Not at all." Tess smiled. "Do you have a pen and paper?"

He rang the bell. Instantly, Litton appeared at the door. "May I help you, sir?"

"Yes, please. Mrs. Bradford requires paper and a pen."

Litton bowed. "I'll only be a moment, m'lord."

True to his word, the butler returned very shortly with the required materials and handed them to Tess. "Will there be anything else, m'lord?"

"No, thank you, Litton."

The man bowed once again and left the room.

"Now," said James. "Explain yourself."

Tess picked up the pen and in a few moments had filled the paper with neat mathematical computations and a shockingly accurate reproduction of the tower wall.

"Here," she said, referring to the lower half of the scaffolding, "this is where your problem lies. I've exaggerated it, of course, but you can see what is likely to happen if something isn't done."

When, at last, she put down her pen she looked up to find him staring at her.

"Who taught you to do this?" he asked.

"My father." She smiled. "He said I had a fine mind."

"He was wrong," Devereaux answered briefly. "Your mind is more than fine. It's excellent."

Apricot color rose in her cheeks. She was very conscious of him standing beside her.

"Thank you," she said.

"Nathanial Harrington must be a very unusual man."

"Yes," his daughter replied, "he is. Forgive me for being rude, but isn't it rather unusual for an English duke to admire an American tradesman?"

James grinned. "I'm beginning to regret sending Georgiana to America. We're not all snobs, you know."

Silence stretched out between them. "No," she said at last. "I apologize. I've been shamefully rude. Please, forgive me."

Looking into the candid eyes, James would have forgiven her anything. From the moment he saw her he knew she was extraordinary. She had a quality that rose above her stunning beauty. It was something that drew him, willing or not, into the dangerous realm of the forbidden. He was no stranger to beautiful women. The ones he preferred were warmhearted and shallow. This woman wasn't shallow. Daniel Bradford's wife was a woman of consummate grace and rare intelligence, the kind of woman a man searched his whole life for, the kind he once imagined would look beyond his enormous fortune to the man behind it. Now, it was too late. Because of a bullet at Badajos, he would never have a woman like Teresa Bradford to call his own.

"You must be a great help to your father," he said quietly.

"He always said so," Tess agreed. "We became very close when my mother died. That was nine years ago. Papa did a wonderful job caring for all of us."

"Why did he never marry again?"

"If you had known my mother, you would never ask such a question."

"I see." His eyes rested on her face. Did the remarkable Mr. Harrington recognize how much of her uniqueness his late wife had given this one particular daughter?

James looked at the chiseled perfection of her features and clear ivory skin against the wine velvet chair. Eyes, grey as rain, stared back at him. He could feel the question in them like a physical thing. Slowly, so as not to startle her, he reached down taking her hands in his own and pulled her to a standing position.

"You may trust me, you know," he said, without relinquishing her hands. "I will help you in any way I can. It is not a thing I would take lightly."

Tess opened her mouth to deny her doubt, but the words wouldn't come. There was strength and compassion in the hard mouth that spoke so gently, compelling her to believe him. But the shadowed planes of his face and the leaping pulse of his blood under her hands held a hidden message. She felt a tenseness within him, a hidden reserve, that made her self-conscious in a way she'd never known before.

"Good morning." The low cultured voice of Leonie Devereaux broke the silence.

Tess flushed and tried to remove her hands from his grasp. They were held fast in an iron grip.

"Good morning, Your Grace," she stammered.

Without a hint of embarrassment, James released her. He walked around the table and pulled out a chair.

"Good morning, Mother," he said, bending to kiss her cheek. "You're up early." He winked at Tess.

"Yes," said the duchess reaching for a cup of coffee. "I went to check on Teresa and when she wasn't in her room, I suspected I'd find her here." She smiled dazzlingly at the younger woman. "James can be such a bore in the morning. I thought I should rescue you."

Tess's eyes widened. Of all the terms she could think of, boring was the last one she would use to describe James Devereaux.

"Do you ride, Mrs. Bradford?" James asked, returning to his own seat.

"Shame on you, m'lord," Tess teased. "To ask a woman from Maryland if she can ride is like asking Lord Liverpool if he's a politician."

James laughed. "I stand corrected. If you would care to join me, I believe we could find a suitable mount for you in the stables."

Tess opened her mouth to accept when the gentle voice of her hostess cut in. "Why don't you wait for Georgiana to join you," Leonie suggested. "You know how disappointed she would be if you didn't invite her."

"You know very well that Georgiana doesn't emerge from her room until noon. She won't even know we've gone and come back," James answered.

"Don't forget, dearest, that Tess is her guest," his mother reminded him. "Perhaps Georgiana had plans to ride this afternoon."

There was a message hidden beneath the gracious words that Tess couldn't identify. It was almost as if the duchess disapproved of her.

"Nonsense. We shall be back before the morning is done." James was too well bred to openly defy his mother but there was steel and more than a little annoyance in his terse reply.

"I really would prefer to wait for Georgiana." Tess pushed her chair away from the table. "If you'll excuse me I have some letters to write."

"Of course, my dear." The duchess smiled in approval as she watched the graceful exit of the American girl. Buttering her biscuit, she turned innocent eyes on her son. "She really is a very sensible girl. Don't you think so, James?"

"Yes, Mother," he agreed dryly. "I only wish I might say the same of you."

Leonie's blue eyes widened. "Whatever do you mean?"

"Teresa Bradford is a married woman," he reminded her. "It

would be quite awkward if you forgot that and treated her as you would Georgiana or Judith."

"I have no intention of forgetting Mrs. Bradford's marital status." She looked up through her lashes at the rigidly controlled expression on her son's face. "I'm extremely relieved to know you haven't forgotten it either."

Five

Tess ran her hands over the cannon bones of the grey mare and looked up at the groom. "She's perfect, Higgins. Are you sure the duke won't object to my riding her?"

"Not at all, madam," he assured her. "His Grace told me himself that I was to choose a mount suitable for you." He looked approvingly at her well-worn riding habit. "I can tell you know what you're about."

She laughed. "I hope I won't disappoint you. May I ride alone if I stay within the park?"

"Aye." he nodded. "As long as you don't go beyond the south wall you'll be perfectly safe. No one would harm a woman on Langley grounds." Lacing his fingers together, he cupped his hands around her instep and boosted Tess into the saddle.

"Handle her gently now," he warned patting the mare on the rear. "She has a mouth like silk."

Twenty minutes later Tess reached the edge of the park. Beyond the manicured lawn and neatly clipped hedges, a wooded forest beckoned her. Urging the mare forward she pushed aside green-leafed branches of white oak and maple, their beauty unfamiliar but still appealing. A stream gurgled beyond the trees. She could barely make out the flash of silver where the water tumbled over the rocks. A movement, white and abrupt, like the flicker of a gull's wing, caught her eye.

Curious, she turned her mare in the direction of the movement and slid to the ground. Winding the reins around one hand she placed the other over the animal's nose. Higgins had told her there was nothing to fear on Langley land, but Tess knew a startled animal, or person for that matter, could be dangerous. Stepping into the darkness of the trees she waited until her eyes adjusted to the light. There, perched on a rock, fishing pole in hand, sat an extremely muddy Lizzie Devereaux.

Tess stifled a laugh as the youngest Devereaux daughter reeled in a respectable trout.

"Hello," she called out, after the fish had been removed from the hook.

Lizzie looked up, startled. Her brow cleared when she recognized Tess. "Oh," she said breathlessly, "it's you."

Lifting the skirt of her habit, Tess waded through the shallow water to the rocks where Lizzie remained seated. "Were you expecting someone?"

"Not exactly," the child explained. "It's just that I'm supposed to be in the schoolroom and I've escaped."

"I see," Tess's lips twitched. "Do you dislike studying?"

"Oh, no," Lizzie smiled when she realized Tess wasn't going to scold her. "It's just that we've had rain for over a week and I couldn't stay inside for another moment."

Tess nodded. "I know exactly what you mean. I was something of a madcap myself at your age and much preferred the outdoors to dabbling in watercolors and playing the pianoforte."

Lizzie looked wonderingly at the chiseled features and silvery coloring of Georgiana's friend. She looked down at her own reflection in a pool of still water. Running her tongue across dry lips she said, "I really do want to behave like a lady, but sometimes it's very hard."

"What is it that you find so difficult?" Tess asked.

"I'll never be like Georgiana or Judith." Lizzie's eyes were suspiciously bright. "I'm not pretty enough," she explained, refusing to let the tears spill over onto her cheeks.

Tess's eyes widened. She looked at the child's thin high-bridged nose and clear translucent skin, at the glossy black hair pulled back into a single plait and the impossibly blue eyes fringed with thick beautiful lashes.

Wrapping the reins around a tree branch, Tess pulled off her boots and rolled up the sleeves of her habit. Barefoot, she climbed up next to Lizzie and reached for a worm to bait the empty hook.

"May I?" she asked, lifting the rod.

The child nodded her head and watched in astonishment as Tess expertly cast her line into the shadowed brook. Within moments a trout was hooked. Lizzie laughed out loud as Tess deposited her catch into the basket.

"How old are you, Lizzie?" Tess asked suddenly.

"Twelve," was the reply. Tess measured off a piece of fishing line and efficiently bit off the end with even white teeth.

"I have a sister just about your age," she said.

"Does she look like you?" The blue eyes were fixed trustingly on her face.

"Good heavens, no!" Tess laughed. "She's a child. A person's appearance changes a great deal between ten and twenty."

"That's what James says, but I wonder if he's telling the truth or merely trying to comfort me because he's my brother." Lizzie looked away again.

"Well," Tess appeared to consider the matter. "It wouldn't be unusual for an older brother to try and make his sister happy."

"That's what I think." The child's voice quavered.

"Lizzie, look at me." She waited until the blue eyes met hers. "If I tell you something will you believe me?"

Lizzie Devereaux looked for a long moment into the lovely clear-eyed face. At last she nodded.

"You aren't the least bit pretty," Tess emphasized every word. "But in less time than you can imagine, you'll be quite beautiful." She tilted her head to the side surveying Lizzie's openmouthed face. "In fact," she continued, "you look more like your mother than any of your sisters and I'm sure you'll agree that to resemble the duchess would be a wonderful thing indeed."

"Do you really think so?" The child's face glowed.

"I'm sure of it."

"I thought you were going to write letters?" an amused voice broke into their conversation.

Startled, Tess lost her precarious balance on the rock and tumbled into the stream. She landed in an upright position. The water wasn't deep, but it was very cold. She gasped in shock as the icy wetness lapped against her knees.

Before she could even think, strong arms lifted her to the bank. James stripped off his coat. Lifting her skirts to her knees, he began rubbing the life back into her calves and feet with the costly wool.

Pain, like the tiny stabs of a thousand needles, followed his touch. She gasped again as his fingers touched the sensitive skin on her inner calf. "I had no idea my presence would affect you so," he teased, maintaining the steady rubbing pressure on her feet.

"You know very well why I fell," she retorted, trying to ignore the dark head so close to her own and the warm fingers massaging her skin. "I think you frightened us on purpose." She looked at Lizzie hovering anxiously nearby. "You weren't expecting him, were you, dear?"

Lizzie shook her head. "You startled us, James." Her lips tightened. "It isn't like you to do such a thing. Tess could have been hurt."

"Perhaps I was paying her back for being dishonest." There was a disturbing glint in his eyes.

"What are you talking about?" Lizzie demanded.

Tess squirmed beneath his gaze.

"Mrs. Bradford refused my company earlier today in favor of writing letters in her room," he explained. "Now, I find that she preferred riding after all." He kept his eyes on her face. "You might have mentioned it was the company and not the ride you objected to."

"Don't be absurd," Tess said, pulling her feet away. "Since you obviously prefer to be direct, so will I. I would have been very glad of company but for some reason your mother did not wish you to ride with me this morning. I've no desire to anger my hostess."

She stood up and looked around for her boots. "We've enough trout for a fine meal, Lizzie. If your mother is anything like my father, the longer you stay away from your studies, the angrier she'll be."

James did not move immediately, watching Tess from beneath lowered lids. He was struck by the natural appeal of the woman beside him. The sight of a lady in a muddied habit and wet hem, her tangled hair down her back should have appalled him, but it didn't. Tess, with her worn clothing and loose hair looked charming, too charming for her own good.

He stood up suddenly. "Lizzie has been gone for the entire morning already," he said. "A bit longer won't make a difference. There's a sunny spot in the meadow where we can rest while your skirt dries."

Afraid of offending him any further, Tess followed behind as he led the horses to a grassy knoll at the edge of a secluded meadow.

Lizzie lay down the fishing gear and stretched out on the grass. Tess joined her, her eyes closed against the light, her hands behind her head. The sweet smell of new grass and the drugging warmth of the sun worked their magic and soon, Lizzie was asleep.

James looked at Tess, free at last to let his eyes move leisurely over the entire length of her body. Lashes, darker than her hair, rested on cheeks the color of warm honey. Anyone with eyes in his head would recognize her as an American. The glowing skin, the sprinkling of freckles on her small straight nose, the confidant vitality of her walk, the lovely drawl of her speech, belonged to a gentler, slower-paced world.

With a shaking hand, he wiped away the moisture collecting on his forehead. Tess stirred, changing position slightly. Her breasts rose and fell under his fascinated gaze.

Tess felt his eyes on her. Her body was drawn tight as a bow, almost as if she were waiting for something. She knew the exact moment he withdrew his gaze and lay back, hands behind his head. She released her breath, finally able to relax.

Much later, a hand on her arm and the duke's familiar low voice woke her. The sun was low in the sky. She looked up to find Lizzie already mounted.

"Wake up, lazybones," the child grinned. "We'll be late for dinner."

Tess rose unsteadily to her feet. She was hungry, and the sun had drained the energy from her body. Walking to the mare she took the reins in her hand and leaned against the animal's warm flanks. As if she weighed no more than his small sister, James encircled her waist with his hands and lifted her to the saddle.

"Thank you," she smiled gratefully. "I'm more tired than I realized."

"You've done nothing but travel for the last several weeks," replied James, climbing up in back of Lizzie. "You need time to recover."

"I really had intended to write those letters, m'lord," she said. "But until I can send some news about Daniel to his father, I hesitate to give him hope." She bit her lip. "Adam Bradford is a very old man."

"He's also a sensible man, if I recall."

"Do you know him?" Tess looked surprised.

"I've met him several times," James replied. "Unless he's changed his mind, he was against a war with England."

"That's right," Tess agreed. "He's an outspoken Federalist. Even now, after what happened to Daniel, he still feels the same. He sees no need for war, not even to help France."

"Didn't Senator Bradford fight in the revolution?"

"Yes, he fought in the Virginia Brigade with George Washington. My father did, as well. Both of them survived the winter at Valley Forge."

"Without the French the Americans would never have been victorious, you know."

Tess looked offended. "Yes, James. It is American history we are speaking of, after all. I know it well."

He returned her look with a level stare. "I'm glad of it. Then you should know something of Napoleon Bonaparte."

"Only a little. What do you think of him?"

"I believe what every sensible Englishman believes. Bonaparte is a madman."

Tess frowned. "I suppose you are bound to feel that way. It is your duty as an Englishman. But Americans feel differently. He has helped our country a great deal."

"Believe in fantasies if you must," replied James curtly. "If you knew one half of what he's done, you would agree that the term butcher describes him perfectly."

"I assume Wellington can do no wrong," she teased.

James smiled. He noticed the change in her tone and recognized it as an attempt to lighten the seriousness of their conversation. "I've enormous respect for the general. There is no one like him in all the world."

"I've heard he is a terrible taskmaster."

James laughed. "You wouldn't say that if you knew him. He has quite a way with the ladies. One look at you and he wouldn't concern himself over something as inconsequential as an absent husband."

Her cheeks burned. "Rumor has it that he shares that same quality with his chief intelligence officer." The words were out before she could stop them.

His eyes were the deep blue of the sun-kissed Atlantic but there was no longer any laughter in them. "You shouldn't listen to rumor, Mrs. Bradford. There is little truth in it."

Lizzie watched in interested silence. James was sad again. He had been that way ever since he came back from Spain. She wondered if his leg hurt. She had overheard her mother say that a piece of leg was a small price to pay if it meant James never had to go back to the army again. Lizzie agreed with her. Nothing was worse than not having James at Langley.

"James," she said, quickly before her nerve deserted her. "Tess thinks I'll grow up to be beautiful."

He smiled down at her. "You know how I feel about that, brat. You're the prettiest female in the entire family."

"No, James." Lizzie refused to be taken lightly. "I'm not pretty now, but someday soon, I shall be beautiful."

"Is that so? His mouth was serious but his eyes were amused. "What makes you say that?"

"Tess told me. She said I'm not pretty now, but someday I'll look exactly like Mama."

An arrested look appeared on his face as he carefully studied his youngest sister's features. "She may have something there, Lizzie," he replied slowly. "Heaven help me if I have that to contend with."

Tess's musical laugh interrupted their conversation. "I don't envy you, James," she said. "A young lady with the fortune of Midas and the face of an angel. You'll not have an easy time of it."

He groaned. Kissing the top of Lizzie's head, he pulled her back into his arms. "At least I've a few years respite before that happens and I intend to enjoy them. Judith is already too sophisticated for my taste. I'd hate to see that happen to you."

Lizzie sighed contentedly. "Oh, James. I'll never be too old to go fishing with you." She smiled. "Even Tess likes to fish. She caught most of the ones in my basket."

"Tess," he said, winking at the blond woman beside him, "is most unusual. In addition to fishing, she can ride like a dream and compute mathematical figures that would make your head spin. If you want to be like her you'll need to spend more time with your books and less roaming the countryside."

Resting against the warmth of her brother's chest, Lizzie closed her eyes. "It isn't any use. I'm sure there's no one in all of England like Tess."

"God help me, if you're right," he muttered under his breath.

Six

Leonie Devereaux felt a headache coming on. The attractive picture of her children conversing in the sitting room with Teresa Bradford didn't help. She wasn't normally a harsh parent but she felt a sudden and irrational anger toward Georgiana. Why hadn't the wretched girl told her Teresa was a diamond of the first water?

Calling upon the iron control carefully cultivated over a lifetime, she stifled her resentment and forced a charming smile to her lips.

"The handicap was unnecessary," the duke admonished Tess as she threatened his queen. "I can't remember when I've played with a more formidable opponent."

She looked at him through lowered lashes. "I'm a poor loser and I couldn't be sure you wouldn't win."

He countered with a knight. "Wherever did you learn to play?"

Tess opened her mouth to answer when he held up his hand.

"Wait," he said, "let me guess. Your estimable father is the culprit."

"Actually, no," she replied, her eyes brimming with laughter. "My husband taught me. Daniel is the finest chess player in Annapolis."

"How fortunate for him." James was no longer smiling. He concentrated on the game, determined to best the ghost of Daniel Bradford.

A slight smile appeared on Leonie's lips. "Tell us about your husband, my dear. He sounds like a delightful young man."

"Mama!" Georgiana's shocked voice emerged from behind

her embroidery. "How could you? Any mention of Daniel must be excessively painful for Tess."

"Not really." Tess smiled warmly at her champion. "I've known Daniel all my life. It's actually quite comforting to speak of him."

"Not now, if you don't mind," Devereaux's dry voice cut in. "We've a game to finish and unless you intend to lose badly, you had better pay attention."

"Don't be overly confident, sir," Tess mocked him, removing his queen. "You are in no position to cry victory."

"Ah, but I am," replied the duke moving his rook into position. "Check."

"I should win this," Tess muttered to herself. "I've both my knights and you've only one." She moved her knight and promptly lost her queen.

"My game, I think," said Devereaux, his eyes glinting with satisfaction. "You are easily distracted, a flaw I'll have to keep in mind."

"Shame on you," she scolded. "A gentleman should never point out a lady's imperfections."

The tea tray arrived, putting an end to their banter. Soon after, Lizzie and Judith were sent to bed and Georgiana followed. The duchess was very tired but she resigned herself to stay as long as necessary. Nothing, short of her own demise, would allow her to leave James and the all-too-charming American, alone together.

"I've decided to have a house party," she announced suddenly, uncomfortable with the proximity of the two heads, one dark and one light, so close to one another.

James looked up from the tower design Tess had advised him to reinforce. "Is that really necessary, Mother?" he asked. "In a few short weeks, we'll be in London."

"It will serve to prepare Tess for the ton," Leonie explained. "She will find it difficult enough attending parties and balls in London after living in Annapolis all of her life."

Tess's lips twitched but she remained silent.

"Don't be absurd," James sighed in exasperation. "Annapolis is a thriving metropolis very close to the capital. It may not be as crowded as London but it has its own grace and elegance. Good God, think of Thomas Jefferson and William Curtis. The ladies and gentlemen of America are not provincials, Mother."

"I never thought they were," Leonie protested, visibly upset. "I merely thought introducing our guest to some influential people ahead of time might make her more comfortable."

She looked at the lovely face illuminated by candlelight. No one would ever take this girl for a backwoods provincial. Her gown was of palest cream over a white satin underskirt and the pearls at her ears and throat were worth a fortune. She was the epitome of taste, from the loosely knotted hair at the back of her head, to the sloping shoulders rising from the bodice of her gown. The delicate rose of her cheeks and the clear grey eyes were the only colors about her.

"I didn't mean to offend you, my dear," Leonie apologized.

"A party sounds lovely, m'lady," Tess reassured her. "It really is a very thoughtful gesture. Don't you think so, James?" She looked directly at Devereaux.

He met her look. Something primitive and intimate blazed between them.

Leonie closed her eyes briefly, admitting defeat. She hadn't missed the familiar address. Few people, other than family, were invited to call the Duke of Langley by his first name. This young beauty, this foreigner, had accomplished the impossible. In only two days she had broken through the reserve and captured the interest of England's most eligible bachelor. Whatever happened now was up to fate. She would have to rely on the character and integrity of her son.

She looked again at Tess. There was something reassuring and implacable in the straight shoulders and lovely tilt of her chin, as if she could only be coerced so far.

Leonie smiled. Her skin felt very tight. "It's late," she said, rising to her feet. "I think I'll retire."

"I'll go up with you," Tess said unexpectedly. "It's been a long day." She linked her arm through Leonie's and smiled enchantingly. "We can lean on each other."

The duchess's blue eyes softened. She patted the small hand tucked beneath her arm. "Thank you, my dear," she whispered. "Thank you, very much."

Tess couldn't sleep. With a curse only her father would recognize, she pulled on her dressing gown and walked downstairs to the library. After selecting a book she curled up in an armchair warmed by the smoldering embers of the fire.

It was there, several hours later, that Devereaux found her. He stood in the doorway watching her. The silvery mane of hair fell past her waist, partly concealing her profile. Her skin looked luminous and very pale against the dark velvet chair. He made no sound, but after a moment she looked around and saw him.

"What are you doing here, at this hour?" she asked.

"I might ask the same of you?"

"I couldn't sleep," she replied. "There is so much on my mind. I can't explain it." Her voice was low and slightly husky. "What about you? Perhaps you heard a noise and began believing in your own ghost stories?"

His lips turned up in a smile. When he spoke, his voice seemed to come from someone else. "Like you, I couldn't sleep." He absorbed every detail of the woman seated so gracefully in his chair. He felt a strange tingling sensation, like a nervous energy, beneath his skin. He ached to touch her. A year ago he would have consigned her husband to the devil and used the considerable charm he was born with to seduce her. In his world it was commonplace for married women to have affairs. But that was a year ago. Now, the hideously scarred stump that served as his left leg stopped him.

Before Badajos, he had never considered the physical appearance of his body. Women had always found him attractive. Now, a newly acquired self-consciousness held him in its grip. He hadn't sought out a woman in over a year.

Recovering from his wound, learning to balance and walk on his wooden leg without a noticeable limp, getting used to the strap and the feel of the uneven weight in his boots, had taken up all of his time. Sex was not a priority. But now he felt it all over again, the wanting, the sense of delicious anticipation, the slow, hot slide into the willing scented body of a woman.

Tess knew something was wrong. James appeared detached, almost angry. Then she saw the tense jaw and grim set of his mouth.

Smiling sympathetically, she stood, holding her place in the book with her finger. Her gown fell in soft folds to the floor. "I'll be going now. Good night, James," she said gently.

The smile devastated him. He heard her speak but the words meant nothing. A startling revelation swept through his consciousness. This was no fleeting passion. She wasn't just one more beautiful woman he desired for an evening's pleasure. This was Tess, a woman whose quick intelligence and lively wit were unparalleled, a woman whose sensitivity and warmth endeared her to everyone she met, a woman whose eyes and skin and hair were the loveliest he'd ever seen, a woman whose loyalty was destroying his sanity and eating out his heart.

She moved toward the door.

He barred the way.

She stopped and looked at him inquiringly.

"Tess," he said softly, his eyes gleaming a deep blue in his dark face.

Her throat tightened and her heart slammed against her ribs. "No," she whispered to his unspoken question.

He closed the distance between them. No power on earth could stop him now. "You don't mean that," he muttered. "I'll show you that you don't." With the inevitability of tomorrow he drew her, unresisting, into his arms. Bending his head he kissed her, gently at first, then with deepening intensity. It seemed, to James, that he had waited all of his life for this moment, this feeling, this woman.

She lifted her hand to push him away. His lips moved from her mouth to the hollow of her throat and back to her mouth. She stood very still fighting the weakness within her. He parted her lips to meet the driving force of his tongue.

The passion and repressed longing of the last several weeks came to a head. She could bear it no longer. Her control snapped and she moaned against his mouth, meeting the slow, heartstopping kisses with her own frenzied desire. The hand she had raised to push him away, curled around his neck. The other slid under his shirt to rake his back with her nails.

Devereaux, filled with his own mounting need, began lowering her to the floor. Outside, rain drummed against the windows. The wind howled, snapped a tree branch and flung it against a diamond-shaped pane. It shattered with a loud pop. She tensed in his arms. Desperate to be free of him, she pushed against his chest.

With enormous effort he released her and moved away, breathing raggedly. "What is it?" he demanded, his voice hoarse, his eyes coal black with desire.

Her face was haunted, her skin flushed. "I can't," she replied brokenly.

All at once it came to him. Georgiana had told her. She found him repulsive. He smiled bitterly. "Of course. Forgive me."

"I must leave here immediately."

"Don't go. I apologize." His eyes were guarded once again, his breathing even. "This was entirely my fault. You came here for a reason that has not yet been resolved. I won't embarrass you again. You have my word." He drew a deep sustaining breath and smiled. "Georgiana would never forgive me if I chased you away."

"I don't know." Her voice betrayed her confusion.

"Think about it," James coaxed her. "Tomorrow this will all be a bad dream."

She laughed shakily. "You underrate yourself, m'lord. I'm sure the right woman would find you extremely charming."

"You needn't patronize me, Tess."

She looked confused. "What—?"

His smile did not reach his eyes. "Good night."

She hurried past him, through the door he held open for her.

For the rest of that night Tess fought a battle with her conscience. She was honest enough to admit the truth. James Devereaux was like no one she'd ever known before. She was terribly attracted to him. Nothing in her nineteen years had prepared her for the overpowering emotions she experienced when he touched her. Her marriage to Daniel seemed unreal and very far away. It was this man, this English duke, who occupied her mind.

She knew he wanted her. Tess was no stranger to the attentions of men. From the time she was fourteen years old, their eyes had followed her admiringly through the shops and streets of Annapolis. Only a healthy respect for Nathanial Harrington had kept their actions within the bounds of propriety. And, of course, there was always Daniel, her childhood companion and dearest friend. They had pledged to marry when Tess was fifteen and Daniel three years older, a children's pledge neither cared to break.

An affair was always a possibility. But Tess had been raised in a strict colonial family. Adultery was wrong and nothing could make it otherwise. Her situation was impossible. How could she remain in this house feeling as she did? But, for Daniel's sake, and Adam Bradford's, how could she do otherwise?

Tess forced herself to go down to the breakfast parlor as usual the following morning. She found Devereaux reading his paper. Her sleepless night had left her dull and out of sorts and the picture of him sitting at the table as coolly as if nothing had happened between them irritated her. Rubbing her aching temples she sat down at the table.

"Good morning, Lord Langley," she said, forcing herself to remain detached.

He looked up from the newspaper, his face completely devoid of expression. "I thought we had progressed beyond Lord Langley and Mrs. Bradford?"

Grey fire flashed from her eyes. "Your manners are dreadful, you know."

"Are you changing the subject?"

"Yes."

"Please answer the question, Mrs. Bradford."

She reached for a cup and bit her lip. He looked polite and faintly bored, not at all dangerous. Perhaps she was being foolish. She smiled tentatively. "You're quite aggravating, you know," she said at last.

Something flickered in his eyes but it was gone too quickly. Saying nothing, he went back to his paper feeling very pleased with himself. After a moment he finished the section he was reading and offered it to her. They passed the rest of the meal in amiable silence.

Tess was about to excuse herself when James folded his paper and announced, "I leave for London directly after Mother's dinner party. Parliament meets on Thursday. I'm to speak on impressment." He waited for her reply. There was none. He hesitated. "If there had been any new developments regarding the matter of your husband, I would have heard, but I'll check once again."

"Thank you, James," she said formally, and left the room.

Devereaux watched her graceful exit with hungry eyes.

Seven

Georgiana yawned and closed her book. "We've been reading for hours," she complained. "I'm going inside to help Mother with the invitations."

"Will there be many?" Tess asked, with a guilty glance at her book.

"Not enough to worry about." Georgiana smiled at her. "You know how it is. If one person is invited, then another must be also. It would never do to offend anyone. Don't worry, Tess," she reassured her. "Finish your novel and I'll help Mother. After all, you're our guest."

"If you're sure."

"Very sure." Georgiana rose from her chair. The soft blue muslin of her gown swirled gracefully around her legs as she walked through the gate to the house.

With a grateful sigh, Tess returned to Jane Austen.

Less than a quarter of an hour later, Georgiana returned to the garden.

"I'm afraid Mama is beside herself. The gowns we ordered won't be ready for our party. Madame Rochelle is ill with influenza. She sent a note this afternoon along with the fabric Mama and I selected." She sighed regretfully. "Poor woman. I'm sorry she's ill but I did so want to wear something new. I suppose it can't be helped."

Tess sat up giving Georgiana her full attention. "Isn't there anyone else in her shop who can sew?"

"That's what my mother is so angry about. Madame had our

order for nearly three weeks which means she left it until the final hour. I'm sure we won't be using her again, which is a shame because her creations are truly lovely and so original."

Tess frowned. "All of my gowns, with the exception of my trousseau, were made at home. I suppose it's natural, with so many girls in the family, that we all learned to sew." She looked thoughtfully at Georgiana. "Maybe I can help."

"How?"

Tess closed her book. "Show me your fabric. If I can't do it, I'll tell you, and nothing will be lost."

Georgiana stared at her friend in wonder. "Can you really sew well enough to design an evening gown?"

"I don't know," Tess replied truthfully, "but I'm an American, remember? We are extremely resourceful."

"Where did you learn?" Georgiana asked. "At home you had servants. I remember them."

"My mother taught my sisters and they taught me. We don't actually have help," Tess reminded her. "There is only Clara who has been with us since before Mother died. She's really more a member of the family than anything else. If you recall, there aren't nearly as many servants in America as you have here."

"I can't wait to see Mama's face when you tell her," said Georgiana. "Let's do it now."

The Langley household dined that night on a simple but delicious meal. Trout, caught by Lizzie and the duke, was served with a delicate buttery lemon sauce, and the chickens, basted to perfection, were pronounced the tenderest anyone at the table had ever tasted. The dessert, a delicious apple meringue confection, was served with a flourish.

Devereaux looked curiously at the flushed faces around his dinner table. "Have I missed out on anything?" he asked.

Feeling unusually charitable, the duchess raised her wineglass in a toast. "To Teresa Bradford," she said warmly, "a woman of unusual talents. Tess has saved us from a fate that would surely have resulted in complete mortification."

Devereaux's right eyebrow lifted in a questioning arc.

"Madame Rochelle was taken ill without finishing the gowns Georgiana and I commissioned for our dinner party," his mother continued. "The result of such negligence is that we would have had nothing at all to wear."

"Surely, *nothing* is an exaggeration, Mama," commented the duke dryly.

"There isn't one evening gown in my clothes press that wouldn't be remembered from last season," she returned. Don't be difficult James. Let me finish."

"I'm anxiously waiting for you to do so."

The duchess beamed at Tess. "It appears that our American guest is a skilled seamstress. Apparently Madame Rochelle has been charging us abominable rates for something that Tess assures us is quite simple. She has agreed to direct the maids in the fashioning of our gowns. Isn't that wonderful?"

Over the rim of his glass Devereaux's eyes met the wide grey ones of Daniel Bradford's wife. Something familiar and disturbing flashed between them, lingered briefly, and then disappeared.

"Is there anything you don't do?" he asked, regarding her thoughtfully.

"What do you mean?"

He checked off her accomplishments using his fingers. "In the few days since you arrived, you've redesigned my tower, caught more fish in a single day than Lizzie and I have in a week, saved my mother an embarrassment too great for words and," his eyes twinkled, "most unusual of all, you're my equal at chess."

"Don't be absurd." Tess laughed self-consciously.

"Is there anything else you haven't told us?"

"Nothing," she assured him, "nothing at all."

Remembering her reply several days later, he looked with amusement at her expert handling of what could have been a very awkward situation.

His mother's dinner party was an enormous success by eve-

ryone's standard. The most important men in English government circles attended with their wives. Political differences were
ignored as Whigs and Tories chatted politely while drinking the
duke's excellent champagne.

Among these were Lord and Lady Holland who arrived with
the Prince Regent's sharp-eyed favorite, Lady Jersey. Viscount
Castlereagh, the Foreign Secretary who had single-handedly run
England's affairs for years, was there with his lady, and even
Lord Liverpool made an unprecedented appearance. To have as-
sembled such a group together under one roof was a feat attrib-
uted directly to the tremendous power and influence of the
Devereauxs of Langley.

Devereaux wasn't concerned that Tess would learn of the hos-
tilities between his country and hers. In addition to their expertise
in diplomacy, every one of his guests had impeccable breeding
and wouldn't dream of embarrassing the lovely young American
with talk of war.

He looked at the slim regal figure seated next to Lord Liverpool. She appeared to be listening intently. Suddenly her eyes
widened. She shook her head and smiled. His heart constricted.
He felt the pull of her, almost as if she'd called his name.

Casually, he extricated himself from the perfectly beautiful,
perfectly cold Miss Davenport and made his way to the prime
minister's side. He arrived in time to hear Lord Liverpool's question.

"What can you tell me about the War Hawks, Mrs. Bradford?
Are they a political force in America?"

Her smile was dazzling. "Yes, sir. According to my father and
Senator Bradford, there is a growing concern among the legis-
lature that America isn't being taken seriously as a sovereign
entity. We are surrounded on all sides by hostile nations whom
we are trying to appease, the French to the North, the Spanish
to the South, and of course, the Indian nations to the West. The
War Hawks are young men, like Andrew Jackson, mostly from
frontier states, who feel we should stand up and be noticed. They

are moving in and taking votes away from the Federalists, who, I understand, have always been friendly with the Tories."

Lord Liverpool, every inch a Tory, lifted his quizzing glass to one eye.

"Indeed," he replied. "And do you agree with them, Mrs. Bradford?"

"Yes." Her voice was filled with conviction. "I, too, would argue for war with England unless trade is resumed and impressment stopped."

"Now, see here, young lady," the prime minister protested. "You can't possibly know what you are proposing. Are you suggesting we give up everything and allow Bonaparte to succeed? It's preposterous."

"There must be another way. Your current policy is nothing more than pure piracy upon another nation's resources." Her eyes, the color of liquid silver, were fixed on his face.

Liverpool looked helplessly at his host. "Help me, James. I'm losing this argument. This woman is a radical."

Devereaux grinned. "You should have remembered her citizenship before you engaged in debate."

"Don't tell me you agree with her?"

"Not at all, but that doesn't stop me from appreciating the strength of her convictions."

"If you don't mind," Tess interrupted. "I would prefer not to be discussed as if I were some inanimate object. If America, a nation without the military might and naval power of England, can solve her problems using her own resources, surely England can as well."

"We have elections here," Lord Liverpool said defensively. "Traditions are not so easily changed."

"Is that what you call them?" She smiled sweetly. "Membership in the House of Lords is hereditary and your House of Commons is not elected by the people."

"Is that so dreadful?" asked Liverpool.

"I won't argue for impressment or infringing upon American rights," Devereaux broke in, "but I will stand up for our system of government. If you will think for a moment, the men Americans elect to office are those of enormous wealth, your very own untitled aristocracy, so to speak. Your leaders are men from the landholding class of Virginia. Men with the leisure time and intellect to undertake the business of government. Perhaps, in time, it will change. As it stands, the system is a good one."

"I think it will change," Tess said quietly. "My father believes that the man I spoke of, Andrew Jackson, will make his mark in American politics. He is as far from landed gentry as you are, m'lord, from a chambermaid."

Devereaux's clipped voice sounded annoyingly patronizing. "Perhaps you are right. However, although we have some inequities, our class system has worked quite well over the centuries. It is up to those with the ability to rule to manage the circumstances of government. Your own founding fathers agreed. After all the American Constitution is based on our Magna Carta."

The creamy curves of her breasts rose and fell rapidly beneath the blue velvet bodice and her eyes were very bright. "Let me rephrase to be sure I understood you correctly. The poor and working classes are incapable of rational judgment and therefore must rely on the wealthy, titled, and therefore more intelligent, to make their decisions for them?"

Devereaux thought for a moment. The prime minister waited with bated breath. How would James salvage this one? She had deliberately made him sound like a pompous bigot.

"An interesting interpretation," James said and smiled brilliantly, effectively disarming both Tess and the prime minister. "I wonder if dinner is ready."

Again, he had minimized the differences between them. Tess hadn't expected to be taken seriously. After all, she was a woman, and women, she reminded herself bitterly, were disregarded in America as well as in Britain. But James had listened to her and so had Lord Liverpool.

The anger, which changed the golden color of her cheeks to a rich apricot, drained from her body. She knew from her friendship with Georgiana and Caroline, that the English temperament was not like an American's. It appeared that the duke, despite his sense of honor and considerable charm, ran true to form. Still, he was a duke and unlike anyone Tess had ever known. Because she was always completely honest with herself, she admitted that his air of noblesse oblige was a very large part of his personal appeal for her.

She placed her gloved hand on Liverpool's arm. "Forgive me, m'lord," she said, looking up through her lashes. "I hope I didn't make you uncomfortable?"

Liverpool looked at her with open admiration. "Not at all, my dear, not at all. Always glad to hear an intelligent opinion." He patted her hand. "This is a difficult time for you. Rest assured we'll do everything we can to right this unfortunate situation."

Devereaux smothered his laughter with a cough. The woman had the finesse of a diplomat. Without apologizing for her beliefs, she managed to convince the prime minister of England that he was the recipient of a very great honor.

Pushing himself away from the wall, he held out his arm to Tess. "Dinner is served. May I escort you?"

"Of course." She looked up at the lean handsome face. His emotions, as usual, were carefully held in check. Hesitating for an instant, she turned back to Lord Liverpool. "That is, if you don't mind, sir?"

"Not at all," he blustered, his strident voice carrying across the room. "James always did have a way of walking off with the loveliest lady around."

Devereaux's eyes glinted as he saw the look of outrage on Cynthia Davenport's narrow face. The evening was turning out much better than expected.

"I hope I didn't offend you with my liberal opinions," Tess's expression was carefully neutral as they made their way to the dining room.

"Would you mind if you had?"

"Yes," she replied. "I'm not totally lost to all propriety. Your family has been very kind to me."

"Does that appreciation extend to me? Have I been very kind to you, also?" His gaze carried a disturbing expression.

She stopped, oblivious to the others around them, and stared up at him. The censure in the clear grey depths of her eyes was unmistakable.

"I'm sorry," he said quickly. "That was unforgivable of me."

"Yes, it was," she agreed.

"Shall we continue, or have I gone past forgiveness?" He smiled, sure of his charm. "We are holding up dinner."

"I don't think the way these people do." The passion in her voice demanded an immediate answer.

"That's understandable. No one expects you to," he answered reasonably. "Your opinions are your own." Lifting her chin, he forced her eyes to meet his. "You are a credit to your country, Tess. It isn't necessary to apologize for that." The white line deepened around his mouth. "In the end it may be I who will ask for your pardon."

She said nothing, noting the air of confidence that emanated from him, the easy assured way he held his head, the pride, so unconscious it was close to arrogance. Taking a deep breath she turned, once again, toward the dining room.

"I hope your mother hasn't seated me near Lord Liverpool. The poor man has had enough discord to spoil his dinner already."

"You really are an innocent, aren't you?" The familiar note of amusement was back in his voice. "His lordship was utterly charmed by your novel ideas. He will be very disappointed to learn that Mother has seated you beside Lady Castlereagh and Lord Holland."

"Good Lord," Tess choked. "What a combination."

"You will find," he said seriously, "if you look past the trappings of Whig and Tory, they share similar philosophies."

The first course, a delicious cream soup, was already being served when Tess slipped into her chair. Sparkling crystal and silver reflected the light from a thousand candles and the food was served on the finest Sèvres china.

Lady Castlereagh, a small birdlike woman with brown hair and eyes the color of sherry, smiled warmly. "I'm so glad we'll have this chance to talk. How are you enjoying England?" Holding her spoon poised at her lips, she waited for Tess's answer.

"It's unbelievably lovely," Tess replied, grateful that she could be honest about this aspect of English life. "I don't know if your husband has mentioned it, m'lady, but he is acquainted with my father-in-law. Lord Castlereagh stayed at Bradford House when he visited America. My father and Senator Bradford were very impressed with him. He is the single British official to seriously accept my country as a sovereign nation."

Lady Castlereagh looked fondly at her husband. "I wish it were so with his peers in England. Unfortunately, many can't see behind his natural reticence." Her eyes clouded. "They see him as cold and aloof when actually he's quite shy."

"My father believes him to be the greatest statesman in England," said Tess softly, moved by the obvious affection in Lady Castlereagh's eyes.

"I think history will eventually agree with your father, my dear. My husband's dream is to restructure Europe so no one will ever again feel the need to engage in war."

She turned glowing eyes toward Tess. "Please call me Emily." She nodded toward Langley. "That young man also has enormous potential. He thinks in terms of all of Europe, not just England. Mark my words," she lifted a napkin and dabbed her lips, "we'll hear a great deal of him in the future."

Tess looked with admiration at the small animated woman beside her. Here was no dimwitted female who did nothing but gossip, entertain, and await the attentions of gentlemen. Her razor-sharp mind was the equal of any man's there that evening. Lord Castlereagh had chosen his political hostess well. She was very deeply involved in her husband's career.

The assembled guests were an interesting assortment, decided Tess. Lady Holland, a notorious philanthropist, was debating land reform with Lord Liverpool. Leonie Devereaux had Lord Castlereagh's undivided attention and, although Tess was too far away to hear their conversation, she was sure from the serious expressions on their faces that it was political in nature. At the far end of the table James Devereaux was sharing conversation with Miss Davenport and her mother, who had been placed on either side of him. He looked bored.

Lady Castlereagh whispered softly. "James will be making a dreadful mistake with that one." She tasted the buttered crab and smiled with pleasure.

"What do you mean?" Tess asked.

"Rumor has it that Cynthia Davenport will be the next Duchess of Langley. She has Leonie's approval, although I must admit, that usually doesn't weigh much with James."

An unexpected pang pierced Tess's heart. "Is it settled then?"

"Not at all." Emily smiled. "If I know Devereaux, he may surprise us yet."

She couldn't keep from staring. James and the classically beautiful blonde made an appealing couple.

Unexpectedly, he turned and looked directly at her. For a brief moment he searched her face, then looked away. For the length of that look, she held her breath until the ache in her chest was almost painful. Good Lord, what was happening to her?

She needed to go home, away from everything English, especially the man at the far end of the table. There was something about him, something elemental and dangerous that set him apart from every other man she had ever known. Perhaps it was his arrogant assurance that frightened her, or his air of command, or the sharp lean planes of his face. His hair, shining and black as a crow's wing, was a sharp contrast to the brilliance of his eyes, the clear impossible blue of the Maryland sky on the cusp of summer.

Tess took a shuddering breath. If Daniel wasn't found soon and she didn't return to America, her husband would find himself married to a very different woman than the one he left behind on his wedding day.

She wondered what it would be like to live a quiet predictable life again, filled with nothing more exciting than neighbors for dinner or a country barbeque, her world defined by green fields and blue water, by the Chesapeake tides lapping against the harsh red soil of the tidewater. It sounded incredibly dull.

Devereaux couldn't keep his mind on Cynthia Davenport's insipid conversation. How could his mother possibly imagine he could endure a lifetime of this woman's sanctimonious prattle? Against his will, his eyes were drawn to the far end of the table where Tess and Lady Castlereagh were deep in discussion.

Teresa Bradford was everything that was lovely and honest and alive. It was more than her undeniable beauty that fascinated him. It was her loyalty, her clear-thinking mind and, oddly enough, that quality that made her different from everyone in his world, her all-encompassing enthusiasm. Tess Bradford did not know the meaning of the word *bored*. The sheer warmth of her personality drew everyone to her, from all stations of life. For the first time James realized that because of Tess he was embarrassed by the class-consciousness of the English aristocracy. He also knew, with a frightening sense of inevitability, that he would never meet another woman like Teresa Bradford.

Later, in the drawing room where the ladies gathered after dinner, Tess took a seat apart from everyone else. The men were in another room lingering over glasses of port. For the last interminable minutes she wished she were in the dining room with them. In America, the antiquated custom of separating men and women after dinner was no longer practiced. With the exception of Lady Castlereagh and Georgiana, Tess felt stifled by the conversation of English women. She tensed as the elder Mrs. Davenport crossed the room and sat by her side.

"Are you looking forward to London?" the woman asked, determined to be kindly condescending to this chit of an American.

"Of course," Tess replied graciously. "London is renowned in America. I'm eager to see the sights."

"I fear it will be overwhelming at first," she said with a vapid smile. "You must ask Cynthia how to go about."

Tess managed to control her amusement. The woman really

was impossible. Nathanial Harrington's daughter had never in her life needed such assistance.

"You needn't concern yourself, Mrs. Davenport. Annapolis isn't exactly a small town."

"Really?" The older woman's double chin quivered. "We hear so very little about America, you know."

Tess's temper flared. "I'm not surprised."

Mrs. Davenport sniffed. She had been prepared to graciously condescend to the Devereaux's houseguest. Never in her wildest dreams had she imagined the young woman had the looks and grace to put her own daughter in the shade.

"I wonder, my dear, how you can bear to accept the hospitality of an enemy?"

"I beg your pardon?"

"Lord Langley is a British statesman. Perhaps it would be less difficult if he had no ties with the government, but under the circumstances, I should think you'd rather leave."

Tess stood, her eyes blazing like twin jewels in her set face. "Under the circumstances, Mrs. Davenport, I believe I will leave."

Just then the door opened and the gentlemen entered the room. With a sigh of relief, she saw Devereaux making his way toward her. She noticed that his limp was more pronounced than usual. She smiled warmly. She waited for him to reach her side. If she had anything to say about it, he need not be plagued by the odious Mrs. Davenport anymore tonight.

James recognized the invitation, ignored the pain in his leg, and increased his pace. More than one person noticed the look in his eyes as they rested on the blond head and slim graceful figure of the American woman.

Cynthia Davenport caught her breath and turned away, a resigned smile on her lips. She could wait. Teresa Bradford was married. Whatever her relationship with Langley, it could never be permanent. It was the nature of men to have their diversions and the nature of women to look the other way.

Eight

No one who happened to encounter James Devereaux two days later at Westminster would have guessed that behind the ice-blue eyes and implacable demeanor was a man as close to elation as he had ever been. France had invaded Moscow and among members of Parliament there was little interest in a prolonged war with America. Most of the statesmen James had polled were in favor of pulling troops out of the United States. Wellington would finally get the support he needed.

At precisely two o'clock, Devereaux presented himself at Downing Street. Lords Liverpool and Castlereagh were already there, and Lord North, accompanied by William Grey, arrived shortly after. One look at Langley's dark, arrogant face told them the matter was of great importance. In the ten years since James had taken his seat in the Lords he had developed an almost legendary reputation. The duke did not often speak to issues unless he was completely prepared to justify his point of view. The four men settled down to listen.

"I wish to speak on the subject of suing for peace with America." He came directly to the point, the clipped, lucid tones of his voice completely without emotion. "Wellington needs help, gentlemen. Without sole concentration of our troops and navy in Europe, we don't stand a chance against Napoleon."

"What about British deserters?" protested Grey. "Are we to turn our backs and ignore our own traitorous seamen?"

"Not at all," answered Devereaux. "We must refrain from trade with America until the war in Europe is settled."

"You can't be serious," Grey's eyebrows lifted to his hairline. "It would break us."

"Is the blockade of her ports and the maintenance of an army on American soil not breaking us?" countered Devereaux.

"Nothing can be worse than the existing situation," Castlereagh spoke firmly. "We are not now benefiting from trade with America, nor are we likely to until the conflict is over. They, on the other hand, may consider sending their ships into British ports if we are no longer enemies." He looked at Devereaux. "Do you think the terms will satisfy Madison and the American Congress?"

"I don't know," replied James frankly. "But our only alternative is to garrison an army overseas permanently. The American people are British descendants, gentlemen. They won't take to subservience easily."

"I have never approved of impressment and embargoes with relation to the United States," said Liverpool unexpectedly. I will do what I can to persuade the Cabinet."

Castlereagh looked with amazement at the dark head and strong hawkish nose of James Devereaux. The mere strength of his personality had persuaded the most powerful men in England to plead his cause. For a moment he experienced a twinge of envy at the sheer magnitude of what had just occurred.

It was late at night when Devereaux reached Langley. He stopped for dinner at the White Horse Inn but decided against staying the night. Everyone had retired for the evening by the time he had stabled his horse and walked wearily into the library at Langley. A glass of something warm and sustaining was needed after his solitary ride.

Pushing open the door, he saw Tess, her figure bathed in moonlight, standing by the window. In her pale embroidered nightdress with her loose silvery hair hanging about her shoulders, she looked like an angel of the dawn welcoming him home.

"Hello," he said, as if only moments had passed since he'd seen her, instead of weeks.

She stared back at him. Moonlight reflected on his black hair and startling blue eyes. The look on that harsh, aristocratic face told her more than anything else, what she had long tried to deny. He wanted her more than ever and, God help her, she wasn't strong enough to withstand him alone, especially when it was something she wanted very much herself.

"How did you fare?" she asked, striving to keep her voice normal.

"Very well. I believe we have a chance at abolishing impressment and once again establishing trade with your country."

She nodded her head, the smoky grey of her eyes intent on his face. "Thank you." She could see the pulse beating evenly in the smooth brown of his throat. His mouth was no longer grim. A frightening sensation consumed her, as if her bones had turned to liquid under her skin.

He took a step toward her.

"Don't," she whispered. Her legs lacked the strength to move away.

Gently, he placed his hands on her shoulders and moved her to the door. "Good night, Tess," he said, his voice strong and sure and faintly amused. "I'll see you in the morning."

Leonie Devereaux was not prone to illness. Her frequently recurring headaches, she was sure, had everything to do with her son's impossibly pigheaded behavior.

"Really, James," she sighed, confronting him across the breakfast table. "How long do you intend to prolong this deception? We leave for London tomorrow and Mrs. Bradford still doesn't know we're at war. How long do you think she'll remain in ignorance once we've reached the city?"

"I'll tell her as soon as I feel it's the right time," answered her son.

"For all your experience, you're really impossibly obtuse."

Leonie's exasperation was leading her into dangerous territory. "Do you think a woman, especially an intelligent woman like Teresa Bradford, will thank you for keeping such a secret?" She rubbed her aching temples.

"I'm not a complete fool, Mother," James answered. "Allow me to handle this in my own way."

"It could be very embarrassing for all of us," she warned. "Remember, there are others involved beside yourself. Georgiana's friendship is something to be considered, and Lizzie's as well. She has formed quite an attachment to Teresa."

"I'm aware of that." James refused to elaborate and sipped his coffee instead.

Sighing in resignation, Leonie stood and left the room without a word. Ten minutes later James left the table and proceeded to his study where he reviewed his correspondence of the last two weeks. He was in the middle of deciphering a wordy Parliamentary motion when a discreet knock on the door interrupted him.

"Come in," he called without looking up.

The door opened and Tess slipped inside, closing it behind her. Devereaux looked up in surprise and stood immediately. Her hair was braided and twisted on top of her head and her gown of peach-colored cambric brought out the delicate apricot color tinting her cheekbones. She looked young and nervous and exceptionally lovely. Clasping her hands tightly in front of her, she hesitated before speaking.

"Surely," Devereaux said gently, "I can't be all that formidable."

Tess smiled. "It isn't that." She took a deep breath. "I forgot to ask you, but have you heard anything of my husband?"

James looked at her for a long moment. "Do you think if I had I would have kept it from you?"

"No," her eyes flew to his deeply tanned face. "Last night it was late and you were very tired."

"Rest assured, if I hear anything you will be the first to know."

"Thank you." She stood there, motionless, looking at him.

"Was there anything else you wanted?" he asked politely,

moving around his desk to stand before her. He was very large, his shoulders blocking out the bookshelves and portraits behind him.

Tess shook her head.

"Come," he persuaded her gently. "It can't be that difficult. I thought you had learned to trust me." His eyes smiled down at her, warm with amusement.

At that moment Tess could have forgotten her citizenship, the pending war and her husband, everything but the brilliant light in those blue eyes, the thudding of her heart against her ribs, and the blood, dark and hot, searing a pathway through her veins.

She closed her eyes briefly. The scent of dust and old leather was familiar and comforting. "I do trust you," she said, surprised that she could find her voice.

He was about to speak when the library door rattled again. "I'm sorry, sir," the butler's dignified voice broke in, "but Captain Mottsinger is here to see you."

James sighed. "I suppose it wouldn't do to keep him waiting." He spoke to Tess. "Wait for me here. I'll return shortly."

She nodded. The library was steeped in shadows and very quiet. Tess walked to the window and pulled back the curtains, leaning her forehead against the cool glass. The clock ticked loudly, the only sound in the oppressive silence. Ten minutes passed. She sighed impatiently. Where was James?

After ten more minutes, she began to pace, her skirt accidentally brushing against a pile of papers perched precariously on the desk. They fluttered to the floor. She stooped to pick them up and caught a glimpse of the return address. It was from Mr. Rush, the American minister. Her eyes widened in disbelief and then narrowed in anger.

The door opened and closed. Tess stared at Devereaux, unable to speak.

He looked at her white face and the paper in her hand and cursed under his breath. Bracing himself, he waited for her to speak.

"How could you?" she said at last.

"Forgive me." He summoned his most charming smile.

Tess remained unmoved. "Tell me how you could possibly imagine I should remain ignorant of such a thing."

"I have no excuse," answered James, surprising her once again with his honesty. "The war began the day I met you at the American minister's residence. My only thought was to spare you grief."

"Are you sure that was your only motive, my lord?"

The skin was drawn very tightly across her bones making the hollows below her cheeks more pronounced than usual. A muscle worked in the tense line of his jaw. "Acquit me of selfishness in this, please. Georgiana wanted you here. I saw no need to upset her plans or yours because of a misguided declaration of war."

She opened her mouth, but he held up his hand to silence her. "You would never have been allowed to leave England," he explained. "I thought you would prefer to spend your time with friends rather than as a political prisoner under security in the minister's residence."

"I would rather that, than have everyone think I'm a traitor to my country," she protested.

"No one who knows you could possibly believe anything of the sort."

"What about those who don't know me?" she countered.

Devereaux smiled, sure of himself once again. "We can easily take care of that."

"What do you mean?"

"You wish to find your husband, is that not so?"

"More than anything else in the world," she replied fervently.

His mouth hardened. "How do you think it would help him if you were locked up in Mr. Rush's apartments for the duration of the war?"

"What choice do I have?"

Deliberately, giving himself time to compose his answer, he walked behind his desk and sat down in the leather chair. Pressing the tips of his fingers together he leaned his elbows on the rich mahogany.

"You could remain with us in London. As my sister's guest you will have the opportunity to mingle with the most influential men and women in England."

"Why would anyone listen to me?" She frowned.

He studied the proud tilt of her head and the silver-blond hair pulled loosely away from the clear, beautiful lines of her brow. His eyes sparkled with mischief.

"In England, men are the ones who vote, and there isn't a man alive who could resist you."

She looked startled, then to his delight, embarrassed. "Don't be absurd," she said.

"Think about it," he suggested, leaning back in his chair. "You needn't decide immediately. I'll ask for an answer when we reach London."

Tess bit her lip. There was something she needed to know and it was abysmally clear that she had nothing to lose by asking it. "James," she began tentatively.

"Yes?"

"You didn't want me to come here, did you?"

He frowned. "No. I did not."

Her voice shook ever so slightly. "Do you still feel that way?"

From across the room she could see the uncompromising stare of his level blue eyes. "More than ever," he replied tersely.

"I see." She forced a smile. "Perhaps your plan will work after all." Closing the door softly behind her, she hurried down the hall, hoping she could make it to the door of her room before bursting into tears.

Nine

Teresa Bradford took London by storm. When she and Georgiana, escorted by the duke, were announced at Lady Jersey's ball, all eyes swung toward the entrance.

The Devereauxs were tremendously popular. Georgiana was a renowned beauty and the duke, a head taller than anyone in the room, was heartbreakingly handsome in an exquisitely cut black coat and dazzling white knee breeches. But it was Tess who drew wondering murmurs from the gathered assembly.

Her gown of white satin was cut high at the waist and low at the bodice, emphasizing her petite slimness and long delicate neck. Diamonds encircled her throat, sparkled in her ears, and glistened in the loosely coiffed silvery hair. The brilliant gems were no brighter than her eyes, clear grey, and calm as the sun-steeped Atlantic after a storm. With her arm on Langley's, she passed through the entrance and into the ballroom, brilliantly lit with ten thousand candles.

A murmur of approval traveled throughout the room. Lady Marjorie Weatherby, a Titian-haired widow who hoped to become the next Duchess of Langley, turned to her companion and whitened under her rouge.

The expression on William Fitzpatrick's narrow, lightly freckled face did not bode well for her plans. He was one of her most loyal admirers, despite the rumors of her association with Langley. To see this blatant defection from her ranks both frightened and enraged her.

"So that is why Langley has kept himself hidden away in the

country," he murmured, his eyes narrowing. "Marjorie, my dear, you've been upstaged." Without even a by-your-leave he pushed his way through the crowd to Tess's side.

"Introduce me, Langley," he commanded, a dazed look on his face.

Devereaux frowned. William Fitzpatrick was twenty-seven years old and heir to a hundred thousand pounds a year. Upon his father's recent death he had inherited a seat in the House of Lords. Possessing a quick intellect, powerful friends, and a certain disreputable sense of humor, he wielded considerable influence among the ton.

James didn't trust him. There had been an incident with a serving maid, years before, and later, another young female of his acquaintance left to visit relatives in America and had never returned. There was something speculative and dangerous in the admiring brown eyes gazing at Tess, something that hinted at dark secrets and a tarnished character.

Tess looked up expectantly. The question in her eyes forced Devereaux to perform the introduction.

"Mrs. Bradford, may I present Lord William Fitzpatrick."

Lord William lifted her hand to his lips. "May I have the honor of the next waltz, Mrs. Bradford?" he asked.

"Of course," Tess smiled. "You've rescued me, m'lord. How dreadful it would be if I were a wallflower at my first London ball."

He looked down at the exquisite face that barely reached his shoulder. "There isn't the slightest possibility of that, Mrs. Bradford," he said wryly. "Devereaux, if you'll excuse us?"

With an arctic smile, the duke bowed his head and turned away.

"James." Marjorie Weatherby's husky voice reached his ears. "I've been waiting an age for you to notice me."

James looked around with a tight smile, trying to ignore the picture of Tess sailing around the room with her besotted partner.

"Nonsense, Marjorie," he teased. "I'm merely waiting for your circle of admirers to thin before I brave the crowds."

"Don't be absurd." She laughed, tapping him lightly with her fan. "Since when have we stood on ceremony with one another. You have only to ask." Pressing herself against him she looked up through her lashes. "Surely you know that by now, m'lord."

The slight smile on his lips did not extend to his eyes. He appraised the slanted green eyes and red hair, his eyes lingering on the ripe curves of her breasts, milk white and almost completely revealed, by the daring décolleté of her gown.

She smelled delicious. He couldn't remember the last time he'd taken a woman to his bed. With the knowledge that he was a cripple, all physical desire had left him, until recently, until Tess. Marjorie was an experienced woman of eight-and-twenty. She knew what she wanted and didn't expect a marriage proposal in the bargain.

Lady Marjorie purred with contentment. She slipped her arm through his. "Dancing is really such a waste of time, isn't it, James, when we could be doing something else?"

James grinned. "Bless you, Marjorie. You have a knack for saying exactly the right thing." Pulling her closer than propriety allowed, he spoke close to her ear. "I'm pledged to stay with Georgiana and her guest."

With a becoming pout, Marjorie pulled away for a brief moment. "Ah, yes," she said slowly. "The young American. How is the search for her husband coming along?"

Devereaux's face assumed its implacable expression. "We've heard nothing yet."

"I'm sure he'll turn up soon." She yawned.

"Perhaps not." Surprising himself with his vehemence, Devereaux lowered his voice. "There is a strong possibility that Daniel Bradford is dead. An impressed seaman's life aboard a battleship isn't worth a great deal."

Marjorie considered him carefully, noting the tight set of his mouth and the look of strain about his eyes. "What happens then?"

"When?" Devereaux forced himself to ignore the brown head bent closely over the blond one as the pair circled the room in an intimate waltz.

"What happens if Mrs. Bradford's husband is dead?" she repeated. "Will she be given safe passage to America?"

James looked startled, as if he had never considered such a thing. "There is no safe passage until the war is over."

"I see." Some of the light died out of the arresting green eyes. "Will she stay with Georgiana until then?"

"Yes," replied the duke. He smiled suddenly, using the strength of the Devereaux charm. "You're very inquisitive tonight. Surely we can find a more interesting subject to discuss."

She caught her breath at the look on his face and did not protest when he maneuvered her behind a large potted plant and lowered his lips to her neck. The heat of his mouth against her bare skin fanned her already ignited passions to a fevered flame. She moaned softly. "I'll go home and wait for you. Do hurry, James," she whispered. "It's been so very long."

Tess sipped her lemonade and looked on the attractive picture of the duke deep in conversation with the redheaded beauty.

"Who is that woman?" she asked Lord William.

"I've noticed no other woman in this entire room since you walked into it."

"How flattering," Tess murmured. "What did you tell Georgiana when you danced with her?"

Lord William placed his hand over his heart. "Dare I hope you were jealous?"

"Not at all," she answered coolly. "Georgiana is one of my closest friends. It is she I was interested in."

"So beautiful but so cruel."

"Please, m'lord," the grey eyes flashed dangerously, "shall we have a serious conversation or shall I go away?"

Lord William frowned. He wasn't accustomed to women who scorned flattery. This slender beauty with the coloring of an angel saw much more than he intended.

"Very well," he replied. "The woman is Marjorie Weatherby. She and Langley have an acquaintance of a longtime standing."

"Do you mean she's his mistress?"

He looked startled and then amused. Leaning against a Grecian pillar he shoved his hands into his pockets. "You are very forthright, aren't you, Mrs. Bradford?"

"Very," replied Tess emphatically. "What happened to the opera dancer?"

"Young ladies aren't supposed to ask questions like that."

Tess sipped her lemonade. "I'm not an English lady, m'lord, I'm an American."

"The duke wouldn't thank me for revealing his secrets."

"How can it be a secret when even Georgiana knows?" Tess asked bluntly. "Besides, I don't think you care whether James is pleased with you or not."

"Not only forthright, you're perceptive," Fitzpatrick murmured. "You're quite right, of course. There is no love lost between us. He dislikes my reputation."

His candor surprised her. More than that, it appealed to her.

"Apparently I'm not respectable enough to associate with the Devereauxs." His smile was tinged with bitterness. "If he sees you here with me, you'll be in for a scold."

Tess stiffened. "I'm not a Devereaux," she reminded him. "I'm a married woman. The duke is not the head of my family."

"How uncharitable of you, my dear." The silky voice of James Devereaux interrupted them. "I've searched everywhere for you, hoping to claim a moment of your time and here you are, maligning my hospitality."

Tess burned with mortification. "It wasn't like that at all," she explained through clenched teeth. "I was merely stating my position. If I choose to befriend Lord William, it is no concern of yours."

"Of course not." His lips smiled in agreement but the eyes were hard as splintered steel.

"Shall we?" He extended his arm.

Tess had no choice but to allow him to lead her away. The musicians took up their instruments. This time it was a waltz. Tess looked expectantly at the dance floor but the duke was taking her the other way, through the door of a small anteroom filled with flowers and upholstered chairs.

Without speaking they sat and watched the dancers glide to the music. Tess wanted to be with them. Her feet moved to the familiar steps and a growing awareness that he had no intention of asking her to dance filled her with impotent rage. How dare he take her away from the gaiety as if she were a recalcitrant child who did not even deserve the courtesy of his conversation, especially after the company he kept? Mutinously, she looked up.

His darkly handsome face regarded her steadily. "What have I done to make you so angry?" he asked.

Tess considered telling him the truth and decided against it. "It isn't anything you've done," she said at last, "but rather what you could do if you wished."

"It isn't like you to speak in riddles," he answered.

"You know nothing about me."

"On the contrary. I know a great deal about you and that is why I would never forbid your friendship with William Fitzpatrick."

"Do you think I would obey if you did?"

He smiled suddenly and her breath caught in her throat. He took the most unfair advantage with that smile.

"If my reasons were good enough." Skillfully he changed the subject. "What were the two of you discussing so seriously?"

Tess smiled wickedly. "You."

Devereaux looked startled. "Me! What could Fitzpatrick tell you that I couldn't?"

"I wondered who the lady was that you were embracing behind the plant."

She couldn't be sure but his dark face seemed suddenly a shade darker. "What lady?" he asked abruptly.

"Was there more than one?" She looked up innocently. "The lady I refer to is Marjorie Weatherby."

"What else did His Lordship tell you?"

She looked up at the sensual, proud mouth. Suddenly she was dangerously, recklessly angry. Ignoring the warning signals ringing in her brain, she plunged on. "Nothing I didn't already know. She's your mistress, isn't she?"

Without warning, he stood and pulled her from the chair and out the nearest set of French doors leading to the garden.

"Are you lost to all sense of decorum?" he demanded furiously when at last they stopped. His blue eyes were narrow and dangerous. "How dare you ask such a thing?"

Tess smiled sweetly. "Does it bother you more that I know of it, m'lord, or that I would say it? Because if it is the former, I should tell you that your relationship with Lady Weatherby is no secret to anyone." She was shocked at the strength of the raging anger flowing through her. The night was cold but she felt nothing, her only awareness was the lean powerful figure standing with clenched hands before her.

Devereaux stared at the pale hair and trembling lips. His own anger dissolved, replaced by something infinitely more dangerous. "Why does the idea of my having a mistress distress you so?" he asked softly.

Tess felt the tears very close to the surface. She blinked rapidly. "It doesn't distress me. Hypocrisy, however, does."

He reached into his pocket and handed her a handkerchief. "I don't understand."

She sniffed, blew her nose and handed it back to him. "You disapprove of William Fitzpatrick for the very same qualities you possess."

"I do not flaunt my private life before the world, Tess."

"No?" Her eyes were very bright. "Then what was that scene I witnessed behind the plants?"

He sighed. "Why don't you tell me what's really bothering you."

She burst into tears. For Tess it was a relief to fling the words at him. "You didn't even dance with me. I thought we were friends. I thought you liked me." She was sobbing in earnest now.

Shocked, he stared at her, the accusing words registering in his brain. She actually believed he didn't want to dance with her, that he preferred Marjorie Wetherby. Ignoring everything but the instinctive need to reassure, he stepped forward and gathered her into his arms.

"Hush, my darling," he murmured, his breath stirring the wisps of hair at her temples. "I would give ten years of my life to stand up with you." He swallowed and continued. "A good part of my left leg was removed at Badajos. I've only recently learned to walk again. Much as I regret it I'm afraid that for now, dancing is impossible, perhaps even forever."

Slowly, she lifted her head from his shoulder and stared at him, searching his face, wondering if it was possible for someone to tell such a tale and not mean it. A deep, humiliating flush traveled from her chest to her throat. What a fool she'd been. The limping gait, the tense muscles in his face, the pain he refused to acknowledge. Time and again she had chided him about his own military record and how he could never understand the conditions under which Daniel was now living. Good Lord! What must he think of her?

"I'm so sorry, James," she began.

He loosened his arms. "I've grown accustomed," he said stiffly. "Pity doesn't help."

She clung to him and shook her head. "It isn't that. I mean I'm sorry to have been so stupid. Please forgive me."

His eyes studied her face. "Of course," he said slowly.

Something was wrong. She could feel it. Something stood between the two of them, something that hadn't yet been resolved. His words came back to her. *Hush, my darling, I would give ten years of my life to stand up with you. Hush, my darling, my darling.*

Suddenly she knew. James was in love with her and if she rejected him now, this proud and brilliant man would believe that he was less than he was because of something as small and insignificant as a missing leg. She had been Nathanial Harrington's daughter long before she was Daniel Bradford's wife and the pull of character was strong within her. Keeping her eyes on James's face, she slipped her arms around his neck and pulled his head down to her mouth. His lips were firm and cool, the kiss soft and exploring.

Surprised, he lifted his head and looked at her, his glance moving to her bodice and the lovely full breasts so temptingly displayed. His throat went dry. With a muffled curse, he pulled her against him, his arms closing tightly around her. Smoothing her hair back with a shaking hand, he waited for the slightest sign of resistance. When none came, he smiled triumphantly. Lowering his mouth to hers, he kissed her again. This time, it was not soft and exploring.

For the space of a heartbeat, she remained unresponsive. Then her arms tightened. Her lips parted under the force of his tongue and she moaned as the unfamiliar roughness invaded her mouth, teasing the soft insides until she gasped with pleasure. Her fingers wove themselves through the shining black hair and she gave herself up to the delicious torment of warm hands caressing her shoulders and demanding lips moving over her face and throat.

Easing the tiny sleeve from her shoulder, his hand dipped inside her bodice, cupping her breast. She gasped. The sharp, involuntary sound inflamed him. Finding her mouth once again he kissed her deeply. Never, in his wildest fantasies, had he dreamed she would respond so completely.

Familiar sensations, long repressed, leaped to life as he breathed in the intoxicating scent of perfumed hair and skin. The meticulously honed edge of his self-control slipped away. Forgetting everything but the incredible softness of lips and skin and breasts, he pulled her tightly against the rock-hard lower half of his body. The pent-up desire of the last several weeks was too much for him. With urgent strength he eased the soft material from her shoulders. Feeling her surrender, he bared her to the waist, his mouth capturing the taut peak of a rounded breast.

Tess stiffened in his arms. It took several seconds for his befogged mind to realize she was pushing him away. With a tremendous effort of will he released her. Backing away toward the door, she pulled up her gown, a look of horror in her eyes.

"Tess," he said, stepping toward her. His eyes were black, not blue.

"No," she said, her breath coming in deep, ragged gasps.

"You must know I have wanted you since the first moment I saw you."

"I know." Her eyes were grey pools in her pale face. "But I am no Marjorie Weatherby."

Devereaux had himself under control now. He would use any power on earth to win this woman.

"Lady Weatherby was my mistress before I left for Spain. I am thirty years old, Tess. There have been a number of women in my life." He looked at her steadily. "Surely you know this is different."

Her shuddering sob tore at his heart. "How?"

"If it were possible, I would marry you," he replied harshly. "As there is little chance of that, I'll take what I can."

She stood very still in the darkness, her silvery hair surrounded by a halo of light from the candles in the ballroom.

"I must decline your hospitality once again, m'lord," she said. "Until my husband is found, I will stay at the American minister's residence."

His expression was severe, implacable, like rigid lines of carved mahogany. "Can you throw away this bit of life that is allowed us?" he asked. "Lament the circumstances, if you must, but don't deny what exists between us."

"Do marriage vows mean so little to you, that you can disregard them without a hint of remorse?" Her voice shook.

"It was you who kissed me first."

She stared at him in disbelief. "Do you think I blame you? The fault is mine. You, at least, are unmarried. It is I who played the harlot."

"You wanted me. You still want me. I won't forget that."

The promise in his words gave her cold comfort. She shivered and used his own against him.

"We have no choice, James." She slipped back through the doors into the lighted room.

For over twenty minutes he stood on the cold balcony. When, at last, he returned to the ballroom, Tess was gone and Marjorie waited.

Ten

Devereaux hailed a hackney cab to Berkeley Square. The forthcoming interview would be difficult. Marjorie had every right to be angry. But there was no help for it. The thought of bedding Lady Weatherby after holding Tess's fine-boned beauty in his arms left a taste like ashes in his mouth.

The flame from the porch lamp flickered on the massive oak-paneled door. Devereaux lifted the knocker and let it fall. Immediately the door opened and the butler ushered him inside.

"How are you, Richards?" inquired the duke. He removed his hat and cloak and handed it to the servant.

"Very well, thank you, m'lord." The dour expression on his face softened slightly. "May I say that it is very good to see you again, sir?"

Devereaux opened his mouth to speak, and hesitated. Changing his mind he asked, "Is Her Ladyship expecting me?"

"Yes, m'lord. She asks that you go straight up."

With the ease of familiarity, the duke climbed the stairs to the second landing. He knocked softly on the third door to the left and, without waiting for an answer, opened it and stepped inside.

Marjorie sat at her dressing table in a thin silk nightdress, her flame-red hair flowing over her shoulders like polished satin.

"James," she purred. "I had about given you up." She looked at him as he stood by the door. Her first thought was that something momentous had occurred. He seemed tense and alert, completely divested of the amused control that usually characterized their encounters.

She grasped the handle of the brush until her knuckles whitened. Something in the steady gaze gave him away. She stood and pulled a nightdress over her gown. Walking over to a chair by the fire, she motioned for him to sit beside her.

"You look lovely, Marjorie," he began.

"Thank you," she replied. Marjorie would not be the one to begin the conversation she knew could culminate in only one way.

He crossed to her side looking faintly embarrassed. "Even lovelier than usual."

Her green eyes flashed. "Why then, are you still wearing your coat?"

His eyes darkened and she was suddenly afraid. Biting her lip, she said, "I'm sorry, James. That was terribly rude of me."

Reaching down, Devereaux took her hands in his and pulled her to a standing position. He looked down into her face for a long moment before speaking.

"We have known each other for a long time," he said gently. "For that reason I cannot pretend something which is no longer there."

Her eyes swam with tears. "You are telling me that our connection is now over?"

"Yes." The blue eyes didn't waver from her face.

She blinked several times and smiled bravely. "Can you tell me why?"

"No," he answered. "Let us say that circumstances have changed."

She searched his face, the green eyes narrowing in dawning comprehension.

"James, what have you embroiled yourself in?"

He stiffened. "I beg your pardon?"

"There is no hope for you in all the world," she warned him. "She will only bring you grief."

"I'll handle my own affairs, Marjorie." His face was shuttered against her. "Never make the mistake of believing otherwise."

It was after two o'clock in the morning when he reached Grosvenor Square. After learning that everyone had returned from the ball, he climbed the stairs, seeking his bed with a deep sense of relief. Passing by Tess's room, he saw a light. At the sound of his footsteps, it disappeared.

Coming to a decision, he walked to the door and knocked softly. There was no answer.

"Tess." Deep and firmly authoritative, his voice penetrated through the thick wood. "Open the door."

Still no answer.

"It's a matter of some urgency." He raised his voice. "It can't wait until morning."

The door cracked slightly. "Go away," she whispered.

"Not until I say what I must."

"You've said enough," she insisted. "Nothing you can say will change anything."

"Then it won't hurt you to listen," he answered reasonably. "I promise it won't take more than a moment."

The door opened wider. Taking advantage of her indecision, he pushed it open still further and slipped inside, closing it tightly behind him.

After his eyes accustomed themselves to the dim candlelight he saw that the room was in complete disarray. Delicate cambrics and linens, shining satins and costly velvets covered the bed, spilled from the wardrobe and lined the huge travel trunk, now open in the center of the room.

"You don't waste time do you?" he observed dryly. "Are you planning to leave tonight?"

"You know I cannot." She was quick to defend herself. "It would hardly be the civil thing to do after everything Georgiana and your mother have done for me."

"I was wondering if that would weigh with you."

"Of course it does. What kind of person do you think I am?" He noticed her accent deepened when she was angry. Ignoring her question, he spoke calmly. "I have lodgings close to Westminister. I frequently stay there when I am in London. No one will be surprised if I do so now."

"How dare you?" Her voice shook with suppressed rage. "You led me to believe what you had to say was of the utmost importance. What have I done that you should insult me so?"

Confusion was quickly replaced by dawning awareness. She had mistaken him completely.

"Tess." In two steps he was standing in front of her, his hands grasping her shoulders. "You have it all wrong," he said urgently. "I merely suggested that you stay here with Georgiana. I'll move to the government lodgings. That way you won't be made uncomfortable by my presence."

Embarrassment deepened the color in her cheeks. She was grateful for the darkness.

"I can't go to parties and balls while my country is at war and my husband a prisoner," she whispered.

"You can do nothing else," he insisted. "Don't you see that the people you meet at those parties and balls are the same people who will decide your country's fate? Campaign for America, Tess. Think of it as winning sympathy for America's right to govern herself. Give us a favorable impression that will convince those who matter that Americans aren't illiterate yokels."

She lifted her chin. "I won't toady to the people who are responsible for Daniel's kidnapping."

He looked at the flawless face reflected in the moonlight, the chiseled, delicate bone structure, the smooth skin and loose pale hair. He thought of the way her mouth felt under his. Suddenly the room seemed uncomfortably hot. "All of us must compromise at some point in our lives," he said wearily.

She hesitated.

He used his final weapon, hoping his instincts were accurate. "My sister cares for you deeply."

Still she said nothing.

Desperation tinged his next words. "You have even managed to win over my mother. Surely you can't wish to hurt either of them."

Tess bit her lip. She had been neatly outmaneuvered. "Very well, m'lord," she sighed. "I'll accept your hospitality until we have word of my husband."

Devereaux released his breath. He hadn't been off the mark, after all. Loosening his hold on her shoulders he walked to the door and opened it.

"Good night, Tess," he said. His wide shoulders filled the doorway for a brief moment. Closing the door behind him, he left her alone in the darkness.

The following morning Tess found Georgiana arguing with Lizzie in the breakfast parlor.

"You promised you would take me." Lizzie's lower lip was pulled down in a definite pout. "Mother is promised to Lady Ashton today and there is no one else."

"Lizzie," Georgiana protested, "Judith isn't at all interested in gadding about London seeing sights she's seen countless times already. I promised to take you and I shall, but not today."

"Where did you wish to go, Lizzie?" Tess helped herself to a cup of coffee.

"To Piccadilly and the Tower of London," replied Lizzie, her eyes shining with excitement. "I haven't been to London since I was seven years old and probably won't again until I'm grown. Georgy promised to take me and now she won't." Her voice had risen to a wail. "She's the meanest thing in the entire world."

"Lizzie!" Georgiana laughingly protested. "That is the outside of enough. What will Tess think of us?"

"Well, it's true," said Lizzie mulishly. "Now that James is gone, I'll never see anything."

Tess's eyes met Georgiana's, a question in their depths.

The dark-haired girl nodded her head. "He's staying at his

lodgings near Westminister. Five women can be a dreadful distraction for him."

"James said he would take me if you couldn't," Lizzie pouted. "Now he isn't even living with us."

Tess flushed guiltily. Setting her cup on the table she looked at Lizzie.

"If you wouldn't mind a replacement, I'll take you," she said. "This is my first visit to London, and I should dearly like to see Piccadilly and the Tower of London."

"Truly, Tess?" Lizzie's blue eyes shone like stars. "That would be just the thing. You are married and even more respectable than Georgy."

Georgiana smothered her laughter. "Tess, you can't possibly want to spend your day with this impossible child."

Tess's eyes sparkled. "I can't think of anyone I'd rather spend my day with."

With a cry of delight, Lizzie pushed back her chair and rushed to Tess's side. Throwing her arms around her she kissed her several times on the cheek.

"We'll have the most wonderful time. I'll be ever so good, you'll see. I'll go and tell Mother." Making a face at Georgiana she ran out the door.

Georgiana sighed and looked at Tess. "You can't possibly realize what you've volunteered for. She'll wear you out before noon."

Tess laughed. "I'll manage. You forget that I have five sisters. Besides, I do want to visit the sights. Lizzie's company will relieve you of an extremely tedious day."

"I wouldn't mind at all, some other day," insisted Georgiana loyally. She looked down at the napkin in her lap. "For some reason I thought James had planned to show you about."

Tess could no more prevent the hot blush that swept across her face than she could stop the evening tides from breaking on the shores of the Chesapeake.

"No," she said, her voice very low.

"We are friends, are we not, Tess?" Georgiana's words, warm and deeply understanding, demanded an answer.

Tess sighed and looked up to meet the sympathetic blue-eyed gaze.

"Yes, Georgy. We are very good friends."

"You could do much worse, you know. My brother is really a wonderful man."

Pain and resignation shone from the wide grey eyes. "Has everyone given up hope of finding Daniel?"

Georgiana bit her lip. Reaching across the table she covered Tess's clenched hand with her own. "The frigates in the Chesapeake that night have all been thoroughly searched. Unless Daniel escaped, there is a strong possibility that he died in battle and was buried at sea."

"He could have escaped."

Georgiana hesitated and then forged ahead. "I have never known you to be a coward, love."

Tess pulled her hand away. "Is it cowardly to hope?" she asked.

"Of course not." Georgiana smiled bracingly. "All we ask is that you be prepared for the worst."

"We?" Tess inquired.

Georgiana nodded. "Would it be so terrible to stay here with us permanently?"

Tess thought of the massive Langley holdings and the icy hauteur of Leonie Devereaux. She thought of the duke's impressive title and generations of aristocratic ancestors, their portraits staring down at her from the walls of the great hall, the thousands of servants spread across nine Langley estates, and the enormous responsibilities of such a lineage.

She closed her eyes and remembered a dark face alive with laughter, a hard mouth tight with pride, softening with tenderness against her own and the blazing passion in eyes as blue as the North Atlantic in summer. Her voice when she spoke was not as firm as she intended.

"I am an American," she whispered. "How can someone without noble blood become a duchess?"

"James would never marry to please anyone other than himself." Georgiana assured her. "If he loves you, nothing else would weigh with him."

"I'm not sure the emotions I inspire in your brother can be called love," replied Tess, dryly.

"Then you are a fool, Tess Harrington," announced Georgiana, pushing herself away from the table and rising to her feet. "Surely you can see for yourself the effect James has on women. If he were only interested in what you suggest, he has the whole of London to choose from. Why would he concern himself with a skinny nobody from America who is bent on making his life difficult?"

Shocked at the lapse in Georgiana's normally beautiful manners, Tess could only stare at her. Then, all at once her lips twitched and she collapsed into gales of laughter.

"Oh, Georgy," she gasped, fighting for breath. "Surely, I'm not skinny."

Georgiana's eyes twinkled, her good humor restored. "You know I didn't mean it," she confessed. "You are the loveliest thing imaginable and I should dearly love to have you for a sister."

"You are rushing things a bit," replied Tess, completely sober once again. "It hardly seems real discussing this with you, but if Daniel is dead, rest assured I shall miss him terribly." Her voice shook. "He was my husband for only one day, but he was my friend for most of my life. To think of replacing him so quickly is indecent, not to mention immoral."

Georgiana hung her head. "Forgive me, love. I didn't even consider that."

Rising from her chair, Tess slipped her arms around her friend's slim waist. "I know what you meant. You have a good heart Georgy, but now I must get ready." She smiled. "Lizzie is waiting."

Georgiana groaned. "You'll be sorry, Tess. Don't say I didn't warn you."

Eleven

Tess and Lizzie were equally dazzled. London was filthy and exciting and incredibly crowded. The noise made their heads ache but the color and glitter bypassed even their wildest dreams.

Tess decided the Langley town carriage with its elegant horses and liveried driver and groom was an extremely comfortable way to see London. She stared out the windows at fashionable Piccadilly Square. Phaetons and barouches crowded the streets, their wheels so close to one another that Tess feared an accident would surely occur. An impressive Household Regiment rode by in perfect synchronization. Red and white brick mansions lined the wide streets, reminding her of Washington, only there were ten times their number.

On Bond Street, ladies in high-waisted gowns escorted by elegant Corinthians made Tess feel decidedly old-fashioned even though her own wardrobe, part of her trousseau, had been fashioned by an expatriated Parisian seamstress. Carlton House, where the Prince Regent lived, was like nothing she had ever seen before. Its impressive portico and lacy columns were even more amazing than the guidebook's description.

By the time they had seen the zoo and Westminister Abbey, Tess was ready to skip the Tower and Hyde Park in favor of home, but one look at Lizzie's disappointed face, changed her mind. She did, however, insist they stop for tea. Fortified with a repast of tiny ham sandwiches, hot tea, and raspberry tarts she felt revived enough to continue.

It was five o'clock when their carriage reached Hyde Park. In the late afternoon sunlight it was a place of glittering color, green foliage, and gaily dressed ladies. Gentlemen in immaculate uniforms pranced about on horses groomed to glossed perfection. Chaises and barouches promenaded terrifyingly near pedestrians who, unaware of the dangers lurking around every corner, were out for an evening stroll.

Although she knew it was extremely unfashionable to appear so provincial, Tess craned her neck as eagerly as Lizzie to gaze at the sights and sounds and smells of London.

Just ahead of their carriage, she recognized a pair of very large shoulders and a familiar dark head. James Devereaux, on a massive chestnut, was smiling down at a lovely young lady Tess recognized as Cynthia Davenport. The odious Mrs. Davenport was with her. Just as Tess was about to look the other way, hoping they hadn't been recognized, Lizzie clutched her arm.

"Tess," she said, "there's James with that hateful woman Mama wants him to marry." She turned a mischievous smile on Tess. "Let's surprise him."

Before Tess could protest, Lizzie leaned out of the carriage window and cried, "James, it's us. Do wait."

Tess flushed with embarrassment at the older woman's outraged expression, but Devereaux only grinned. Excusing himself, he missed the look of pure venom on Cynthia Davenport's face.

"How are you, brat?" he said affectionately, maneuvering his horse close to the carriage. "I see you finally arranged a chaperone for your sightseeing." He smiled at Tess.

"Oh, you mean Tess." Lizzie smiled sunnily. "She's a great sport, James. We've had the loveliest day. You can't imagine all the things we seen." She went on to describe in infinite detail the horrors of the Tower.

Throwing back his head, Devereaux shouted with laughter. "You never fail to amaze me, love," he said. "What I don't understand is that Tess looks as pleased as you do." He looked appreciatively at the tasteful burgundy pelisse molding Tess's slender figure. A chip hat, complete with matching ribbons, rested stylishly on her head. He noticed that her smile was softer than usual and those incredible eyes had lost their look of suspicion.

"Why shouldn't she look pleased?" Lizzie turned innocent eyes to the older girl. "You did have a good time, didn't you, Tess?"

"I had a wonderful time," Tess assured her. "You were very well-behaved and by far the finest tour guide I could have asked for."

Devereaux smiled indulgently and was about to speak when a well-dressed gentleman on an energetic bay rode up to the carriage and stopped. Sweeping the glossy beaver from his head, he bowed.

"How fortunate to see you again so soon, Mrs. Bradford. Devereaux, I hope I didn't interrupt."

"Not at all, Fitzpatrick." Devereaux's tone was cool. "Do you know my sister Lizzie?"

"Never had the pleasure. Glad to make your acquaintance, Miss Devereaux."

"Thank you." Lizzie, confused at the sudden change in her brother's manner, looked from James back to the newcomer and then at Tess. Seeing nothing that would give her the slightest clue, she turned away, bored with the conversation.

"James," she interrupted. "I should like to get down and walk by the lake. May I?"

"Why not?" he replied. Dismounting, he handed the reins to the groom and lifted his sister from the carriage. "A walk might do us all good."

"You won't mind if I join you?" Fitzpatrick's question hung on the air, unanswered.

Breaking the silence, Tess answered politely. "Of course not, m'lord. Please join us."

Lizzie ran ahead while Tess, walking between the two gentlemen, followed. Three children were playing with a small monkey near the edge of the lake. Their nurse hovered nearby. Lizzie ran to join them and soon her happy laughter was echoed by the two younger girls. Tess, drawn by the laughter, excused herself and walked toward the children.

Just as she reached them, the monkey pulled away from Lizzie's hold and darted into the path of a high-perched phaeton pulled by an enormous grey stallion. The child, unaware of her danger, chased after him.

Without thinking, Tess cried out and threw herself in the path of the horse, pushing Lizzie to the ground, rolling her away from the terrifying hooves. Somewhere in the background she heard a woman scream.

Devereaux, his face rigid with terror, forgot his leg and broke into a run. He fell and dragged himself up again, his only thought to stop the frightened horse with his bare hands. The animal reared up and swung aside, controlled, once again, by the strong arms of the driver.

Tess never heard his stammering questions. She held Lizzie in a gentle embrace, her gown torn and muddied, her eyes wide with horror. The child was unconscious, and blood seeped from a deep gash in her temple.

Without a word, Devereaux lifted his sister into his arms and walked to the carriage. Stepping inside, he cradled her in his arms and ordered the driver to proceed quickly to Grosvenor Square. Leaning his head out the window he shouted to Fitzpatrick.

"See Mrs. Bradford home and for God's sake, send a physician."

Tess, seeing the terrible fear in his eyes, lowered her head into blood-smeared hands and sobbed.

A steady voice attempted to soothe her. "She was merely stunned from the fall, Mrs. Bradford. I'm sure she's not seriously hurt."

"Please," Tess wiped away the tears that continued to stream down her cheeks, "take me home."

"Of course." Fitzpatrick hurried to hail a hackney. Helping her inside, he tied his mount to the rear and rode with her to the

Langley town house. At the door he stopped and lifted her hand to his lips. His eyes were warm with affection.

"Never have I seen a lady act with such selflessness. You are an amazing woman, Mrs. Bradford."

"Thank you, m'lord," answered Tess. "I only hope Lady Langley can bring herself to forgive me."

Fitzpatrick lifted his eyebrows. "You saved her child's life."

"She was in my care," Tess reminded him. "If only I had watched her more carefully, this would never have happened."

"Nonsense," Fitzpatrick spoke briskly. "You underestimate Her Ladyship. She would not be so foolish as to blame you."

"You don't understand, m'lord." Tess looked very young and forlorn standing there in her disheveled state. "I blame myself."

He ached to comfort her. Obeying the impulse of the moment, he reached out to pull her into his arms. At that moment the door opened. Litton, his face inscrutable, ushered her inside, leaving Fitzpatrick staring at the massive oak-carved entrance.

Tess lifted agonized eyes to his face. "Is she all right?" she whispered.

He pointed to the drawing room. "In there, madam."

Straightening her shoulders, Tess walked to the open door and peered inside. There, leaning against the mantel, his face an iron mask, stood Langley. On the sofa near her daughter sat the duchess, anxiously watching the doctor run his hands over the child's body.

"She seems all right," he pronounced at last. "Nothing is broken. The cut on her head will have to be stitched."

Leonie pressed the handkerchief she carried in her hand to her lips.

Lizzie's lashes fluttered. She opened her eyes and began to cry.

"Hush, love," her mother soothed her. "Everything will be all right. Are you in pain, my darling?"

"My head hurts," she whimpered.

Devereaux moved across the room to stand near his sister.

"Lizzie," his voice commanded her attention, "the doctor says your cut will need to be sewn up."

Lizzie's face went chalk white. "No!" she shrieked, "Please, no!"

Tess cringed and a strange black cloud seemed to hover about her head removing all sensation. She sat down heavily on the nearest chair and bent to rest her head in her lap. A gentle hand stroked her arm. She looked up into the sympathetic blue eyes of Leonie Devereaux. "Come, child," she said. "James has her in hand. We can do no more here."

Tess allowed the duchess to lead her out of the room into the library.

"Litton," Leonie said to the butler, "Mrs. Bradford and I should very much like a pot of tea."

"Right away, Your Grace," the butler replied and disappeared, leaving them alone.

Leonie sat down beside Tess and smiled at her disheveled appearance. The lovely burgundy pelisse was stained with blood and grime from the road. Several strands of hair had escaped from her chignon and dirt marked her cheeks and chin.

"It seems I owe you more than I can ever repay." Leonie's voice shook.

"I'm so sorry, m'lady." The grey eyes filled with tears. "I should have watched her more carefully."

The duchess reached over to squeeze Tess's hand. "James told me the entire story," she said warmly. "The fault was Lizzie's. If you hadn't acted so swiftly, she would not have survived." Her eyes filled with rare emotion. "My husband died ten years ago leaving me with five children. You may have heard that ours was a marriage of convenience, but that isn't so. He was a rare man and I miss him very much. My children are all I have left. You have given me what all the wealth and power in England could not." Her eyes burned with the effort of holding back the tears. "Bless you, my dear," she whispered, holding out her arms.

Tess responded to the warmth of the older woman's embrace with all the longing of a girl who had spent her childhood without a mother. For a timeless interval the two heads, one dark, one light, gathered comfort from each other.

Later, when the tea tray came, they sat together for almost an hour before James came into the room with the message that Lizzie was asking for her mother. Leonie rose to her feet and hurried to her daughter's side.

Devereaux stood before her, his eyes steady and reassuring. "Thank you," he said. "I don't believe I said that."

"No," her laugh was shaky. "You didn't, but it isn't necessary."

He stared at her, noting the haunted eyes framed by purple shadows, the cameo paleness of her skin, the trembling mouth, the taut, desperate pride in the set shoulders and straight back. James Devereaux had spent three years in the peninsula. He knew suffering when he saw it.

"Tess," he said, his voice firm. "Lizzie is not injured badly. She'll be up and about again in a few days."

For an embarrassing moment Tess felt like crying. She stood and walked to the mantel, blinking hack the telltale tears. James had seen enough of tears.

A strong hand, warm and comforting, grasped her arm. "Tess," he commanded, "look at me."

There was no way of avoiding him. She lifted her chin, defiantly. Let him see that she had no more control over her emotions than a child.

"You are an extraordinary woman," he said gently. "There is no disgrace in tears."

Drawing her into his arms, he pressed her cheek against the solid wall of his chest. She stood quietly allowing the fear to drain from her body. Her pulse stopped its erratic throbbing and the fierce pain in her chest subsided. The warmth of his embrace and the steady beating of his heart were the only sensations in the universe.

Slowly, Tess recovered her poise and lifted her head. "Thank you," she said, smiling.

He grinned and her legs turned to jelly. "Your servant, ma'am," was all he said.

Later, in the quiet of her room she remembered his words. His effect on her was far too devastating for comfort. In the future she must take hold of herself more carefully. Before long, she would feel as if she actually belonged here in England with the haughty Devereauxs of Langley.

Twelve

The prime minister summoned Devereaux to his office at Whitehall. He had struggled with his conscience for the better part of two days and finally came to a decision. There behind the closed door, amidst the leatherbound books and large comfortable armchairs, he would tell him, and let him deal with the matter as he saw fit. James would manage. He always had. A knock sounded on the door.

"Come in." Liverpool's gruff voice penetrated the oak paneling.

Devereaux walked in. Smiling pleasantly, he seated himself in a chair opposite the prime minister and warmed his hands at the crackling fire.

"How are you, my lord?" he asked politely.

Liverpool took in the serious, relaxed figure of the duke of Langley, observing his capable hands and quiet strength. Immediately he felt better.

"I've news for you, James. Unfortunately, it isn't good."

Devereaux liked Lord Liverpool. He respected his honesty and admired his abilities. Whatever happened, he knew the prime minister would hold nothing back.

"Go on," he said.

"Mottsinger has lost *The Macedonian*. An American privateer shot away all of her top masts."

James thought of Charles Mottsinger as he last saw him, the merry brown eyes and jubilant smile. His hands clenched.

"What of her captain?" he asked quietly.

"Charles has been taken prisoner," replied the prime minister. "It's probably just as well. He'll be court-martialed for his actions. Never in the history of the world has a British frigate struck her colors to an American ship."

"How many does this make? asked James.

"What do you mean?"

Devereaux was brutally honest. "First *The Constitution* escaped five British vessels by damping her sails and starting her water, tricks as old as time. Nevertheless, our own exemplary captains have never even heard of them. In August," the relentless voice continued, "she came up against our own *Guerriere,* off the coast of Nova Scotia, and within ten minutes our ship had lost her mizzenmast and was so badly damaged she had to be set afire and abandoned. Now, we've lost *The Macedonian.*" His blue eyes blazed contemptuously. "When will you realize we have neither the manpower nor the inclination for a war with America?"

"We haven't lost yet," replied Liverpool.

"Given enough time we'll manage that as well," promised Devereaux.

"They've ten frigates and eight small cruisers," protested Liverpool. "We've over a thousand vessels."

"All employed in Europe," Devereaux retorted. "We've also no one to compare with officers like Isaac Hull and Stephen Decatur." The flickering light from the flames cast dark shadows across his face. "The Admiralty finds it difficult to send even a squadron to the western Atlantic. When and if the time ever comes, our Navy will be so demoralized it won't be worth the effort."

"This conversation is most edifying," the prime minister snapped, "but it isn't why I sent for you."

Devereaux looked up in surprise. His voice was surprisingly humble. "Why did you send for me, sir?"

Liverpool spared him nothing. "The American frigate, *The United States,* came up against *The Java* three weeks ago. Among the prisoners of war was one Daniel Bradford."

Devereaux's eyes were sharp as splintered glass. *"The Java* was outfitted in England less than eight weeks ago," he said. "Mr. Bradford was not on board."

"He was on the American ship," explained the prime minister. "Apparently he was exchanged some weeks before and had not yet reached port."

"I see." The cryptic words spoke volumes.

"No," contradicted Liverpool. "I don't think you do. Mr. Bradford was taken to Dartmoor prison. He died of pneumonia two weeks ago."

A muscle jumped in the taut skin of Devereaux's jaw. Given the enormity of the information he had received, there was nothing left to say. His face completely expressionless, he rose from his chair and bowed.

"Good day, my lord," he said and left the room.

Tess sat on a low stool near the couch where Lizzie lay propped up on pillows. The two were playing a game of cards in the sitting room. Devereaux paused near the door. His first thought was that she looked very young, almost as young as his sister, and very happy. The next was that he would be the one to destroy her.

James Devereaux waged a bitter battle within himself. With the candor that was part of his nature, he admitted the death of Daniel Bradford was a welcome relief. The elusive Mr. Bradford stood in the way of something he wanted more than anything in the world. He knew now, why none of the women who had thrown out lures to him since his first season held any permanent appeal. He had waited, wanting something different, something he hadn't known existed, until that day in the American minister's sitting room when Teresa Bradford held out her hand.

That very quality that drew him, the one that made her unique from every other woman he had known, was the very thing that would make her deny him. She was beautiful and brilliant. She was also loyal and principled. Devereaux knew, as surely as he knew himself, that she would run from him as quickly as a ship could be found to brave the blockade, and spirit her across the Atlantic to the safety of Nathanial Harrington's house on the Chesapeake. Taking a deep breath, he stepped into the room.

"Hello," he said softly.

Lizzie turned her head, a delighted smile on her face. "James," she showed him her cards. "See, I'm winning."

He had eyes only for Tess. His answer to Lizzie was sensible enough, but it lacked the warmth she was accustomed to.

"So you are," he replied, "but if Tess is as skilled at cards as she is at chess, you are only fooling yourself, brat."

Lizzie frowned. James was thinking of something else as he was so often lately.

Tess searched his face and knew at once that something was wrong. He looked tense, as if his nerves were on edge, like a tightly strung bow. She sensed that the slightest pressure would cause him to snap in two.

Gathering her cards together, she gave Lizzie a meaningful look. "I think we've had enough of card games for now. I've letters to write." She rose gracefully to her feet. "If you'll excuse me."

"Not yet." James looked at Lizzie. "I'll carry you back to your room," he said, "and later I'll come up. But now, I must speak to Tess privately."

Lizzie looked carefully at her brother's face and then nodded without protesting. With no apparent effort, he lifted her into his arms and carried her up the stairs.

Tess walked to the window and looked out on the square. She was still there when Devereaux came back into the room. He was reminded of the first time they met. She looked at him then, as she did now, her eyes mirroring the same mixture of suspicion and anxiety. He came directly to the point.

"I'm terribly sorry, Tess. The news isn't good."

Her face whitened. "What is it?"

"Daniel died two weeks ago."

"How?" The single word came out as a harsh gasp.

Devereaux, fearful of the bleached white of her face, stepped forward and gripped her arms above the elbow. He would give anything to spare her further pain. But he knew of no way to soften the truth.

"He contracted pneumonia at Dartmoor Prison."

Horrified eyes met his. Her mind went numb as she recalled the rumors of that dreadful prison in Devonshire where damp fog and freezing rains reduced even the healthiest man to a skeleton of his former self. At Dartmoor men ate rats for lack of food, drank from muddy puddles of rainwater that collected in their cells and eventually died of smallpox.

"All this time, he was here in England and I never knew? We might have found him, if we'd only known." She bit back a sob. "I'll never forgive myself for this."

Devereaux shook her slightly. "Stop it, Tess. Your husband was a grown man. He was captured by a British frigate while fighting on an American ship. If he had been a mere passenger, he would have been exchanged." His eyes narrowed, searching her face. There was something familiar and disturbing in the pale cheeks and pinched blue lips. Cursing fluently, he slid his arm beneath her knees just as they buckled and she collapsed against his chest.

Lifting her into his arms, he shouted for Litton as he carried Tess's limp body up the stairs. She barely weighed more than Lizzie. Miraculously the butler appeared at his elbow.

"Send for the physician," he ordered. "Mrs. Bradford is in shock."

"Right away, sir."

"James," Leonie appeared at the top of the landing. "What on earth is the matter?" Her eyes widened in alarm as she spied the unconscious form supported in his arms.

"Quickly," she hurried to the door of Tess's bedchamber and threw it open. "In here." Pulling off the satin spread, she moved aside for James to lay Tess on the bed and watched him remove her leather half-boots and tuck the blankets around her.

"The doctor should be here shortly," he said, moving to the grate to stir the embers to greater warmth.

"What happened?" Leonie asked.

"Daniel Bradford died two weeks ago."

Leonie sat down on the side of the bed and smoothed the pale hair from Tess's forehead.

"The poor child," she murmured.

Devereaux stared at his mother. Rarely were her emotions stirred by anyone outside her immediate family. Tess had indeed worked a miracle if she could invoke sympathy in the outwardly cold and unapproachable Duchess of Langley.

Twenty minutes later Tess was awake and the doctor was checking her pulse.

"You've given everyone a scare, young lady," he said. "What have you got to say for yourself?"

Tess smiled faintly and turned her head to the wall. Frowning, the doctor motioned for Devereaux to follow him out of the room.

"Is there somewhere we can speak privately?" he asked.

James led the way to the drawing room where Leonie waited with Georgiana and Judith. Georgiana stood immediately and ran toward him clutching at his coat.

"Will she be all right?" she asked anxiously.

Devereaux smiled down at her and covered her hands with his. "The doctor is here to tell us what we must do to make her feel better."

The doctor cleared his throat. "She's had a nasty shock. From what I understand she's no more than a girl, without her family and quite alone."

"She's not alone," protested Judith. "She has us."

"Hush, dear," her mother warned. "The doctor is merely telling us what he perceives." She turned her wonderful smile on the gentleman. "Isn't that so, Doctor?"

He blushed furiously. "Just so, Your Grace. It was not my intent to offend."

"Of course not," Leonie reassured him. "Now, please tell us what we must do for our guest."

"She needs absolute quiet, Your Grace, and rest. London, at the height of the season, isn't the place for her at all. With the proper care, she should be herself in no time."

"I see." Leonie walked to the door and held it open. "May I offer you something to drink before you leave?"

He blinked in surprise. "If you don't mind, Your Grace. I am rather parched."

The butler suddenly appeared out of nowhere. "Litton will take care of that." Leonie's smile was frosty as she closed the door behind him.

"That wasn't kind of you," Devereaux's amused voice chided her.

"He was odious," broke in Georgiana. "Imagine, telling us that Tess feels alone in England." Her nostrils quivered with indignation.

"He was positively insulting," Judith agreed.

Devereaux walked to the mantel. Propping his boot on the fender he stared into the fire. "Perhaps she does feel that way," he suggested, his voice troubled and low.

"James!" cried Georgiana, "You can't be serious. We love Tess dearly. She knows that." She turned toward her mother. "Doesn't she, Mama?"

Leonie was silent, her eyes on the ravaged face of her son. The lines around his mouth were deep with suffering.

"She is little more than a girl," he said slowly. "Alone, she crossed an ocean hoping to find her husband at the end of her journey. Instead her country declared war, virtually banishing her from her family for an indefinite period. Now, her husband is dead and her future unsure." A shadow crossed his face and he continued with difficulty. "Tess may need more than kindness in the weeks and months to come. Her husband died in an English prison. Despite our efforts she may never forgive us."

The silence was oppressive. No one moved for what seemed an eternity. Finally Leonie spoke.

"Tell us what to do, James?"

He flashed his brilliant smile. Crossing the room he took her hands in his and kissed her cheek. "Bless you, Mother. That streak of obstinacy in your character may be just the medicine Tess needs."

"Nonsense." Leonie sniffed. "I merely know my duty."

"Very well." He was all business, once again, thoroughly in command of the situation. "You and the girls will return to Langley." He turned toward his sister, his face softening.

"I know it will be disappointing for you, Georgy, but if Tess is feeling better, you'll be back before the season is over."

"I don't mind," answered Georgiana loyally.

Devereaux smiled. "Good girl."

"Will you return with us?" The question was innocent enough, but Devereaux didn't miss the challenge in his mother's words.

"No," he answered. "I'll stay here in London."

Relief reflected itself in the duchess's blue eyes. "We'll miss you, but I do believe that would be best for all of us."

Thirteen

The lines around Devereaux's eyes deepened in amusement as he read the letter from Nathanial Harrington.

"It rather sounds like he means to call you out," Castlereagh observed from his seat by the window.

The two men were at White's, an exclusive gentlemen's club, furnished with heavy dark furniture, muted crimson carpeting and an air of elegance that spoke of thin blue blood and generations of tradition.

"I wouldn't blame him if he did," Devereaux remarked. "I wrote to him after war was declared. Apparently he wasn't satisfied with my credentials. If it wasn't for Caroline, I'm sure he would have found a way to arrive on my doorstep."

It was obvious that Mr. Harrington was torn between raging anger and his own reasonable practicality. Despite the duke's assurances that Tess would be well cared for, her father was furious and demanded that his daughter be returned as soon as it was safely possible.

Devereaux, trying to decipher Harrington's less-than-legible penmanship, finally managed to make out the remainder of the letter. He paraphrased it for Castlereagh.

"I am to carry a message to Tess from her father. The British, according to Mr. Harrington, are presumptuous beasts and Mr. Madison a fool to allow honest Americans to embroil themselves in a fight that isn't theirs." James frowned, hesitating before continuing the next sentence. Clearing his throat, he went on.

"He is devastated over the news of Daniel's death, but Tess is young yet, and will find her own happiness. He ends by saying that she is his dearly beloved daughter and anyone who dares take advantage of her unprotected status will answer to him. She must take care and not be a bother to the Devereauxs, but remember that an American citizen may hold up her head with pride anywhere in the world. He remains her affectionate father and looks forward to her return."

"I'm afraid your letter did little to reassure him," Castlereagh remarked, pouring himself a glass of claret. "He seems a rather violent fellow."

"He also happens to be the most progressive shipbuilder in America," Devereaux replied. "Mark my words, we'll hear much of him once trade is reestablished."

Castlereagh sipped his wine and looked at his friend. Devereaux was dressed for the evening in a black coat and snow-white waistcoat, shirt and cravat. The grim look on his face did not belong to a man bent on a night of pleasure.

"What is wrong, James?" The calm voice demanded an answer.

Devereaux looked startled for a moment and then laughed. His voice sounded harsh to his own ears.

"I've been too long from Langley. London doesn't suit me."

"Then, why not go home?" Castlereagh asked.

Lifting his wineglass to eye level Devereaux stared at the ruby liquid. His thoughts, behind the shuttered blue eyes, were his own. Finally, he turned to meet his friend's sympathetic gaze.

"I had thought to give a certain young woman more time. Perhaps you are right and I should try my hand."

Castlereagh twisted the stem of his glass between thin fingers. "Why do I know, without a doubt, you aren't speaking of Cynthia Davenport?"

Devereaux grinned. "Because you have seen Teresa Bradford."

Nodding his head, Castlereagh smiled. "She would be a fool to refuse you."

Laughing unsteadily, Devereaux shook his head. "The strange

thing is, it is my title and fortune she objects to. Otherwise she would have me, missing leg and all."

Lord Castlereagh did not think it proper to bring up his wife's comment when he had mentioned that James's having only one leg, might cause him to suffer for female companionship. *If James Devereaux were missing both legs and an arm, he would still be the most desirable man in the room,* she had said quite emphatically. "What an odd young woman," Castlereagh remarked instead.

"Tess is an American," he explained. "Nathanial Harrington didn't inherit his money, he earned it. For Tess, there is no dishonor in trade. She doesn't care for titles and considers it vulgar to have more than one estate."

"If what you say is true," Castlereagh's dark eyes gleamed, "and she accepts your offer, you may have found the one woman in the world who wants you for yourself. That is a rare privilege, James. Don't let it slip away."

Devereaux swallowed the rest of his wine in one gulp and stood up. "I don't intend to, m'lord. Wish me luck."

"You have it. Take care, James."

October passed unnoticed by Tess. At first it had been pleasant to do nothing but sit in the sun-warmed grass and wallow in her pain. It was harvest time at Langley. The air was filled with smells of autumn, of apples and cider and cinnamon and baking. Tess sat in the garden eating apple meringues and apple turnovers, apple cakes laced with spice and apple tarts topped with cream, until even Georgiana protested.

"You can't go on like this. It may not show now, but soon you'll need a seamstress to let out your gowns. James won't believe it when he sees you."

At the mention of his name, Tess suddenly lost her appetite. Abandoning the last bite of her tart, she asked, "Do you expect him home soon?"

Georgiana closed her eyes, allowing her head to fall back against the chair. The sun was comfortably warm.

"He hasn't said. But Langley is his home. He'll turn up soon enough."

Dusting the powdered sugar from her skirt, Tess pulled her straw hat down shielding her face from Georgiana's curious eyes. Her heart pounded. The serene, closed-in garden suddenly seemed a prison. His very name, spoken aloud for the first time in two months, broke down the barriers. Forcing herself to admit the truth, she faced her private terror.

The long sleepless nights, the frustrated tears, the pain of her loss, the leaping fire in her veins and the tearful prayer that life couldn't be so cruel, not when so much was still new and unexplored, were not all for Daniel Bradford. Her love for Daniel was the love of a girl for a lifelong friend. Perhaps it would have deepened into more as time marched on, or if she had never met James Devereaux. But she had.

With her usual uncompromising honesty, Tess admitted to herself that she missed him dreadfully. He was the life and breath and heartbeat of the female household that revolved around his presence. Everything became brighter and more intense when James was around. Leonie glowed from within. Georgiana, Judith, and Lizzie exerted themselves to be charming. Even the cook managed culinary masterpieces when his master was in residence. And now, Tess knew, she also had been captured in the net of his aura.

Her need was far greater than the natural longing of a mother for her son, or sisters for their brother, or even that of a woman for a male companion. It was a desire far more intense and impossibly dangerous. Tess wanted James Devereaux with the craving hunger of a woman who had tasted the promise of passion only to be pulled back from fulfillment, time after frustrating time.

November dragged more slowly as the pain of her grief dulled. The sun came out in an unusual burst of warmth and for a week the inhabitants of Langley basked in the lovely weather. The air was crisp, the skies blue, and the sunshine brilliant. The last of the autumn leaves were a dark crimson and the wild mustard glowed golden in the lingering sunsets.

Leonie and the girls were kind and understanding, never leaving her alone until her need for privacy became so great, she begged a mount from the stables and took long, invigorating rides around the countryside. The tenants of Langley clucked with sympathy as they watched the slim, blue-clad figure roam the estate day after day, for hours at a time, seeking no particular destination.

One morning at breakfast, the duchess handed her a letter. The penmanship was bold and masculine, a hand Tess didn't recognize. Tearing it open, she saw that it carried a letter from her father and a short message from James. Excusing herself, she made her way to the privacy of the library before reading either correspondence.

Nathanial Harrington's words brought tears of laughter to her eyes and a warm flush to her cheeks. Plain-speaking and blessedly predictable, her father ferreted through the trappings of the whole tangled mess to the very heart of the matter, managing to bring order and calm to her world.

The message from James shattered her newly found peace of mind.

My Dear Tess,

   I shall return to Langley before Christmas. There is a matter of some importance which must be settled between us.

James

As Christmas neared, Tess was so restless and filled with such anxiety that even the tears wouldn't come. She lay at night in her bed staring into the lonely darkness with hot cheeks, remember-

ing the taste of firm lips against her own and the comforting feel
of strong arms holding her close.

Dreams of the graceful white house on the banks of the
Chesapeake intruded into her shameful thoughts. What she
wouldn't give for one deep breath of salty air, laced with the
scent of mussels and crayfish. Closing her eyes, she would imagine lights flashing across the misty bay and the soft keening moan
of the wind as it filled the clippers' sails, whipping the slim-
hulled boats across the channel and out to sea.

When winter finally descended upon the countryside, the residents of Langley confined themselves indoors. Fires crackled in
the hearths. Rain and wind slanted against stone gables. The
colors of the countryside faded to a dreary, lifeless grey.

Tess chafed at the endless waiting, the desolate ceaseless rain
and the uncertainty of her future. The golden cast of her skin
had faded, emphasizing the smattering of freckles across her
small, straight nose. Wrapped in a warm shawl, she spent long
silent days by the fire in the library, her eyes staring at the same
page for hours on end.

Late one night, less than a week before Christmas, when sleep
again eluded her, she heard a sound downstairs. Straining her
ears she listened again. There was nothing. Throwing aside the
covers, she lit a candle and opened the door. Tiptoeing to the
landing she peered down the stairs.

Litton and the valet were whispering softly and arming themselves with luggage. But Tess shook with trembling awareness
for only one man.

His coat and boots were wet with rain. Those massive shoulders and the unconscious arrogance he carried with him at all
times were exactly as she remembered. He looked vital and
brown and painfully alive.

Tess moved slightly, her candle adding to the flickering shadows on the tapestried wall.

Devereaux glanced up and saw her. Immediately he started
toward the stairs. For a brief instant she saw the question in the
blue eyes and then she saw his smile. It was filled with something

that stole the breath from her lungs. With no thought other than the incredible pleasure of touching him, she ran down the stairs and threw herself into his arms.

He held her tightly against his heart. "Be careful," he warned, his voice muffled against her hair, "I'm wet. I've already doused your candle."

She cared nothing for the wetness that was already dampening the linen of her nightshift. She heard only the hammering of a heart that beat in unison with hers and the whispered murmur of words against her throat proclaiming beyond all doubt that his longing was as great as her own.

Slipping his arm beneath her knees, he lifted her against his chest and climbed the stairs. He was very tired and his gait was awkward, but the warmth of her welcome gave him strength.

Tess clasped her arms around his neck and lay her head on the wide shoulder. With every step toward her chamber she quivered in anticipation. Her thin night shift, damp from rainwater, clung to the curves of her breasts and hips, revealing the lovely lines of her legs.

Setting his jaw, Devereaux waged a battle with himself. This was the only woman in the world he wanted. From her response he knew she needed only the slightest encouragement and she would submit to him. The temptation was great. He looked at the long slender neck, the fall of silvery hair and the clear, thickly lashed eyes, slanted and filled with desire. Her lips trembled.

Succumbing to an instinct older than time, he bent his head, seeking her mouth. A low moan from the back of her throat enflamed him, and all resolutions dissolved at the velvet softness of her touch. His control snapped. Parting her lips with his tongue he plundered the soft recesses of her mouth, deepening his kisses, refusing to allow her even to breathe until, heart pounding, she pulled away, drinking in deep, rasping lungsful of air.

Pushing aside the door of her room, he lay her on the bed, breathing harshly, staring down at her. The pupils of her eyes were completely dilated, the invitation unmistakable.

She looked very young and very vulnerable. Sanity returned. Clenching his jaw, he pulled the bedcovers around her and ran his forefinger down the delicate bridge of her nose. Kissing her brow lightly, he relaxed and smiled, in control once more.

"Sleep well, my love," he said, and stood up to leave.

Tess clutched his hand in a desperate grip.

"Why?" she demanded.

Fingers of moonlight crept through the window bathing her face in a netherworld glow. The humiliation in her eyes haunted him. He wanted nothing more than to assuage the tension burning through every fiber of his being and bury himself in the heat of her golden flesh. Calling forth the self-discipline of a soldier, he returned the pressure of her hand before releasing it. He stood above her, his eyes intent on her face.

"I want more from you than this." His voice was strained. "Perhaps it would be better to give you more time, but I find I cannot wait any longer and still retain my sanity. Since you are neither a fool nor a dissembler, and by far the most direct female I've ever known, you won't pretend to misunderstand me." His eyes glinted steel-blue in the moonlight. "You were correct all along, my love. Marriage vows are very important to me. Anything less, between us, is impossible." Without waiting for an answer, he left the room.

Numb with disbelief, Tess stared for a long time at the closed door.

Fourteen

Tess didn't come down to breakfast the next morning. Instead, she requested coffee and toast sent up on a tray to her room. While the enthusiastic Devereauxs welcomed back the head of their household, she busied herself in the stables practicing the art of applying a bran poultice to an open wound. Wrapped in a muffler and coat, she spent the afternoon riding across the frozen fields of Langley, returning too late for tea. Pleading a headache, she retired to her room carving a path in the expensive carpet with her nervous pacing.

The duke, attempting to plead his case, found her polite, charming and maddeningly elusive. As she continued to find excuses for her absence, his amusement deepened. Knowing the battle she fought with herself, he bided his time. The moment came sooner than he expected.

Several mornings later, while reading over a dispatch in his office, he heard a discreet knock. Without waiting for an answer, Tess opened the door and slipped inside.

Devereaux rose to his feet. "Hello," he said moving toward her.

Involuntarily, she stepped backward, losing some of her courage. He was very large standing over her, his face dark and unsmiling.

"Do I make you uncomfortable, Tess?"

She shook her head.

"I returned to Langley because I thought there was hope for me. Was I wrong?"

YOU ARE CORDIALLY INVITED TO GE SWEPT AWAY INTO NEW WORLDS OI PASSION AND ADVENTURE.

AND IT WON'T COST YOU A PENNY!

Receive 4 Zebra Historical Romances, Absolutely Free!
(A $19.96 value)

Now you can have your pick of handsome, noble adventurers with romance in their hearts and you on their minds. Zebra publishes Historical Romances That Burn With The Fire Of History by the world's finest romance authors.

This very special FREE offer entitles you to 4 Zebra novels at absolutely no cost, with no obligation to buy anything, ever. It's an offer designed to excite your most vivid dreams and desires...and save you almost $20!

And that's not all you get...

Your Home Subscription Saves You Money Every Month.

After you've enjoyed your initial FREE package of 4 books, you'll begin receive monthly shipments of new Zebra titles. These novels are delivered direct to your home as soon as they are published...sometimes even before th bookstores get them! Each monthly shipment of 4 books will be yours to examine for 10 days. Then if you decide to keep the books, you'll pay the pr ferred subscriber's price of just $4.00 per title. That's $16 for all 4 books...a savings of almost $4 off the publisher's price.

We Also Add To Your Savings With FREE Home Delivery!
There Is No Minimum Purchase. And Your Continued Satisfaction Is Guarantee

We're so sure that you'll appreciate the money-saving convenience of home delivery that we guarantee your complete satisfaction. You may return any shipment...for any reason...within 10 days and pay nothing that month. And if you want us to stop sending books, just say the word. There is no min mum number of books you must buy.

It's a no-lose proposition, so send for your 4 FREE books today!

*A $19.96
value.
FREE!*

*No obligation
to buy
anything, ever.*

ZEBRA HOME SUBSCRIPTION SERVICE, INC.

120 BRIGHTON ROAD

P.O. BOX 5214

CLIFTON, NEW JERSEY 07015-5214

"No," she whispered, her voice deserting her.

The blue eyes were alight with something that took her breath away.

"I once asked you a question that is very important to my happiness. Have you come to give me an answer?"

"You never asked me anything," she protested. "From the beginning you said I was an obligation. Then, you spoke of taking what you could get." She flushed, the words tumbling across her tongue. "When you returned and it was obvious how I felt, you changed your mind and would have none of it." He was very close. She fastened her eyes on the leaping blood in the brown column of his throat. "I'm not at all sure of your intentions."

His eyes warmed with laughter. "Shall I show you?" he asked.

Reassured by the expression on his face, she smiled and held out her arms. "Yes, please. I've missed you dreadfully."

He reached for her, his arms tightening possessively as he bent his head to kiss her. The feel of his lips, warm and firm, on her mouth, the strength of his hands and the hard lean body pressed close to her own, was an exquisite torment she wanted never to end.

He pulled away at last, smoothing the hair away from her face. "I fell in love with you from the very first moment I saw you. I'm sorry about Daniel, Tess, but I don't know what I would have done had you not been widowed." He sounded very unlike himself. "You've put me through the worst kind of hell."

"I know," she whispered. "It was that way for me, too."

He kissed the tip of her nose. "When shall we set the date?"

Tess closed her eyes and swallowed. Leonie Devereaux's thin, disapproving face appeared before her. "What about your family?"

"They love you nearly as much as I do."

"As a guest perhaps, or a friend, but not as your wife." Tess's eyes clouded.

"You will not be marrying my family."

"How can I become an English lady?"

He looked at the proud, straight back, the thin, finely drawn features and the regal way she held her head. If he searched through all the stuffy drawing rooms in England, he would never find another more suited to be his duchess.

"You will be the most unusual duchess England has ever known," he assured her.

She was not convinced.

The warmth left his face. "Is there another reason you don't wish to marry me, Tess?"

She looked confused. "What do you mean?"

He searched her face for a long time and then he smiled again. Sliding his hands up her shoulders, he bent his head and pressed his mouth to her neck.

"I love you," he murmured, his breath warm against her throat. "Please, say yes."

She closed her eyes. Slipping her arms around his neck, Tess wove her fingers through the velvety, black hair. Melting against him, her skin absorbed the heat of his lean, muscled frame. It was difficult to breathe.

He bent her back across his arm, his mouth finding the pulse point at the base of her throat.

"Say yes," he demanded, deepening his kiss. "Damn you, Tess, say it." His hand closed over her breast.

She gasped and opened her eyes, pale and clear as water. His expression was transparent, no longer guarded, the emotions clearly spelled out for her to see. He breathed as though he had been running.

A brilliant smile curved her lips. "Yes, James," she said. "I will marry you."

The radiant happiness on his face was a difficult thing to look upon. Tess blinked back tears. She pressed her cheek against his lapel.

"Finish your work," she whispered. "I'll see you at dinner."

"Shouldn't we announce our news?" he asked.

"Not yet." There was a breathless quality to her voice, as if she held something back. "Dinner is a better time. The entire family will be together."

"Very well." He lifted her hand to his lips. "Then, we'll discuss a wedding date. You won't keep me waiting longer than necessary, will you, darling?"

She shook her head, smoothed back her hair and left the study.

Devereaux stared at the closed door. The once comfortable room seemed dark and gloomy. Picking up the letter, he settled back in his chair. It was difficult to concentrate. An unsettled feeling, as if something were not quite finished, came over him.

"What is it, child?" Leonie set down her pruning shears, her lovely voice reflecting concern.

Tess was acting most unlike herself. Her flushed face and the rapid rise and fall of her chest indicated a state of agitation totally unlike the calm serenity with which she normally faced the world.

"Please, Your Grace," she clasped her hands tightly before her. "There is something I wish to ask you."

"Of course, dear."

"I think you should be seated."

Leonie's eyes narrowed. She removed her gloves and obediently moved toward the bench near the door of the conservatory. Tess followed and sat down beside her.

"James has asked me to marry him."

"I see." Leonie's mouth was very severe. "And what was your answer?"

Tess spoke in a low steady voice. "I said yes."

The duchess felt as though a very large and heavy boot had kicked her in the stomach. It was one thing to harbor suspicions, it was another to have them confirmed without a doubt.

"Then there is nothing more to say," she replied.

"He has told me a marriage between us is possible. Is that so?"

There was a moment's silence as the duchess considered Tess. Her mouth softened. The girl was lovely and honest and proud.

If she were English and of noble blood, the match would be cause for great celebration.

"If you truly care for my son," Leonie said gently, "you will not marry him."

"I see."

Leonie forced herself to ignore the hurt in Tess's eyes. "No, I don't think you do. If James were anyone other than he is, the marriage would have my complete approval. If I had a second son, there is no one I would rather have for my daughter-in-law than you."

"Say no more, Your Grace." Tess moved as if to stand up. Leonie's hand detained her.

"James is not like other men," she explained. "He's certainly not perfect. But, he has a sense of purpose that is entirely missing in most wealthy young men of his generation." She searched for words. "The wildness, the drinking, the utter boredom that characterizes our nobility isn't necessary for James. He has it in him to become a very powerful force in the country. He needs a wife from his own order, one who agrees with his political convictions." She squeezed her hand. "Do you understand what I'm trying to tell you?"

Tess stared at the blue fire in Leonie Devereaux's eyes and thought what a terrible waste it was that a woman could not run for political office.

"You needn't worry, ma'am. I shall not marry him."

The look on her face caused Leonie to avert her eyes. "I'm terribly sorry, my dear."

"So am I," Tess replied softly.

Her meeting with James was even more difficult. She found him on the way to the stables. Following him into the empty tack room, Tess came directly to the point.

"I made a mistake. I can't marry you. I'm sorry."

"You damn well are going to marry me!" The grooves in his

cheeks were stark and forbidding, as if they had been carved from stone.

Tess lifted a trembling hand to her temple. "Must we prolong this pain? Can't you see I'm not the proper wife for a British politician?"

"What is the proper wife for a politician?" Like knife blades, his words sliced through her argument.

The pearl-like skin tightened across her cheekbones. She clenched her hands into tight fists.

"Someone who knows about your way of life. Someone who was born to be regal and dignified and spends her days holding teas and her nights giving parties. Someone who can speak to servants and heads of state without embarrassing you." Her voice carried a sharp, bitter quality. "Someone who can single-handedly run your disgustingly massive estates, give you sons to carry on your precious line, and most important of all, someone who can live up to your mother."

Devereaux stared at her, fascinated. The tight rein, with which she held her emotions in check, had broken at last. She was furiously, splendidly angry. His lips twitched.

"Then I'm destined to remain a bachelor."

"Why?"

"The paragon you described doesn't exist. If you won't have me, I won't marry at all."

"Nonsense."

"I mean it, Tess."

The anger drained from her. "I can't marry you, James."

His heart ached at the hopelessness in her words. He ran his hand through his hair. Never before had he come up against a force he could not move. He tried once more.

"Tell me you don't love me."

Her face was too pale. "I don't love you," she repeated automatically.

His grin pierced her heart. "You'll have to do better than that."

She lost her temper and turned her back on him. "I don't have to do anything at all. Go away and leave me alone."

"Tess." His voice was low, caressing. "Do you think love goes away because one denies that it exists?"

"I don't love you." She refused to look at him.

"Yes, you do," he said gently. "One day I'll make you admit it."

Without another word he walked out of the room leaving her alone. Tess was utterly miserable. She never dreamed he would give up so easily.

Snow crunched under Devereaux's boots as he walked back to the castle. His mouth was grim. Under no circumstances would he allow Tess to have her way in this. Her sense of morality was completely American and he intended to use it to his advantage.

When James Devereaux wanted something he inevitably got it and he wanted Tess Bradford with a passion that consumed his waking hours and left his sleep haunted with dreams of pale gold hair and water-clear eyes. She was almost within his grasp and this time he would ensure that she wouldn't slip through his fingers.

The evening began as usual. The family gathered for dinner and later retired to the drawing room where Georgiana played the piano. Lady Langley kept up a light, easy flow of conversation and, at nine o'clock, the tea tray was brought in. Lizzie yawned and was sent up to bed while Tess and Judith played an uninspired game of chess.

James was pleasant and charming, as if his marriage proposals were refused every day, Tess thought bitterly. How dare he act as if everything were normal? She recklessly moved her rook into a new position.

"Check." Judith clapped her hands in delight. "I'm actually going to win this time."

James stifled a grin. He took a perverse pleasure in watching Tess's composure crumble. Despite the troubled eyes and pale cheeks, she looked magnificent. The gown of cream Italian silk brought out the slender elegance of her figure and the golden highlights in her hair. Pearl combs pulled the shining mass away from her face allowing it to fall in a silken curtain to her waist.

At ten o'clock, Tess could stand it no longer. Complaining of fatigue she went up to bed. Rosie brushed out her hair and helped her into a cotton nightgown. Blowing out the candle she wished her mistress good-night and closed the door behind her.

Tess was still lying sleepless at one o'clock, when the door opened and James walked in. Moonlight streamed in from the window, illuminating his head. His hair was so black it shone blue in the shadowy darkness. It was his face that frightened her. There was a look of determination, so intense on the tight-lipped features, that she knew nothing could stop him from his purpose.

"What are you doing?" she asked, her voice breathless.

He walked over to the bed and sat down, his eyes taking in the sloping shoulders and delicate lines of her breasts above the nightdress. Reaching out he traced a path down the milk-white curve.

She shivered. Her skin burned where he touched her.

"You've become my obsession," he said, softly drinking in the beauty of her still, watchful face. "Since the first moment I saw you, I have been unable to get you out of my mind. For five months I've behaved like a cloistered monk. While you were married to another man I could do nothing else and still live with my conscience," he continued. "But now, I've grown weary of playing the gentleman." His hand reached out to touch the smooth column of her throat. "I'm a man, Tess." His voice was huskier than usual and his eyes glittered as he threaded the fingers of his other hand through her hair. "I told you that once before. Tonight I'll prove it."

Fascinated, unable to deny the force of his will, she watched the deliberate, unhurried descent of his mouth as he bent his head to her throat. Whimpering in protest, she stiffened as his lips touched her skin. He deepened his kiss and the protest changed to something else. Her body melted against him and she gave herself up to the exquisite pleasure of his mouth on hers and the feel of his hands as they caressed her face and shoulders.

Fumbling with the buttons of her nightdress, he moved the thin material aside, baring her to the waist. Sucking in his breath, he stared down at the perfection of high, proud breasts, their rosy peaks, taut with desire.

Shrugging out of his shirt and trousers, he fumbled with the strap of his wooden leg, unbuckling the clasp and stripping away the leather that attached it to his body. He lay down beside her, reaching out to pull her beneath him. Instinctively, she arched her back and his control broke. Parting her lips he drove his tongue deep into her mouth, desperately seeking the response he'd dreamed of for such an endless length of days and weeks.

She cried out deep in her throat, answering the demand of his mouth with a need as great as his own. Consciousness slipped away. The smooth sheets, the frosty air, the shadowed room bathed in moonlight disappeared, leaving only strong arms holding her in a grip of steel. The delicious tension mounted and she knew, once more, the heartstopping pleasure of his words, muffled against her throat. Shivering with passion, she met his lips in a kiss so deep and long that, she was forced to break away, gasping for air.

His mouth moved down, finding the pulse point where her neck and shoulder met. Moving still lower, his hand cupped a swollen breast. Tracing the nipple with the edge of his tongue he took the peak in his mouth and suckled deeply.

Tess moaned and raked his back. Waves of pleasure consumed her. His muscles rippled as her hands moved down the whipcord strength of his back and hips. He was satin and steel, fire and raging tide. She couldn't get enough of his slick, hot flesh and searching mouth. The unfamiliar hardness of the weight between her legs both frightened and fascinated her. Moving up the inside of her calf, his hand caressed the smooth skin of her thighs. She stiffened and pushed against him.

It was several moments before he felt it. Such was the flame of his own desire that her fear was complete before he realized it was even there. Frowning he lifted his head. Her eyes were wide and dark with terror

"What's the matter?" he asked.

She shook her head wordlessly.

"Tess," his voice was very gentle. "I know fear when I see it. Won't you trust me?"

Her words were so low he had to bend his head to hear them. "I've never done this before."

His breathing altered. A piercing joy stabbed his heart. Smoothing the hair away from her damp forehead, he kissed her nose.

"Why not?" he asked.

She bit her lip. "The morning of the wedding, we heard that Adam Bradford was very ill and probably wouldn't last the night. Because everything was all arranged we decided to go ahead with the ceremony. Daniel left immediately after."

James stroked her throat and the sensitive skin below her breasts with gentle exploring fingers.

She blushed, grateful for the darkness. "There wasn't time for anything else."

His mouth took hers in a kiss so intimate it shook her to the core. She wove trembling fingers through his hair, holding him against her. His lips touched her throat. His words were a whisper of air.

"I'll be very careful."

Closing her eyes, Tess was conscious of the large lean body pressed against hers. She heard the reassurance in his voice and the warmth of his hand exploring her hips and breasts, occasionally dipping down to caress the lower part of her belly. The familiar magic of his nearness wove its spell and the fear receded.

He was a skilled lover. Deliberately, he set out, for the first time, to woo a woman he loved. He went very slowly, very gently until he felt her tension disappear.

Tess willed herself to relax. She never dreamed a man could make her feel this way. The incredible ache returned and she moved against his hand as it slipped between her legs. His fingers dipped into her moist heat and she jumped in surprise. "No." The indignant whisper burst from her.

A hoarse muffled laugh escaped his lips. He shifted upward and kissed her mouth with raw, dizzying hunger. "Yes," he murmured moving back and forth against her lips. His fingers tangled themselves in the silky triangle between her legs until he could feel the tension flow out of her thighs. She moved against him, her hips arching against his hand. He moved on top of her and his control broke.

"Tess," he murmured against her throat, "this may hurt you." Parting her legs with his knee, he entered her.

A sharp burning pain replaced the tension. She struggled against him. He held her in a vise-like grip, murmuring words of comfort until the pain receded.

Perspiration beaded his brow. She was warm and sweet and tasted of honey. Afraid of hurting her, he throbbed with the effort of holding back. She shifted beneath him and he lost all sense of time and place. Groaning, he thrust deeply inside her, again and again, until the raging need of five long months was sated at last. Collapsing on top of her, he buried his face in her hair and closed his eyes.

Fifteen

Propping himself up on one elbow, Devereaux looked down at the sleeping woman beside him. Curled on one side, she slept like a child, the golden-tipped lashes resting on her cheek. He reached out to push the weight of her hair from her face, his eyes resting on the exquisite line of her chin and throat.

He was unusually moved by the sight of her, so small and vulnerable, her smooth golden skin very pale against the darker hue of his chest. He had never stayed the entire night with a woman once the physical encounter was past, but this time he had no desire to leave. This odd feeling of tenderness was unfamiliar to him. His arms tightened possessively around her.

She stirred and opened her eyes.

He kissed her forehead. "Did I hurt you?"

"No," she lied. Resting her head against his chest, she listened to the firm steady beating of his heart.

"You will marry me?"

"Yes." Her voice sounded strained. "I'll marry you."

His lips brushed against her temple. "You'll never be happy without me, you know."

"I know."

He frowned. "Tell me you love me."

Tess sat up, holding the comforter in front of her. "Surely, you can't doubt me now."

The careful, guarded look was in his eyes. "Is it so difficult to admit?" he asked, trying without success, to mask his hurt.

Her grave expression faded, replaced by a look of tender

amusement. Could the arrogant, self-confident Duke of Langley harbor the same insecurities as any ordinary man?

Tess leaned forward, placing her hands on his shoulders. The comforter slid to her waist. Touching the tip of her tongue to his lips, she explored the still, firm mouth. Gaining courage, she nibbled at the sensitive contours forcing his lips apart. Her tongue tentatively touched the rough edge of his.

Devereaux held his breath, afraid to move, afraid she would stop. Rigid with the effort of maintaining his control, the sweet torment of her breasts brushing against his chest was almost more than he could bear. His hands clenched.

Moving down from his mouth, Tess trailed moist kisses across his shoulders and the flat ropy muscles of his chest and stomach. He tasted like salt. She felt tremors, powerful yet controlled, wherever her mouth met the heated skin. Her fingers, cool and caressing, played across his flat belly, moving in gently circular motions until, by accident, she brushed against the hardness between his legs.

White heat consumed him. The raging flames seared his flesh and fired his blood, wiping all conscious thought from his mind. Instinctively, he sought relief in the cool fragrant softness of the woman in his arms. Pulling her beneath him, he thrust into her tight warmth, crushing her lips with his mouth. He made no attempt to caress her, holding her still with arms of steel.

Trembling, she arched up against him. A delicious warmth spread through her and she moved to his rhythm.

"My God, Tess," he groaned.

The warmth became an ache. Moving urgently against him, she wrapped her legs around his. Nothing mattered any longer, nothing but the sweat-drenched skin, the weight of his muscled body covering hers and the incredible pressure that started deep inside the very center of her being, threatening to explode and devour her.

Lifting her against him, he bent his head to her breast. Tess gasped and cried out, drowning in the power of her first climax.

His fingers bruised her shoulders. Shuddering, he drove still deeper, until at last, with a hoarse cry, he found his own release.

Devereaux awoke in the darkness of early dawn to find Tess staring at him. The grey eyes were wide and very serious as they searched his face.

"You don't look at all like yourself when you sleep," she said at last.

"How do I look?"

She considered the question carefully before answering. "Younger, I think, and more vulnerable. Probably the way you must have looked when you were a child and hadn't taken the weight of the world on your shoulders."

His mouth quirked. "I'm flattered, but aren't you exaggerating a bit?"

"I want to see you, James, all of you."

He stiffened. "You are seeing me."

Tess shook her head. "I want to see your leg. I want to know how you're able to move the way you do with only one leg." Her hands slowly pulled the quilt down.

"Don't Tess."

She ignored him. As the quilt exposed new skin her mouth followed, nibbling, sucking, tentatively exploring down the flat expanse of chest and tight stomach, the protrusion of hip bone, the length of his straining sex. When he would have reached for her again, she stopped him.

Frustrated, throbbing, humiliated, he lay down again, waiting for her mouth to continue its downward journey. Heated softness touched his thigh, his knee and the calf of his good leg. She moved down to his foot, licking the arch, sucking each toe. James could hardly breathe. He had never been so hard or so sore. He had never wanted a woman more. Christ, he had never been so afraid.

She shifted over him, working her way down the other leg. Again, he felt her mouth on his thigh, the back of his knee and then unbelievably on the aching swollen stump that served as his left leg. Gently she laved him, her mouth and tongue healing the hot flesh, pressing tiny kisses on the smoothness where there should be none. Then she made her way up again, over the long expanse of muscled flesh, until her lips found his heat. Covering the tip with her mouth, she sucked experimentally. James gasped, lost the last remnants of his control, and came immediately.

Later, she rested her head against his chest inhaling the clean scent that always clung to him. "I'm worried about your mother," she confessed.

He could feel her eyelashes tickle his skin. James faced an interesting dilemma and he didn't quite know how to behave. In Tess, he had found a rare combination of innocence and sensuality, the perfect lady, the wanton mistress. He wanted to hold and protect her, yet the sight of her lovely golden body drove him to dizzying heights of desire. From the moment he set eyes on her he had thought of marriage and children. At the same time, the merest touch of her hand heated his blood, making him white-lipped with frustrated need. The frustration was over. His hands roamed possessively over her breasts and he lowered his mouth to the curve of her throat. "My mother need not concern you, Tess.

Her head fell back, answering the demand of his lips. All thoughts of Leonie Devereaux disappeared in the sudden, blinding rush of passion.

Several hours later, Devereaux walked into his mother's sitting room and smiled at her with frosty blue eyes.

"Wish me happy, Mama. Tess has accepted my offer of marriage. The wedding will take place on Christmas Day."

Her face whitened. "You can't be serious."

"On the contrary. I've never been more serious about anything in my life."

Leonie placed the menus she had been looking at on a nearby table. Lifting her eyes to her son's face, she gave him her full attention.

"Isn't this rather sudden, James? When I last spoke to Tess, she had decided to refuse your proposal."

"I can be very persuasive."

Leonie wet her lips nervously. "I see."

"I'm relieved that you do. Because if you do anything to cause Tess to change her mind, I shall be forced to send you away."

"James!" she cried angrily. "How can you do this? The girl is an American, a commoner. Her father is a tradesman and God knows who her mother was." Hot color rose in her cheeks and her lips thinned. "This is the woman you expect me to receive as the duchess of Langley? I'd rather die."

There was a long silence. Leonie was frightened at the expression on her son's face.

"You will receive Tess as the duchess of Langley, Mother." His voice was soft and very dangerous. "If you do not, I will remove you from this house. You will never see me nor any children born to me again."

Leonie lifted a shaking hand to her throat. Never, even in their most difficult moments, had he spoken to her like this.

He came closer and bent so that his eyes were level on her face. "You shall take back the words you spoke about my betrothed or," he waited a moment, emphasizing the last words, "I shall be forced to actions you will regret more than I. Which shall it be, Mother?"

Leonie swallowed. "I shall welcome Tess as your wife."

He smiled with his lips only and straightened. "Excellent." Laying his hand on the door, he was about to turn the knob when her voice stopped him.

"Wouldn't it be more prudent to wait a bit longer?" She used her final argument. "After all, Mr. Bradford has just been declared dead. At least six months of mourning is required."

"Tess has been in England for nearly that length of time," he replied tersely. "For all anyone knows, he could have been dead."

"James," Leonie pleaded. "Why the hurry? Surely, if you love each other, a waiting period won't harm you. Think of the scandal."

"The wedding will be in two days as scheduled. It isn't possible to wait any longer."

"But why?" Leonie stamped her foot, her magnificent eyes flashing blue sparks.

He turned to face her, speaking deliberately. "Unless you want your first grandchild to carry the name of Bradford, the wedding will take place as soon as possible."

Leonie flinched as if she had been slapped. "That was brutal as well as unnecessary."

The level blue eyes burned with anger. "No more brutal than what you tried to do to me."

Tears filled her eyes and spilled down her cheeks. She let them fall, the clear drops forming small dark patches on the blue cambric of her dress.

"I only want you to be happy," she said in a choked whisper.

His face softened. In the space of a second he had crossed the room and taken her in his arms. "I am happy, Mama," he murmured. "Without Tess, there is no happiness for me in all the world. Can't you see that?"

Her heart ached at the unfamiliar tenderness in his voice. She reached up to cup his cheek in her hand. His face swam before her through a mist of tears. This was her son. A leaner, harder, version of the little boy who shrieked with delight and clung to her with smudged cheeks and dirty hands when she walked into the nursery so many years ago. For a long time now he had been withdrawn and preoccupied. Not even Lizzie could penetrate that aura of deep reserve behind which he held his most private thoughts.

Leonie had thought a wife was what he needed. Someone gracious and lovely who would bring him out of his distracted aloofness and provide Langley with a desperately needed heir. It appeared she was right. James was no longer remote. He was a man in love. And although his choice was not her choice, she had no recourse but to accept it. Leonie was an intelligent woman.

She was also sincerely attached to her children. Raising her eyes to his face, she smiled.

"Two days isn't much time to prepare," she said, "but we'll manage."

James grinned for the first time since he entered the room. "Thank you, Mama. I knew I could count on you."

Sixteen

They were married two days later in the chapel at Langley. It was an afternoon ceremony. The bride wore a deep red velvet gown that brought out the iridescent quality of her ivory skin. Her mother's pearl earrings and the gold band Devereaux placed upon her finger were her only jewelry. The couple exchanged their vows in calm, confident voices and although the guest list was comprised of family only, everyone agreed that never had they attended a ceremony so meaningful and so filled with joy.

Even Lizzie was overcome. She clung to Tess and whispered in her ear. "You are really and truly my sister now. I'm so glad it was you. I don't think I could bear it if James had brought home anyone else."

Leonie had feared her first encounter with Tess after James's announcement would be awkward. She needn't have worried. The girl's excellent breeding and calm serenity prevailed, and the occasion passed without incident. At the ceremony, one look at Tess's face and another at her son's made her heart rejoice. Gone was the cool remoteness of the last two years. His face was vivid with youth. The look of intense pride in his eyes when he gazed at his lovely wife, brought the swift rush of tears to Leonie's eyes. She breathed a sigh of relief. Langley would have an heir at last.

After a sumptuous luncheon, the bride and groom left to spend several weeks at their small estate in Stratford.

Tess's eyes widened as the gables of Surrey Manor came into full view. Langley was a castle, beautifully refurbished, but a castle all the same. Surrey was a palace. The rose-colored stone walls gleamed in the dying sunset and deep, long windows welcomed them with light and warmth from the lamps within. Built of mellow brick, it was graceful and lovely, obviously the design of a master architect.

Tess was enchanted. Lifting glowing eyes to her husband's face, she laughed out loud. "Thank you, James," she said. "I feel at home for the first time since setting foot in England."

"You are home, my love," he said gently, "and I have weeks to prove it to you."

He pulled her into the circle of his arms, resting his head against her shining hair. His voice shook slightly.

"For the first time I have you all to myself. I feel as if I've waited a lifetime for this day."

She smiled into the wool-covered shoulder. Drawing a deep shuddering breath, she lifted her head and looked into his eyes. "I feel the same," she answered.

"Tess," he groaned in a strangled voice, "don't look at me like that or I won't be responsible for my actions."

She smiled a wide, lovely smile. "I'll grant a reprieve now, m'lord," she replied, moving to the safety of the far end of the carriage, "but later, I expect you to honor your word."

Something dark and elemental flickered in the pupils of his eyes. "I won't disappoint you," he promised.

Tess swallowed and looked out the carriage window.

The servants were taken aback by the slender American beauty who greeted them with such careful gravity. Reared in an English class system that strictly separated servants from their superiors, the duke's staff was hesitant to accept an outsider. Prepared to tolerate Tess for their master's sake, they were all, without exception, agreeably surprised. From the housekeeper down to the cook's kitchen helper, they fell instantly in love, charmed by the sincerity and good manners of the American girl who was now the duchess of Langley.

At dinner, that night, the cook outdid himself. The duke and duchess feasted on a meal of asparagus and buttered crab, roast beef and Christmas pudding, washed down with an excellent vintage champagne.

Devereaux couldn't keep his eyes off his wife. The creamy skin of her shoulders and breasts gleamed against the rich, green satin of her gown. Her silvery hair was piled on top of her head with one lock pulled free to rest against the bare skin of her shoulder. The thick shining mass seemed almost too heavy for her slender neck. She seemed brighter somehow, more vibrant, as if lit from within by a thousand candles. His heart pounded in anticipation of what would follow.

Reaching into the pocket of his coat, he pulled out a small flat box and placed it in front of her.

"Merry Christmas, Tess," he said.

She opened the box and gasped. An emerald necklace and matching earrings, their magnificent stones brilliantly cut to catch the light, blinked up at her.

"James," she stammered. "These are priceless. I can't possibly wear anything like this."

"Of course you can," he replied, rising to stand behind her. Lifting the necklace from its box, he fastened it around her neck. The jewels glowed richly green against the flawless, ivory skin.

"It's traditional for every Devereaux bride to receive them on her wedding day," he explained.

Tess turned to look at him. "Are you telling me that your mother willingly gave up these incredible jewels merely to uphold family tradition?"

He grinned. "Something like that."

"You really are amazing, m'lord." A smile lurked in the depths of her eyes. "Is anything beyond your persuasive powers?"

His hands slid up her arms to rest on her shoulders. He could feel her tremble under his touch. "Shall we go upstairs?" His voice was thick with desire. The candlelight shone on the night black hair, glinting with blue sparks. His eyes were startlingly light against his dark face.

Her breath caught in her throat. "Give me a moment to get ready," she whispered. "I'll dismiss the maid."

He nodded and watched her climb the stairs.

Tess was conscious of nothing but thoughts of her husband as the maid silently dressed her in a thin, lawn nightgown and brushed out her hair. This was the man she loved. She knew it now, without a doubt. The deep, inner reserve behind which she concealed her innermost feelings had crumbled beneath the strength of his passion. He held her happiness, her future, her very soul in the palm of his hand.

The door opened and he walked in dressed in trousers and a white shirt. The maid left the room.

Devereaux looked at his wife, taking in the grace of her body, the straight slim beauty of her legs visible beneath the nightgown.

"You are very beautiful, Tess," he said.

She smiled. "I was thinking the same about you."

He looked surprised and then laughed. Walking over to where she sat, he reached out to touch her hair.

"It's the color of moonlight," he whispered, his voice huskier than usual. Bending his head, he kissed her.

Tess moaned and slid her hands under his shirt, feeling the smooth hard muscles of his back and chest. He was hard against her thigh. Her hands dipped lower. With a harsh exclamation, he lifted her into his arms and carried her to the bed. Shrugging off his shirt, he looked down at her. Her eyes were wide and dark with desire. He pulled her gown over her head and tossed it to the floor. Slowly, his hand traced a path from her cheek to her throat to her breast.

She melted as soon as he touched her. Her arms went up around his neck and she pulled his head to her mouth.

James felt her shudder and tried desperately to slow the rhythm of his own mounting passion.

"For two days, I've wanted nothing but this," he muttered, caressing her bare skin. When she gasped and arched up against him, his control broke and he waited no longer. Dousing the candle, he lifted himself from his breeches and thrust into the warm, willing body of his wife.

When he awoke the room was flooded with sunlight and Tess was propped up on one elbow looking at him.

He smiled. "What are you thinking about so seriously?"

She moved closer to lay her lips against his chest. "I'm thinking how lucky I am to have you." Her beautiful face was grave. "I love you very much."

All thoughts of sleep vanished. The contented look in the blue eyes disappeared and quite another expression crept in.

"Kiss me," he murmured, sliding his arms around her.

Slowly, her lips met his. White heat flamed inside her. She abandoned all thoughts but the sudden rushing pleasure of his mouth on hers and his hands roaming across her skin, lifting her to sensual heights she'd only imagined.

The business of government didn't stop because the duke of Langley was on his honeymoon. After several days of idyllic solitude, the young couple was interrupted by carriages containing messengers from Westminister traveling the wide avenue leading to Surrey Manor.

Tess enjoyed watching her husband with these gentlemen. There was something about James that was difficult to describe. There was a stillness about him, a sense of authority that set him apart, a distinguishing personal charm different from everyone around him.

She knew he was a powerful political figure, but she hadn't realized, until recently, just how powerful. The level of her feelings for her husband grew deeper as the weeks went by, until she could think of little else. She studied every expression on his face, every gesture of his hand, until she knew it as intimately as she knew her own. She could feel his presence when he entered the room.

Their nights were filled with a passion that both frightened and inflamed her. Once, when she halfheartedly protested that the servants would gossip if they retired so early, he led her into the library, pulled the ribbon from her hair and proceeded to make love to her so effectively, that she begged him to carry her upstairs to bed.

But James was much more than a skilled lover. It soon became very clear to Tess that next to Lord Liverpool and Viscount Castlereagh and even General Wellington, he was a very important man in England.

Again, she had misgivings about her decision to marry him. She couldn't be the political hostess of a man whose beliefs she did not share. When she mentioned her fears to James, he laughed them away.

"You aren't English. No one can possibly expect you to think the way I do."

"But, as your wife," she argued, "how can I support you when I feel as I do?"

He reached over to take her hand. "You may say and do as you wish. Politics need not concern you."

"But you see, James, I am political. Every American must be or we are doomed."

"It isn't the same here," he reassured her. "You are a woman and, unfortunately, a woman's principles aren't given the same regard as a man's. It isn't right. I don't agree with it, but the situation exists."

As the time to return to London drew nearer, James became more and more involved in his work leaving Tess to fend for herself. Gradually she became interested in the running of her household. Mrs. Greely, the housekeeper, was anxious to please her lovely new mistress and explained everything in great detail.

Tess was warm and sympathetic and truly friendly. She ordered new hangings for the drawing room and had the grates repaired in the servants' quarters. In the morning, she played cards with the footmen, or discussed horses with the groom, and on baking day she could be found in the kitchen eating her measure of raisin-filled dough. At night, she lay curled against her husband's lean body, listening to the beating of his heart against her own, his skin slightly damp from their exertions.

She looked upon their return to society with growing apprehension. Here, at Surrey, in the quiet of her bedchamber, he was completely hers. In London there would be parties and balls, concerts and teas. They would scarcely see each other, a daunting prospect for a woman who six months before had measured the annual Bladensburg barbeque as the height of her social season. Worst of all would be the speculative whispers as to how an innocuous American widow with no fortune had walked off with the prize of the marriage mart.

The last night before they were to return, Devereaux found his wife in the library. A blazing fire gave off the only heat and light in the room. Tess sat on the floor in her dressing gown, her legs curled beneath her. He stretched out on the carpet beside her, his hands clasped behind his head, making no move to touch her or to speak.

Tess broke the silence. "Are you happy with me, James?"

He looked at her in surprise. "Very happy, my love. Why do you ask?"

She shook her head. "No particular reason. I'm just feeling strange now that it's time to return to London. I wish I had you to myself for a bit longer."

Devereaux smiled. "I'm flattered that after a month of my company, you aren't tired of me."

Her eyes widened in amazement. "What a ridiculous thing to say. I could never be tired of you."

He reached out and pulled her down into his arms. Her cheek rested against his shoulder.

"What is troubling you, Tess?" he asked gently.

"It's silly." She took a deep breath. The words came out in a rush of air. "I just wish you weren't embroiled in all this government work." She waved her arm vaguely at the papers scattered across the desk. "I'm not a fashionable person, James. My life in Maryland wasn't like this. I feel unprepared. Being married to the duke of Langley takes a bit of getting used to."

The hands stroking her back were still.

"Why?" he asked evenly.

Her words were muffled against his shoulder. "I'm afraid of embarrassing you."

"You weren't afraid of embarrassing Daniel Bradford. Surely he would have followed his father into politics."

"That was different."

"Why?" he asked again.

She shrugged. This vulnerability she felt was new to her. "I knew how to go about in Washington. Here I don't."

His lips found the sensitive skin of her throat before traveling to her shoulder. She gasped as his hands slipped under her gown to caress her bare skin.

"You could never embarrass me," he muttered against her neck. "You're everything I've ever wanted."

He meant every word of it. Devereaux was delighted with his wife. He considered it an act of God that she was Georgiana's friend and that she had come to England searching for her husband. He loved her spirit, her vibrance, her beautiful body. He did not doubt that she had married him because she loved him. There was no one in the world like Tess.

Her hair, spilling across her shoulders, was a sheet of silver in the firelight. Laying her down on the carpet, he removed her gown and stared down at her.

She watched him silently, waiting. Slowly, his hands cupped her breasts at the same moment his mouth came down hard on hers. This would be no gentle coupling. He couldn't get enough of her.

Her lips parted, eager for the invasion of his tongue. Under his exploring fingers her breasts tightened and swelled. She shuddered and reached up to hold his head as his lips claimed a taut nipple. Sliding her hands down the length of his back, she reveled in the corded muscles and powerful thighs. They were slick with moisture. She could feel him heavy and throbbing against her. His breath came in short ragged gasps. Instinctively she parted her legs. Taking him in her hand, she guided him to the entrance of her warmth.

He tensed. Perspiration dripped from his body and all movement stopped. He shook with the effort of holding himself back.

Deliberately, she pressed against him, running her hands over the rigid angles and planes of his body.

"Holy Christ, Tess," he groaned. Plunging into her, he drove with a desperate abandon that was terrifying in its power to move her.

Later, after he had collapsed against her in the great bed they shared, she thought again of the obstacles in the path of her happiness. She would be herself, she resolved fiercely, and she would keep her husband's love. She stroked his hair. In sleep, his face had a vulnerable quality, much like a small boy. As long as the fire flamed between them, she was safe.

Seventeen

There was little conversation between the duke and duchess of Langley on their way back to London. James, preoccupied with Wellington's latest defeat in the peninsula, allowed Tess to suffer her misgivings alone.

It was late January and the season was in full swing. The couple had barely settled into their house in Grosvenor Square when Leonie and her daughters arrived and invitations began pouring in.

Tess made her debut as the duchess of Langley at a ball given by Lady Maria Sefton at Sefton House. At the top of a sweeping staircase, dressed in a gown glittering with diamonds, her ladyship greeted her guests.

"Lord and Lady Dinsdale," the majordomo droned, "the earl and countess of Locksley."

Tess stood perfectly still, her arm through her husband's, waiting to be announced. "The duke and duchess of Langley," the monotonous voice continued.

James looked down at his wife. She returned the look with a smile and lifted her skirts to step into the ballroom.

Marjorie Weatherby, witnessing the intimate exchange, experienced a flash of jealousy. She had planned on resuming her relationship with James. The warmth in his expression when he looked at his wife dashed her hopes.

William Fitzpatrick, also, did not miss the glow on the faces of the handsome young couple. Jealousy was a new sensation for him. His brief interludes with women were not affairs of the heart. The feelings he had for Tess went beyond the shallow encounters he'd had with other women. He knew from the moment he looked across the room, at Lady Jersey's ball, and seen her lovely, serious face, that Teresa Bradford was something out of the ordinary. That feeling grew as he came to know her better. By the time she threw herself in front of the stallion's hooves to save Lizzie Devereaux's life, he was smitten.

For the first time in his life, Lord William found himself in the grip of an honest emotion. Tess Bradford would have brought him no fortune or influence. Worse than that, she was an American. The Fitzpatricks had come to England with the Conqueror. Not since receiving the title, five hundred years before, had a Fitzpatrick allied himself with a commoner. And yet, William had seriously considered it. He had been delighted to hear of Daniel Bradford's death. Her subsequent marriage to Langley was a bitter blow.

Swallowing the last of his champagne, he left his glass on a low table, crossed the floor to her side and bowed.

"Your Grace," he said. "May I hope that you will save me a dance?"

Pleased to see someone she recognized, Tess smiled brilliantly. "It's lovely to see you again, William. Of course I'll dance with you. You don't mind, do you, James?" She looked up, confident of her husband's approval.

James hesitated for a fraction of a second. "Not at all," he replied, his expression bland. "I shall rely on you to take care of my wife, Fitzpatrick."

The slight emphasis on the words "my wife" did not escape Lord William. "My pleasure, m'lord," he replied, leading Tess to the dance floor.

The orchestra struck up a waltz. Fitzpatrick looked down at the bright head close to his shoulder. He hadn't intended to reproach her or even to mention her marital status, but the moment her slim body relaxed in his arms, his resolution dissolved.

"How could you, Tess?" he demanded angrily.

She raised confused eyes to his face. "I beg your pardon?"

"Tell me you married him because you were grateful, or that you had nowhere else to go," he pleaded.

Fitzpatrick could feel her stiffen in his arms.

"I do not discuss my husband with you or anyone, m'lord."

"Forgive me." The pain in his voice was unmistakable. "I did not mean to distress you."

Tess softened. "You have been a loyal friend to me, William. Please wish me happy."

William Fitzpatrick looked into the clear, grey eyes. They sparkled with light and her skin had a special glow he had never seen before.

"Congratulations on your marriage, Tess," he said, through clenched teeth. "I hope you will be very happy."

"Thank you, m'lord." She smiled her wide, lovely smile. "That was nicely done."

He pulled her closer into the circle of his arms. "Remember, if you ever need a friend, I am here."

Her eyes warmed and she lifted her hand to his cheek. "That means a great deal to me. I shan't forget it."

Later in the evening she stopped near her mother-in-law to catch her breath. Leonie smiled and patted the empty seat beside her.

"Are you enjoying the ball, my love?" she asked.

Tess nodded her head. "Very much, but I'm exhausted. I never realized how much stamina is required to last through a London season."

"This is only the beginning," Leonie assured her. "There are breakfasts and picnics and teas, concerts and plays and the opera." She waved her fan in front of her face. "Of course, James will attend political dinner parties and host them as well." She smiled at Tess. "Don't worry, my dear. I'll be here to help you. The Devereauxs have always cut a fine dash. We must uphold our reputation."

Tess felt a familiar rush of panic begin to take hold. She barely heard her mother-in-law's next words. Only when Leonie repeated them, did she shake her absorption and pay attention.

"You are very popular tonight," the older woman observed with a pleased smile. "This is the first time all evening I've seen you sit down. You will be a tremendous asset to James's career."

Tess frowned. "Is my every action weighed as to whether it will aid or hinder my husband's career?"

Leonie's head tilted to one side as she considered the question. "In public, everything you do will be judged," she replied. "For instance, dancing two dances with young Fitzpatrick was not wise." She nodded at William making his way around the floor with a tall, dark-haired young lady. "He is given to excessive behavior. If it weren't for his fortune, he wouldn't be received in our circles."

Tess's hands clenched in her lap. Leonie Devereaux's haughty presumption that everyone thought as she did was annoying.

"William Fitzpatrick has been very kind to me." Tess's eyes, pure and grey as brook water, held her mother-in-law's gaze. "I allow no one to dictate my friends."

Leonie sniffed. "Perhaps James will have something to say about that."

Tess's voice was so low, Leonie strained to hear it. "That would be a foolish thing to do," she said. "And we both know James is not a fool."

"Did I hear my name?" Devereaux's quiet voice interrupted their conversation.

"I was explaining to Tess the necessity of public appearances," his mother replied. "Perhaps you will have more luck with her than I."

A hint of impatience flickered in his eyes and then disappeared. "You know me better than that, Mother. A ball is not the place to discuss politics." Holding out his hands, he pulled Tess from her seat. "I believe this is our dance, my love."

Tess looked surprised. "But James, you don't dance."

He grinned. "Will you come with me anyway?"

Although she was promised to Lord Holland for the set, she nodded. Anxious to escape further admonition, Tess stood up quickly. Tucking her hand in her husband's arm she walked with him to the refreshment table.

Devereaux, aware that the becoming shade of apricot staining her cheeks was caused by anger, wisely remained silent.

Tess's eyes smoldered. "Do you also wish to lecture me on my choice of friends, m'lord?"

"Have I ever done so?" He positioned himself across from her, sipping his punch.

Taken aback by the reasonable words, she looked up. The blue eyes were tender and loving and slightly amused. Instantly, Tess was ashamed of herself.

"No, you haven't. I'm sorry, James. Sometimes your mother is very hard to bear."

He threw back his head and laughed. Every eye in the room was immediately riveted on the handsome couple. "I've often thought the very same thing myself," he admitted.

Tess grinned reluctantly. "I suppose I should learn to control my temper."

"Not on my account," he said. "I like a woman with spirit. In fact, there isn't anything about you I would change."

"Do you really mean that?" Her eyes were wide and very serious.

His eyes darkened. He looked at her mouth. An insistent warmth spread through his veins.

"Let's go home," he said softly.

Correctly interpreting the look in his eyes, she blushed. "What will your mother say? She thinks we spend too much time alone together already."

"My mother will say nothing at all. I'll see to that." He turned her toward the door. "I won't be a moment. I'll just tell her that we are leaving."

Lord Dinsdale had just returned Leonie to her seat when James sat down beside her. "Tess and I are leaving, Mother. I'll send the carriage back to bring you home."

Two spots of color warmed Leonie's olive complexion. "I realize the two of you are newly married, but must you be so disgustingly obvious about your preference for each other?"

James grinned. "You said you wanted a Langley heir," he reminded her.

"Other people have heirs and they don't leave in the middle of social obligations to get them," she observed.

The smile faded from his face. "This is not an obligation. It is a ball where people are supposed to enjoy themselves." He held his mother's gaze with eyes of steel. "In the future," he added, "please allow me to instruct my wife on her duties."

"James," Leonie protested. "I was only trying to help. The child knows nothing about what is required of her."

He sighed, striving for patience. "Tess is not a child. She is a woman of unusual intelligence and compassion. She is also a republican. If you understood her at all you would know that she does not respond to badgering. To tell her someone isn't exalted enough to associate with our family is like forbidding Lizzie to speak at the dinner table. It only increases her desire to do the opposite."

Leonie sighed. "Very well, James. It shall be as you wish."

Frowning, she watched him leave. She did not miss the appreciative female eyes that followed his lean, handsome figure as he crossed the ballroom. Why, of all the women in the world, she asked herself for the thousandth time, had he chosen someone so entirely unsuitable?

Although the conversation was almost nonexistent, Tess was very aware of her husband sitting across from her in the carriage. The air between them was filled with an electric excitement that charged her nerves and sensitized her skin. When they reached Grosvenor Square, she went directly upstairs to her bedchamber.

Her maid brushed out her hair and after helping her into a beautifully embroidered nightgown, left the room. Tess sat down at her nightstand and waited. The minutes crept by slowly. Then, the door opened and James stepped inside.

Tess looked at him. Suddenly, she found it difficult to breathe. He was shirtless, dressed only in trousers and a pair of leather slippers. His hair, black and shining, fell across his forehead and his eyes were narrowed, a thin, glittering line of blue. From the high cheekbones to broad shoulders, he was all sharp planes and angles, tapering to a vee at his waist. Compared to her insignificant height, he seemed very tall, with the long legs and lean hips of a cavalryman. Her eyes lingered on his chest, smooth and tanned, without an ounce of spare flesh.

She stood and walked over to him. Reaching out she ran her hands experimentally over the muscles of his chest. He felt warm and smooth and hard. A muscle jumped under her exploring fingers.

He reached for her, but she slipped out of his grasp, moving behind him. Her hands moved down from his waist to the corded muscles of his buttocks and upper thighs. She smiled as his breathing became louder and more strained.

"I spoke to Lady Weatherby at the ball," she said, keeping her voice deliberately casual.

He tensed. "Might I ask about the subject of your conversation?"

"She told me that several young ladies were inconsolable over our marriage, and that Cynthia Davenport has retired to the country with a broken heart."

He laughed, relieved. "Surely you recognize an exaggerated account when you hear it."

"I'm not sure it is an exaggeration. You are quite a catch, m'lord." Her hands moved to the buttons of his trousers. She unfastened the top one and lightly touched the sensitive skin beneath his navel.

He sucked in his breath and covered her hands with his. "Do you know what you are doing to me, Tess?" he asked, his voice hoarse.

She pressed her lips to his shoulder. "I think so." Her hand dipped lower closing around the pulsing heat of his shaft.

White fire consumed him, wiping everything from his mind but a raging inferno of need, demanding release. Blindly, he turned, and lifting her in his arms, carried her to the bed. Stepping out of his trousers he pushed the gown from her shoulders and covered her body with his own.

Tess wound her arms around his neck. The satin of her skin rubbed against his heated flesh. Urging him on with whispered words, she parted her legs and pulled him inside her, gasping as the steel-like length of him exploded immediately. Filled with his warmth, she moved beneath him, answering the demand of her own clamoring need, until at last they lay still, spent and exhausted, their bodies entwined.

"That was wonderful," she said much later, after awakening to the feel of his lips on her breast. "Your wooden leg is still on. Do you want me to take it off?"

"Uh-hum," he answered, without lifting his head.

"James?" She unbuckled the strap and eased it down over his knee.

Reluctantly, he propped himself up on one elbow. "What is it, Tess?"

She examined the wood piece before placing it gently on the floor. "Will you always be faithful to me?"

Startled, he sat up completely. "Why would you ask such a question?" he asked.

"Must I repeat it?" She looked very young and vulnerable, with her eyes wide on his face and her unbound hair fanned across her shoulders.

"I have never been a womanizer, Tess. If I've done something to make you distrust me, just say so." His voice was cold.

"I am not an Englishwoman, James. I have been brought up to believe that marriage is sacred."

He was silent for a long moment. At last, he said, "Tell me what is troubling you?"

She studied his expression to see if he was merely humoring her. Satisfied, she explained. "What happens here, between married men and women is outrageous. Here in London, a lady may take a lover and, if she is discreet, still remain respectable. That would never happen in Annapolis." She looked at the stern, implacable face of the man she loved. "For me, marriage means one man, forever."

He looked down at the still beauty of her face, her eyes brimming with emotion. Where could he find the words to dispel her fears?

"Tess," he said gently. "I'm thirty years old. It would be a remarkable thing if you were the first woman I'd taken to bed." He turned her face so that she looked directly at him. "You are, however, the only woman I have ever asked to marry me. Our marriage, unlike most of the ton, is a love match." He kissed her nose. "What I'm trying to tell you, my heart, is that for me, marriage means only you."

Tess was unprepared for the surging relief that left her weak. She clung to him as if he were her only strength in the world. When his mouth claimed hers and his hands moved over her breasts, she responded with a passion he had never known before.

"You are everything I've ever wanted," he murmured, his voice shaken. "There isn't a man in London, or the entire world for that matter, who wouldn't give up everything to be here in my place."

She smiled against his throat. Burrowing her head in his shoulder, she slept.

Eighteen

As the weeks went by and news of Wellington's losses in Europe became public, Tess noticed a change in her husband. She couldn't be sure exactly when it began, but she knew James was avoiding her. His days were spent at Westminster or closeted in his study and she had no idea where he spent his nights. He came and went at odd hours and it was obvious, when they did meet, that he had been drinking. Something serious was troubling him. When she asked him to confide in her, he brushed her questions aside, accusing her of an overly active imagination. Hurt, she withdrew behind a curtain of silence, closing off all further communication.

Tess wasn't the only one who noticed a change in the duke of Langley. Lord Castlereagh was also worried. The tight, angry look that had been on James's face, after he returned from Spain and before his marriage, was back again. The foreign minister thought he knew what the problem was, but it had to be brought out in the open. He arranged a meeting with the prime minister.

"Why must we meet here, of all places?" Liverpool tightened both hands around his walking stick and looked around with obvious distaste. "Does Devereaux want every prizefighter in the nation to witness our conversation?"

Castlereagh grinned. "I should think you would be grateful that James was capable of frequenting Cribb's Parlor once again.

The prime minister smiled one of his rare smiles. "He did have a punishing right, didn't he? I'll wager James had the advantage of some of the best prizefighters in England." The smile faded. "But that was before Badajos. What is he up to, Castle-reagh?"

"I'm as much in the dark as you are"

Liverpool lifted his quizzing glass to his eye. "I say, isn't that Tom Cribb? Where in the devil is James?" He grabbed the sleeve of Castlereagh's coat. "The crowd is bound to get ugly. Is he mad, suggesting that we meet here?"

His words were drowned out by catcalls and whistles from the crowd. Tom Cribb, accompanied by his seconds, waved and threw his hat. Then he stepped into the ring. The crowd cheered.

A young man in top form and stripped to the waist, joined his opponent. Taller than Cribb, he had the lean grace of a seasoned cavalryman. Cribb, with his pugilist's frame, looked awkward in comparison. Castlereagh caught his breath. Accompanying him into the ring was James Devereaux.

"What the—?" Liverpool stood, but Castlereagh detained him with a hand on his shoulder.

"Easy, my friend. Let us wait this one out."

"What does he have to prove?" The prime minister asked in amazement.

"More than either of us know, m'lord," answered Castlereagh. "Perhaps James believes that he has nothing left of himself."

Both men breathed a sigh of relief as James spoke earnestly to the young amateur and stepped back outside of the ring.

The fight began in earnest. The younger man hit Cribb in the chin with his right and the champion went down. He was up again on the count of three, and after a fierce struggle threw his opponent to the ground. Now, the newcomer was up and threw a flush hit to Cribb's mouth. The crowd roared. Blood flowed from his cut lip. Both bodies gleamed with sweat. Liverpool closed his eyes in resignation and waited for the inevitable outcome.

At the end of the agreed-upon six rounds, both men were still up. The crowd went wild. At no time in Tom Cribb's illustrious career had an amateur lasted the distance against him. With a wide grin on his face, the challenger threw his arms around James who was now in the ring again and lifted him into the air. The bystanders cheered.

Again, Liverpool breathed a sigh of relief and stretched out his aching fingers. He hadn't realized his hands had been clenched the entire time.

Moments later, Devereaux joined Castlereagh and the prime minister at a small table in the corner of the tavern. His hair and face were damp as if he had just come out of the rain. He looked young and gay and unusually proud of himself.

"Well done, James," Castlereagh said, his eyes shining with excitement. "I never would have believed it if I hadn't seen it with my own eyes."

"Whatever possessed you, lad?" Liverpool surveyed the younger man's face.

Devereaux's smile flashed white in the dim tavern light. "I may no longer be able to spar myself, but I can help others who wish to take up the sport. I haven't felt so alive since I left Spain." He looked from Liverpool to Castlereagh. "Why are you here, gentlemen?"

The prime minister drew a deep breath. "It has to do with Spain and the rest of Europe," he explained. "Wellington's plan is terrifying the Whigs. We need your help in Vienna, James. It is vital that we convince the European powers to remain in Portugal with the general. As soon as the American problem is settled, our troops will relieve them."

"I've sold out," Devereaux replied, his eyes hard as stone. He lifted his glass to his lips and swallowed a long draught. "And what is more to the point, I believe you already know what I think of your foreign policy."

"Damn it, James," Liverpool's fist slammed down on the table. "I need you. England needs you. Why must you be so stubborn?" He looked from Devereaux to the tall, thin man sitting quietly by his side. "Help me, Castlereagh. You have more influence than I."

The foreign minister rubbed his chin thoughtfully before speaking. "I don't think James can be persuaded this time, m'lord. He hasn't forgiven us for allying ourselves with the rest of Europe."

"Do you mean to tell me he is sulking because he didn't get his way?" Liverpool's horrified expression would have been comical had the matter not been so serious.

Castlereagh grinned. "Exactly."

"My thanks, gentlemen," interrupted Devereaux, "for maligning my character and misinterpreting my motives."

"What is it then?" asked Castlereagh. "Why do you refuse to leave England?"

"My reasons are my own," the wooden expression on the duke's face hardened still further.

"That isn't good enough, m'lord," the prime minister's blustery voice softened. "I need time to replace you. Wellington won't accept just anyone. He trusts you. If you're bluffing, I need to know it now. Lay your cards on the table, James. Perhaps we can work something out."

Devereaux dropped his eyes and stared down at the mug of ale on the table. A year ago he had agreed to be Wellington's messenger. The general would retreat to Portugal to await the end of the American conflict. At this very moment, English troops, now stationed in France, were being deployed across the Atlantic to join Admiral Cochrane. After securing the United States, the full power of the British military would concentrate on winning the war in Europe.

Originally, he had supported the plan. But that was before Tess. He had tried, for her sake, to find a peaceful solution to the war in America, without compromising his obligation to Wellington. He had been unsuccessful. She wouldn't blame him for that. She would, however, never forgive him for supporting this betrayal of her country.

He looked up to face the foreign secretary and the prime minister. Castlereagh and Liverpool, the two most powerful political figures in the country, perhaps even in all of Europe, men who had it in their power to ordain the course of history. He couldn't help them. And all because of a woman. Irrational resentment swept through him.

His voice was tight and angry. "I'm sorry, gentlemen, but I can do nothing for you. Contrary to what you may believe, my reasons have nothing to do with England's alliance with Russia and Austria. I still maintain that autocratic powers who care little for their own people have nothing of value to offer us. But that has nothing to do with my decision. My excuse is a personal one." Pushing back his chair, he stood up. Without saying good-bye, he crossed the room and walked out the door.

"What the devil was that all about?" Liverpool asked.

Lord Castlereagh stared at the door for several moments without answering. Finally he spoke. "I think his lordship finds himself in somewhat of a dilemma. For a long time, he has managed to keep his position on the fence. Now he must make his choice."

"Go on," the prime minister demanded.

"His wife is an American."

Liverpool exploded. "What has that got to do with anything? She is now married to an English duke. A woman's loyalties should be to her husband."

Castlereagh thought of his own intelligent, opinionated wife, and grinned. "You don't know the duchess very well, do you, my lord?"

"I don't know her at all," Liverpool roared. "But I'll be damned if I will allow her to dictate the affairs of British government."

The dark eyes narrowed with laughter. "By all means," replied Castlereagh. "Be sure to tell her that. And please, invite me to watch when you do."

The scowl on the prime minister's face faded to a reluctant grin. He stood up and pushed in his chair. "Do you think I can't handle a slip of a woman?" he demanded. "Is that it?"

"I admire your resolution, sir," Castlereagh answered with a straight face. "You are an example to us all."

* * *

Devereaux intended to walk the twelve blocks to Grosvenor Square but the pain in his leg wouldn't allow it. Cursing, he waved down a hackney and proceeded to castigate himself for putting his weak limb through such punishment. He needed an outlet for his anger. Wherever he looked, there was none.

When he arrived at the door of his own home, he was almost relieved to find Lord William Fitzpatrick helping Tess from her carriage. Lamplight shone down on her fair hair. She looked up at Fitzpatrick and smiled. James did not miss the tender look on the man's face as he responded. Rage, primitive and uncontrollable, surged through him.

"May I ask where you've been with my wife?" The words were spoken softly, but the meaning was clear.

The obvious hostility in his voice startled Tess. She studied his face. He couldn't be drunk. He had spoken quite clearly. His movements were perfectly normal but there was a terrifying purpose in his eyes.

"William and I have been driving in the park, James," she said. "You said you would take me, but since you weren't here and William was, I went with him instead."

"Have I been ignoring you, my love?" The irony in his tone was laced with anger.

William moved protectively nearer to Tess. James's fists clenched.

Tess stared at him, her forehead creased in a frown. "Why don't we go inside," she suggested. "I'm cold and it's getting late."

"An excellent idea." James moved to the door. "Good night, Fitzpatrick."

"Would you like company, Tess?" William's face was set with anger.

Devereaux's words cracked like a whip. "You aren't welcome here, m'lord. Don't meddle in my affairs and keep away from my wife."

Tess looked at them both in exasperation. "Please go, William," she begged. "This isn't the place for a scene."

"I'm not leaving you now," William insisted stubbornly. "He's obviously drunk."

"Please," she pleaded. "I'll be all right."

Reluctantly, William stepped away and walked down the street. Devereaux rang the bell and waited, in controlled rage, for Tess to precede him into the house.

"I think I'll dine upstairs tonight, James," she said, after handing her coat to Litton. "I'm very tired."

"Do as you please," answered James, turning away. "Litton," he called out. "Bring a bottle of port to my study."

"James!" Tess's alarmed voice stopped him. "Won't you tell me what is disturbing you?"

His shoulders slumped and he turned back to answer her. Her heart went out to him.

His face was haggard and his eyes burned with anger, but his voice was completely flat when he spoke. "I gave my word to a man I respect more than anyone else on earth. Now, I'm forced to break it, because the woman I love more than life itself, refuses to understand that I am an Englishman. Not even for you, my love, can I change my loyalties."

Her eyes were the color of liquid silver. She lifted her chin and met his glance, contempt etched in every feature of her lovely face.

"Does keeping your word mean blockading Annapolis, m'lord? Does it mean soldiers burning our farms and frightening our people so that it is no longer safe to walk the streets of our cities? Does it mean British control of our ports and British flags flying over our government buildings?" Her voice cracked. "You made a promise to me as well, James. Do what you must, but never expect me to give you permission to end the existence of my country."

She turned and started up the stairs to her room. Halfway up, she heard heavy footsteps on the marble entry and the door slam.

James had gone out. Straightening to her full height, she bit her lip and walked the rest of the way to her room.

Dressed in a burgundy velvet robe with her hair hanging down her back, she sat by the fire and faced her fears. James was miserable. She had known it for some time. Part of it was her fault. She was afraid of losing him, but had no idea how to prevent it. His restlessness, his distracted air, and now the drinking, proved it. He was a man whose energies should be taken up with government affairs. Now, that he had married her, that was denied to him. Only two things mattered to Tess. The preservation of a way of life that was as necessary to her as breathing, and keeping her husband's love.

She closed her eyes and remembered the blissful feel of his arms closing around her. Sighing, she stood up and removed her robe. Climbing into bed, she pulled the covers over her. Where was James? she wondered. Images of Marjorie Weatherby's beautiful face flitted through her mind. She drifted into a troubled sleep.

Nineteen

At dinner, the next night, Tess was very aware of her husband sitting across from her. He had promised to escort her to Lady Bridgewater's ball, but she knew that if Georgiana hadn't been going as well, he would have cried off.

It was the first time in several weeks that the entire family had gathered together. Devereaux was unusually charming and well mannered. His flowing conversation and witty anecdotes were as effective a screen as his former icy aloofness. Tess wanted to scream and throw her soup at him, anything to wipe the smug arrogance from his handsome face.

Her fingers curled around her fork in a desperate grip. "Perhaps you have something else you would rather do this evening, James," she suggested. The sweetness of her words was in direct contrast to the fury flashing from her winter-grey eyes.

"Nonsense," he replied. "There is nothing else I would rather do than escort the two loveliest ladies in London to a ball."

"Are you quite sure?"

"Quite." He smiled mockingly. "Come, Tess. First you complain that I ignore you and now you can hardly wait to be rid of me."

"James." Leonie's shocked voice interrupted them. "Tess merely asked you a question. What has come over you?"

His eyes glittered. "Nothing, Mother. Nothing at all."

Against her better judgment, Tess attended the Bridgewater ball. Pain over her husband's coldness and anxiety over the war weakened her calm control. She was tense, strung tightly like the string of a bow, waiting for the exact moment when too much pressure was applied and she would snap.

Devereaux disappeared almost immediately into the card room. William Fitzpatrick watched him leave and crossed the room to stand by her side.

"Good lord, Tess, you look dreadful."

"Thank you, William. You can't imagine how cheerful that makes me feel."

"Do you have a headache?" he asked. "Let me find a carriage to take you home."

Touched by the concern in his voice, she smiled and placed her hand on his arm. "It's nothing, really. I'll be fine."

"Will you tell me what is bothering you? Perhaps I can help."

"No one can help."

They were interrupted by Lord Burrell. "How are you, Your Grace?" he bellowed. "You promised to ride in the park with me but every time I call, you aren't home. Is that any way to treat an old man?"

Tess truly liked him, but at that moment she was in no mood to listen to an aging war hero extol the glories of the British army. His loud voice grated on her sensitive nerves.

"I haven't been feeling well, m'lord." Her clear voice carried to others around them. "I'm concerned about the state of my country. I'm an American, or have you forgotten?"

Out of the corner of her eye she could see that James had come out of the card room. He leaned against the wall, his arms crossed against his chest, watching her silently.

"My dear child," protested Lord Burrell. "I don't think of you as an American. You are the duchess of Langley." He glanced nervously around the room, looking for a chance to escape. "If you will excuse me," he said, backing away. "I must see our hostess."

Tess looked around at the glittering assembly, dismissing the haughty, jewel-laden ladies and elegant gentlemen in their knee breeches and black coats. Her gaze focused on her husband's lean, powerful figure. Something snapped inside of her. The smoldering fury of her rage erupted at last.

Her voice shook and she grasped Fitzpatrick's arm. "You ask what ails me, William. I shall tell you. Your country has violated mine and even now your armies are invading American cities. Incredible as it seems, no one here feels the least bit responsible."

The blustery voice of the prime minister broke in. "I believe this war was one that your countrymen began, Your Grace."

She lifted her chin and looked defiantly at the elegant nobleman standing before her. Her voice was firm and clear in the sudden stillness of the room. "You are wrong m'lord. This war is England's fault. All America asked was to be allowed the rights of an independent nation and to be left alone. Since our War for Independence, you have refused to accept the United States as a sovereign country." Her eyes returned to her husband's stoic face. "You can win this war with sheer might. You can blockade our ports and starve our people. You can even annex our country so that it is once again a British colony. But, rest assured, your victory will be temporary. We are a proud and independent people. Never again will we bow to an English king or accept the dictates of an English Parliament."

Eyes wide with shock and more than a little shame, they stared at her. This lovely woman, no more than a girl, with her straight back and tear-bright eyes humbled them all.

Tess appealed to her husband. "I wish to go home, James. Will you take me?"

All eyes turned to Devereaux, splendidly handsome, coldly furious, his lean, immaculately clad figure slouching against the card-room door. In fascinated horror they watched as he stared at his wife, immobile and silent, ignoring her plea.

It seemed, to all who were there, that she shrank before them, the fire dying from her eyes. They watched her, cheeks aflame, cross the room and walk out the door into the night.

Not a sound could be heard in the ballroom. Fitzpatrick glared at James Devereaux in outraged silence, willing that he do something. From across the room he could see the brilliant piercing blue of his eyes. Minutes passed and still James didn't move.

Muttering a foul expletive, William walked across the room to the door. The tapping of his shoes was very loud on the polished marble. Glancing back one last time, he turned to follow Tess.

Marjorie Weatherby moved to Devereaux's side. Laying her hand on his shoulder, she whispered something into his ear. He looked at her luscious figure in the low cut gown and nodded. Pushing himself away from the wall, he held out his arm for her hand. Smiling triumphantly, she hardly noticed the pointed stares as they moved toward the door.

Castlereagh stopped them halfway. "You aren't leaving, James?"

"Lord Devereaux has offered to escort me home," Marjorie said. "I feel a headache coming on."

"Indeed." Castlereagh looked faintly amused. "You won't mind if I speak to him for a moment in private."

Marjorie smiled and stepped aside. She could afford to be gracious.

"What the devil are you doing, James?" Castlereagh whispered furiously.

The duke's eyes glittered. "I'm going to spend time in the company of a woman who understands me."

Castlereagh clutched his arm. "Don't do this. Leave now and make your peace with Tess."

James looked down at the hand on his sleeve. He laughed bitterly. "There is no peace with Tess. She doesn't know the meaning of the word."

"You're a fool, James Devereaux." Castlereagh sighed. "Why must you always take the difficult road?"

"Marjorie is waiting," said the duke softly. "Was there anything else?"

"No." The word was barely audible. "Nothing else."

James walked across the room to rejoin Marjorie. Her head was very close to his as they disappeared out the door.

At Berkeley Square, he helped her from the carriage. Leading her up the stairs he stopped at the massive front door.

Turning her toward him, he said, "I'll leave you here, Marjorie."

"You're not coming in?" Hurt was evident in the outraged expression on her face.

Bending his head, he kissed her gently on the lips. "As tempting as the suggestion is, I must decline. I wouldn't be good company tonight."

"Stay with me, James," Marjorie pleaded. "I can make you happy. I know I can."

His face hardened. "Good night, Marjorie."

Fitzpatrick didn't want to leave Tess. He was afraid of what James might do to her.

"I'll be all right," she insisted. "Even if James were to be violent, the duchess will be here. He can hardly murder me without everyone knowing."

"Tess." He clasped her hands. "Come away with me. I'll make you happy. I promise I will."

The corners of her lips turned up in a smile. "You're a dear friend, William. What would I do without you?"

He looked down into her vulnerable, delicate face and groaned. Pulling her to him, he kissed her with hard, insistent lips.

She remained stiff in his arms, neither responding nor resisting.

"Fitzpatrick," a quiet voice, terrifying in its clarity, interrupted them. "Unless I have taken leave of my senses, this is my house and the woman you are mauling is my wife."

Tess looked up, startled. Her husband's figure filled the doorway. He was dangerously angry. Quickly she ran to him.

"It was nothing, James," she stammered, laying her hand on his arm. "William was worried about me. That is all it was."

"Go upstairs," he ordered.

"James," she pleaded.

"Go! Now!"

She stopped before him on her way to her room. "If you hurt him, I shall never forgive you."

His mouth twisted bitterly, but he didn't reply. Fitzpatrick, white-faced and defiant, was equally as silent.

Tess allowed her maid to pull a nightgown over her head and brush out her hair. Climbing into bed, she pulled the covers over her, praying for sleep. It didn't come. The hours crept by. It was almost morning when she heard a step outside her door. She sat up and waited.

The knob turned and James stepped in. He was still dressed in evening clothes. The lamp from the hall shone on his ink-black hair, lighting his face. His features were controlled but his eyes blazed with fury. Tess hid her fear.

"What happened?" she asked, her head tilted defiantly.

Ignoring her question, he moved toward the bed. Her eyes, bruised and dark in her too-white face, stared up at him.

"Did you hurt William?"

Reaching out, he traced her delicate bones with gentle fingers.

"Were you afraid for him?" he asked, jealousy searing a fiery path across his chest.

"I would fear for anyone you were terribly angry with," she admitted.

"But not for yourself." His exploring fingers reached the buttons of her nightdress. He unfastened the top one. "You aren't afraid of me, are you, Tess? If you were, you would never have made such a scene in public."

She melted under his touch. It had been such a long time. "No. I'm not afraid of you." She lifted her head proudly. "I love you."

"You might have thought of that earlier." He slipped the gown from her shoulders, staring hungrily at her body in the moonlight.

She raised her arms to pull him close to her. "You told me to say what I felt. You said it wouldn't matter." She gasped as his mouth found the sensitive spot between her neck and shoulder. "You told me I didn't have to change my politics."

"Holy Christ, Tess," he groaned, pulling off his clothes and sliding into bed beside her. "You can't be that naive. You insulted the prime minister of England."

"He insulted me first." She smiled into the darkness, pressing her lips to his shoulder as he fitted his body to hers.

"You're supposed to be my wife."

"But I don't agree with your politics."

He didn't answer, his eyes intent on her face. "I never knew love could be like this," he murmured, smoothing back her hair. "We're as different as oil and water. Like a moth to your flame, I'm incapable of living too near or too far from your glow."

She touched his face with shaking hands. "Shall we cry truce, my love?"

With arms of steel, he locked her beneath him and without further preliminaries, slid into her.

Tess forgot the prime minister and Lady Bridgewater's ball. She forgot she was an American and her husband a British aristocrat and that Annapolis was an ocean away from London. She forgot that she missed her father and sisters and the lovely tranquil monotony of life on the tidewater. Nothing mattered but the feel of the hard body against hers, the clean soap-like smell that clung to his skin, the warm rush of pleasure evoked by his caressing hands, and the incredible dizzying passion that never failed to claim her.

Later, while she slept, he watched her. Blue shadows showed under the long lashes. Remorse smote him. He had tried to force her to his will with arctic aloofness. It hadn't worked. There was a steel-like quality, an inner strength in the fragile woman lying beside him. He had hoped to make her admit she needed him. In the end, he couldn't stand their emotional separation any longer. He had come to her.

Finding her in William Fitzpatrick's arms shocked him. Not for a moment did he believe Tess would be unfaithful to him. He knew her too well, and her rigid stance told him she had not encouraged the embrace. But the sight of another man holding his wife had wiped all sanity from his mind. It had taken the combined efforts of Litton and his mother, who arrived in time to witness the entire scene, to convince him to leave Fitzpatrick unharmed.

Tess stirred and opened her eyes. The question in them could not be ignored.

"I'm so sorry, my darling." Devereaux kissed her forehead. "Have you been as miserable as I?"

"Yes," she said. "I have." Her pale hair covered the pillow, framing her face like a portrait. "Has anything changed?"

"Only my perspective." He laughed harshly. "I've never been more miserable in my life as I have this past month. Shutting you out isn't the answer."

"What is?"

He breathed a deep, shaking breath. "I'll give it up," he said, "all of it. We'll go back to Langley. I'll play the role of a gentleman farmer and put all of my efforts into producing the grandson my mother wants so desperately."

Tess blushed, but her eyes never wavered from his face. "Can you do it? Give up the world of politics you've been a part of for ten years? Can you disappoint General Wellington?

"Yes," he said softly, "but only if you promise to do the same."

Her eyes were the grey of smoke and filled with love. She reached up, her lips seeking his. "You are my life, James Devereaux," she whispered against his mouth. "There is nothing for me without you."

Twenty

Leonie Devereaux was relieved that her son and daughter-in-law had settled their differences. Their decision to return to the country alone had her unqualified approval. Because their hasty wedding had been such a private affair, she decided to combine the annual Devereaux ball with a public reception, formally introducing Tess as the new duchess of Langley. She insisted they delay their departure until then. The couple reluctantly agreed.

Invitations were sent out to the most elite members of the ton, and although the event was scheduled for only one week away, there wasn't a single refusal.

Leonie was flushed with excitement and nervous tension. The ballroom was cleaned from ceiling to floor. Musicians were hired, flowers ordered and menus planned. Workmen entered and exited the servants' entrance at impossible hours, sawing and hammering until, finally, she pronounced everything perfect.

The decorations were a well-guarded secret. The day before the ball, she led Tess to the huge double doors closing off the ballroom from the rest of the house. With a sweep of her hand she ushered her inside.

"What do you think?" she asked, smiling proudly.

Tess stared at the scene before her, a lump forming in her throat. She couldn't speak.

Mimosa and honeysuckle filled the room and the air was perfumed with the scent of roses. Tall white columns, thick with bougainvillea, supported graceful arches. A huge wooden porch, painted white, had been constructed against the far wall for the orchestra. The room was a perfect replica of the entrance to Harrington House.

Her hand rose to her throat. Tess turned toward her mother-in-law, tears stinging her eyelids.

"This is beautiful," she whispered. "I can't believe it. How could you know exactly what it looks like?"

Leonie looked surprised. "By listening to you, of course. You've described your home to all of us, countless times. What you didn't say, Georgiana filled in for me." She looked around her. "It really is lovely, isn't it?"

Tess's sweeping glance took in colors of moss green, purple, crimson, and bright yellow. She looked again at the ceiling, painted a robin's egg blue and dotted with white clouds. A mural of the bay and Annapolis Harbor, covering one wall, was so lifelike she could almost smell the tangy odors of mussels and crayfish.

She turned to see Leonie anxiously watching her. "Thank you." She smiled. "This is the loveliest gift I've ever received."

Leonie sighed with relief. "I'm so glad you like it." She reached out to take Tess's hand and hesitated. "It hasn't been easy for you these last few months," she said. "I hope you know that we want you to be happy here."

Deeply touched, Tess reached up to kiss the older woman's cheek. Leonie's uncharacteristic display of affection dissolved the remaining awkwardness between them.

"I am happy" she assured her. "And also very lucky to have such a kind and thoughtful family."

Leonie looked into the shining grey eyes. Her last doubt disappeared. Slipping her arm into Tess's, she led her out of the room.

"Shall we show the others or keep it a surprise?" she asked, closing the doors behind her.

Tess tilted her head to one side, giving the matter serious thought.

"Show them now," she decided, after a lengthy pause. "When

the room is filled with people, the full effect won't be the same. I want James to see it as it is, right now."

"Very well." Leonie answered. "We'll take the others through tonight, after dinner."

Harmony between the two women was short-lived. The subject of clothing was an area where Tess and her mother-in-law still could not agree. It was the Langley ball that brought their differing philosophies to a head.

The price of a gown in London was abhorrent to the American girl. Raised by fiscally conservative Nathanial Harrington, Tess understood the value of money. To her, a ball gown worn only once, should not cost as much as the average man earned in a year's time. The clothing she brought from Annapolis was well-made and stylish. Even if she wore a gown not nearly as expensive as one designed in London, her figure and coloring gave everything she wore a special appeal. She also had a much smaller wardrobe than Leonie or Georgiana. Rather than relegate a gown to the back of her closet, she wore it until the fabric was faded or worn through.

Leonie was appalled that the new duchess of Langley was content to wear inferior garments.

"You simply must have a new gown," Leonie insisted.

Tess looked up from the book she was reading to answer her mother-in-law.

"I'll wear my green satin," she said.

Leonie looked scandalized. "You can't wear the same gown twice in a row! It is absolutely out of the question."

She looked at her son, who entered the room at exactly that moment. "Your wife is being extremely unreasonable," she complained. "I've gone to considerable trouble to make this event perfect and she won't listen to reason."

James looked amused. Seating himself beside Tess, he casually placed his arm across the back of the sofa, his fingers caressing the nape of her neck.

"Are you being unreasonable, my love?" he teased.

Tess smiled, trying to ignore the gentle, insistent pressure against her skin. His touch aroused feelings that had no place in Leonie Devereaux's sitting room.

"I see no reason to incur the expense of a new ball gown," she explained. "It may be years before I'll be able to wear it again and I've bought enough clothes already."

"Do you have news for us, my dear?" There was an edge of excitement to Leonie's voice.

"What do you mean?" Tess looked confused.

James translated for her. "What Mother wants to know, is whether or not we are expecting a child?"

Color flamed across Tess's cheeks. "No, I don't think so," she answered, her eyes meeting her husband's. "But soon, perhaps."

"All the more reason for you to have this gown," argued Leonie. "Who knows how long it will be before you have another like it. Sometimes a second child arrives soon after the first." She looked to her son for help. "What do you think, James?"

"I think Tess looks beautiful in whatever she wears." He continued to look at the exquisite face beside him. "And, although I can certainly afford to dress my wife in anything she chooses, the decision is hers."

Leonie lifted her hands, in a gesture of defeat. "Very well," she sighed. "Do what you will. I wash my hands of it. Don't be surprised if the gossips say you are miserly in the treatment of your wife."

Neither James nor Tess deigned to answer. Her eyes narrowing, Leonie assessed the expression on their faces. Without another word, she tactfully left the room.

"I thought she would never go away," James murmured, pulling the pins from Tess's bright hair, until it lay like a sheet of spun silver across her shoulders. Cradling her face in his hands, his mouth came down hard on hers.

Responding to the urgency of his kiss, Tess parted her lips and moaned at the familiar intimacy invading her mouth. Her arms reached up to encircle his neck at the same time his hand reached into her gown, cupping her breast. Heat coursed through her veins. She pulled away, breathing rapidly.

"It's the middle of the day." Her voice was breathless, her protest halfhearted.

His eyes were dark with desire. "Didn't I hear you say you hoped to be expecting a child soon?"

"That was for your mother."

His lips twitched. "Then, you don't want a child?"

"No," she stammered. "I mean, yes." Tess pushed him away and stood up, hands on her hips. "You're teasing me," she accused.

James stood and pulled her into his arms. "Only a little," he said, trailing light kisses from her ear to her shoulder. "You're magnificent when you're angry."

She melted against him, feeling the planes of his body harden as he molded her against him.

"I'm not angry anymore," she whispered.

"Good." He lifted her against his chest. "Let's go upstairs."

In the end, Tess agreed to a new gown. It was a small price to pay, she decided, after Leonie had gone to the trouble and expense of the flower-filled ballroom.

That night, as she looked at her reflection in the full-length mirror, she knew that it wasn't only a wish to please Leonie that prompted her decision. It was a very natural feminine desire to wear her first London-made gown. The effect was breathtaking.

She had selected a fabric of cream-colored silk, shot with silver. The dressmaker had worked it into a starkly simple, classically cut sheath, that sparkled like stardust when Tess moved. The Langley diamonds glittered in her ears and around her throat. The bodice was lower than she'd ever worn before and a single large pendant, worth a king's ransom, rested between her breasts. Her hair, too straight to curl, was dressed in a high chignon, its simplicity setting off the purity of her profile and the long, lovely line of her neck.

She looked, Leonie thought, as she watched the fair-haired beauty descend the stairs, like a princess.

Although he made no comment, the look on her husband's face was worth everything to Tess. Later, as he stood next to her, greeting their guests, he murmured under his breath. "You humble me, my love. Not in my wildest dreams did I imagine I would have the good fortune to find someone like you."

Tess met his glance, her heart in her eyes. "It is the same for me," she whispered. "Every day, I thank God it was you who was Georgiana's brother."

Lord Castlereagh, stepping forward to greet the duke and duchess did not miss the look that passed between them. With genuine pleasure, he shook Devereaux's hand as Lady Castlereagh spoke with Tess.

"My faith in you has been reaffirmed, m'lord," he said in a low voice. "I'm glad of it."

James did not pretend to misunderstand. "That relieves me." His eyes danced. "However, your concern was unnecessary. I can always handle my own affairs."

Castlereagh grinned. "Again, I'm glad of it," he repeated, before moving into the brilliantly lighted room.

After greeting their remaining guests, the duke and duchess made their way through the people clustered in small groups throughout the ballroom. More than one admiring glance followed the attractive couple as they took their places beside a large banquet table. The massive chandelier brought out hidden blue lights in the duke's black hair, a perfect complement to the silvery fairness of his wife.

As Tess stared at her husband, she was struck, once again, by his striking appearance. The light eyes, so arresting against the black hair and dark skin, were intent on her face. The familiar glint in their depths weakened her knees and brought a flush of anticipation to her cheeks.

His features were lean and hard, meticulously sculpted, as if chiseled from marble. The white cravat against his black coat brought out the contrast of dark skin and white teeth, of steel-blue eyes and black hair, unrelieved by even the slightest shade of brown.

Suddenly he grinned. Tess took a deep shuddering breath as he expertly guided her through the dancing couples. God help her. He was devastatingly handsome. She was thankful he had wanted to marry her, thankful it was love they shared, as well as the searing passion that threatened to consume her heart and soul whenever he touched her. She knew with a dreadful certainty, that even if he hadn't been a gentleman, even if he hadn't offered marriage, there was nothing she would have refused him.

In public, James wasn't a demonstrative man. He preferred to show his affection in the privacy of his bedchamber. But the look in Tess's clear eyes couldn't be denied. Just as the last note died away, he bent down and brushed her lips with his.

The intimate caress was missed by almost everyone except the stranger who stood in the doorway. His appearance caused a stir among the guests in the ballroom.

"Good heavens," Leonie whispered to Georgiana, who stood beside her. "Who is that? I'm sure he wasn't on the guest list."

Georgiana turned to look. Her face whitened with shock and she lifted her hand to her throat.

The boy who stood at the door was young, and of no more than medium height and weight. But his lean, athletic grace gave the appearance of controlled strength. He was dressed correctly, in a dark coat and knee breeches, but the clothing didn't suit him. His skin was deeply tanned, his hair the color of sunlight on cornsilk. His eyes were a tawny gold, angry and accusing, like those of an enraged predator.

He searched the room, the molten gaze stopping, now and then, to look carefully at the features of a fair-haired woman before moving on. He found Tess at the exact moment James bent to kiss her lips.

Stepping back from Devereaux's embrace, she looked toward the door. Her gaze locked with the golden eyes and the impact shook her. She gasped in disbelief.

Tess's eyes widened and her throat went dry. All around her, the light began to fade. Drinking in deep gulps of air she fought against the faintness threatening to envelop her.

Unconscious of the staring eyes, the young man crossed the floor with long, deliberate steps. His head was up and his brows drew together in an angry, defiant line.

"Tess?" James's worried voice broke through the fog clouding her brain. "Are you ill?" He looked at the man bearing down on them. "Do you know this man?"

The boy stopped directly in front of Tess. His eyes gleamed with contempt and rage, and something else James couldn't identify.

In the distinctive tones of the American tidewater, he spoke. "Are you ill, Tess?" he mocked her. "Tell the duke of Langley who I am." His lips pulled away from his teeth in a savage grimace. "That is, if you can remember. How long has it been?" The relentless voice showed no mercy as he answered his own question. "All of seven months, I believe. For some women, seven months is long enough to forget one husband and marry another."

There wasn't a hint of color in the pale ivory of Tess's cheeks. She turned to look at Devereaux. Beneath the drawn mask of his face, his expression was unreadable. All at once, she was violently, bitterly angry. She wanted to lash out, to hurt him.

"This," she said, waving her hand at the young man, "is a ghost, Your Grace. Meet the remains of Daniel Bradford, the man you swore was dead at Dartmoor Prison."

A horrified gasp broke the silence. James watched his mother slide to the floor. He didn't move. A horrifying despair held him in its grip. He looked at the still, cold face of the woman he loved. She believed he had lied to her. He could read it in her eyes. Desperation seized him. He tried to make her understand.

"I didn't know, Tess. I swear I didn't." His voice was hoarse. "I believed he was dead."

Fearless and straight as a lance, she moved quickly. He saw it coming and winced even before the contact was made. Like the crack of a gunshot, her hand came up and slapped his cheek. The sound shattered the stillness.

A red welt stained his skin. Still, James didn't move.

Without a word, Tess walked past the assembled guests and out of the ballroom.

Daniel Bradford followed her.

Twenty-one

Walking quickly down the hall, Tess had almost reached the stairs when Daniel caught up with her. Reaching out he grabbed her arm, pulling her around to face him.

"Where are you going?" he asked.

Her eyes were huge and stormy grey. "To get my things."

"You're coming with me?"

Tess heard the question in his voice. She searched his face. He was terribly thin, the bones prominent under the taut skin. Guilt flooded through her and she clenched her fists.

"Did you doubt that I would?"

"Of course." His smile was bitter. "Once, I thought I knew you better than anyone. That was before you married an English duke, barely five months after I was reported missing. The Teresa Harrington I knew would never have done such a thing."

Tess winced, but refused to look away from the censure in his eyes.

"You were not reported missing, Daniel. We thought you were dead."

Against his will, the words burst forth. "How could you do it, Tess? Did you care so little for what we had?"

She shook her head. "I loved you very much," she whispered. "I still do."

He reached for her hands. "Were you forced to wed? Did he threaten you?" Hope shone from the golden eyes.

For the space of a heartbeat, Tess hesitated. A lie would wipe the torment from his face.

"No," she said, at last. "I married Lord Langley of my own free will."

He waited for her explanation. There was none. Finally, he dropped her hands.

"If you've no objection," he said, "I'll wait for you at the American minister's residence."

Tess nodded her head. "Very well. I won't be long."

He opened his mouth to speak and then changed his mind.

Tess watched him open the door and disappear into the night. A blessed numbness took hold of her. She climbed the stairs to her rose-scented bedchamber. Lamplight bathed the room in a welcoming glow. Deliberately ignoring the bed, she threw open the wardrobe searching for the gowns she brought with her from Annapolis. Working quickly, she dragged a trunk from against the wall, and haphazardly began to pack.

A knock on the door froze the blood in her veins. She couldn't face James. Not now. Not ever. On leaden feet, she walked to the door. Bracing herself, she opened it. Lizzie Devereaux peered back at her.

Tess sighed with relief. "Lizzie," she breathed, "what on earth are you doing up at this hour?"

The child's lip quivered. "I heard loud voices and Judith told me Mama is sick." Tears formed in the corners of her eyes. "Is it true, Tess? Georgiana said you are going away."

Heedless of her gown, Tess knelt on the floor and held out her arms. Lizzie fell into them. The tears she had been holding back, now flowed freely down her cheeks, wetting Tess's bare shoulder.

"Hush, dear," Tess murmured, kissing the top of Lizzie's dark head. "Please, don't cry."

"Why are you leaving us?" she cried. "Aren't you happy here?" She lifted her head and looked accusingly at Tess.

"Oh, Lizzie," Tess began. "If only I could make you understand."

Lizzie sniffed and buried her face against Tess's neck. "I don't want you to leave," she whimpered.

"I don't want to leave," Tess cried, "but I have no choice.

Please try and understand, Lizzie. I made a promise that I must keep."

The child's wet eyelashes brushed against her neck. Tess tightened her arms around the small body.

"Will I ever see you again?" Lizzie asked.

"Yes," she said. "Caroline lives in America. When you are older, we'll see each other again."

"I'll never forget you," she murmured, the words muffled against Tess's throat. "I wish you could truly be my sister."

The numbness dissolved and pain, like the searing of a slow burn, twisted her heart. "Oh, Lizzie," she sobbed, clutching the small girl to her breast, "so do I."

Leonie lay on her bed with a handkerchief soaked in lavender water pressed to her brow. She watched her son with worried eyes. He faced away from her, toward the window, but the tight set of his shoulders, and the balled fists in his pockets, gave him away. His silence was frightening.

"Are you going to stop her?" she asked, unable to keep still any longer.

He turned toward his mother. Leonie gasped. His ravaged expression, the haunted eyes, the mouth tight with a pain she had never seen before, couldn't possibly belong to her son. Her heart ached for him.

For a long time he said nothing. She waited for him to speak. When he did, the despair in his voice nearly broke her control.

"No," he replied. "I am not going to stop her."

She dropped the handkerchief and sat up. "James," she began, wetting her lips, "you must listen to me." She fixed serious blue eyes on her son. "For years you've gone your own way, refusing to do as I asked, but this time I insist that you listen."

He stared at her without answering, his mouth grim with suppressed rage. For a moment, Leonie doubted her courage to continue. Recklessly, she proceeded.

"Tess is the kind of woman who does not give her heart easily.

I know she loves you. Can you send her away with a man she no longer cares for?"

His lips twisted. "How can you have lived with her for all this time and not come to know her at all?"

Leonie frowned. "What do you mean?"

"Tess will never forgive me for this," he answered. "She believes I lied to her."

Leonie's eyes widened in disbelief. "She can't be foolish enough to think you would actually marry a woman who already had a husband."

His smile mocked her. "Tess is no fool, Mother. Unlike you, she knows me for what I am."

The ice in his voice chilled her. She shivered. Rubbing her arms, she forced the question from her lips.

"What does she know, that I do not?"

The firelight flickered across his angry mouth and high cheekbones. He looked up suddenly, startling Leonie with the deadly purpose reflected in his eyes.

"Nothing would have kept me from marrying Tess," the soft voice answered her. "If I had known that Daniel Bradford had survived his impressment, he would no longer be alive."

Shock drained the color from her face. Leaning back against the cushions, she shaded her eyes with her hand.

"May God have mercy on your soul," she whispered.

As the sound of his footsteps died away, she turned her face into the pillows and wept.

The vessel Daniel had secured for them to return to Maryland was an American privateer. Tess knew the moment she saw it that the slim beautiful hull and proud bow could have been crafted by only one man. Nathanial Harrington's mark was there in the clean lines and graceful sails. Tears filled her eyes. She would sail home on a ship designed and built by her own father.

Because of Adam Bradford's failing health, Lord Liverpool had arranged for Tess and Daniel to be given the right of safe

passage across the Atlantic to Annapolis. Tess was sure this act
of unprecedented kindness had more to do with consideration
for the Devereauxs than any concern for the troublesome son
and daughter-in-law of a dying American senator.

Tess looked at the sober cut of Thomas Waverly's clothing
and the carefully neutral expression on his handsome face when
he conversed with Daniel or Mr. Rush. The captain's gentlemanly
manners were in direct contrast to the way he treated her when
no one else was around. The dark eyes stared boldly into hers,
admiring her beauty, teasing her, daring her to respond. His teeth
were very white against his dark face, and his sensual mouth
slanted with laughter as he whispered improper suggestions into
her ear. The earring in his ear and his deep tan reminded her of
a pirate, rather than a respectable patriot loyal to the United States
of America.

Although she treated him with icy disdain, Tess couldn't help
liking him. He was completely obvious about his intent and went
about achieving its end with a single-mindedness that took her
breath away. Unlike Daniel, he made it very clear that he desired
her company.

It mattered little to Thomas Waverly that the beautiful young
woman on his ship had a husband. Early in the voyage, he con-
cluded that the couple were not on intimate terms. The details
were unimportant to him. Whatever their difficulties, he hoped
they would not be reconciled before their journey ended. He
found her alone on the deck, one evening, staring at the white
foam breaking against the bow.

Tess was worried about Daniel. They had been at sea for over
a week and still he could not bear the sight of her. They shared
a cabin, but each night he waited for her to fall asleep before
stretching himself out, fully clothed, on the far side of the bunk.
Other than a brief explanation of his rescue by the crew of *The
United States* and *The Java*, Daniel had revealed little of his
difficulties during the past year. When Tess asked him why his
name had appeared on Dartmoor Prison's roll of the dead, he
refused to discuss it. Finally she gave up. When he was ready,

he would explain. She hoped it would be soon. Annapolis and their future loomed closer every day.

"Why so melancholy, little one?" The low, vibrant tones of the captain interrupted her thoughts. He leaned on the railing beside her.

Feeling more miserable than usual, Tess answered him honestly. "I wish that we would never reach home and I might sail the seas forever."

Waverly looked at her, a strange expression on his face. "That's an odd wish for a beautiful young bride."

"Not so odd," she replied, "when you consider the circumstances."

"May I know these unusual circumstances?"

Tess shook her head, brushing the hair from her face. "No, I'm sorry. I've said too much already."

He looked at the proud set of her chin, the anguished eyes and trembling lips. A surge of possessiveness swept through him. Without thinking, he put his hands on her shoulders, pulling her against him. "Tell me what troubles you, Tess?" he whispered. "I can't bear to see you miserable."

Shocked at his presumption, Tess tried to move away but he was too strong. "Please release me," she said, holding her arms stiffly at her sides. She would not compromise her dignity by struggling.

Instead of complying, the captain tightened his arms, holding her immobile against his chest.

Suddenly it was too much. The humiliating public disgrace, the contemptuous stranger waiting in her cabin, the aching pain of a loss she hadn't even begun to come to terms with and now, this final insult. Perhaps Waverly had heard her shameful story. Perhaps he thought that a woman who had been unfaithful once would be so again. Tears spilled down her cheeks wetting his shoulder.

His hands moved up and down her back. "I'm a man, little one. And if you don't say something very soon, I'll forget that you're particularly vulnerable tonight and show you."

"May I interrupt?" Daniel's cold voice cut through the silence.

Waverly raised his head. Smiling down at Tess, he put her behind him.

"By all means, Mr. Bradford." He waited for the challenge he was sure would come.

"It's late, Tess." Daniel stared pointedly at her.

She nodded and disappeared down the companionway.

Shock registered on the captain's face as Daniel turned to follow her. The captain's hand shot out to grab his sleeve.

"What kind of man are you?" he demanded, as Daniel turned to face him. "Your wife takes comfort in my arms and you go calmly off to bed."

" Stay out of this, Waverly," Daniel warned him. "You know nothing about it."

"I know this." Thomas Waverly couldn't remember when he'd been so angry. "If she were my wife, I would make sure she had no need for anyone but me."

Daniel's eyes blazed a brilliant gold. "I am growing accustomed to finding my wife in the arms of other men, Captain. Unless you wish to take your place in line, I suggest you leave her alone."

The silence drew out between them. Just as Daniel was about to turn away, Waverly's words stopped him.

"I know something about the nature of women, lad," he said softly. "Your wife is no harlot."

Daniel's bitter laugh floated across the quiet deck. "Can't you see that makes it even worse."

When he opened the door to the cabin, Daniel could barely make out Tess's form under the bedclothes. She was huddled against the wall, her body curled into a tight ball, as if to discourage any contact between them.

He cursed under his breath. Shrugging out of his coat, he untied his cravat and walked over to the bed. Reaching out, he touched her shoulder.

She tensed and pulled away.

Daniel looked down at the bright hair loose on the pillow. He wound his fingers through its silken softness. Her cheek, barely visible behind the silvery mane, was wet with tears. He felt instant remorse. This was Tess, his wife. How had they come to this?

His earliest memories were of her. She was his friend, his confidante, his childhood sweetheart, his love. From the time she was fourteen years old, he had wanted to marry her. Raging jealousy had consumed him when men, older and more sophisticated than he, had squired her to local parties and barbeques. He lived in fear of her falling in love with one of them.

She had laughed away his doubts and, true to her word, married him shortly after her nineteenth birthday. He had been the happiest man on earth. The thought of her lovely face, and slim golden body, had kept him alive and sane through his impressment on the British man-o'war, and during the long months of hell in Dartmoor Prison.

Obeying his instincts, he bent his head and kissed her tear-stained cheek.

Tess turned to look at him. He was struck, once again, by the perfect symmetry of her features and the clear slate-grey beauty of her eyes.

With a groan, he gathered her into his arms, blindly seeking her mouth. After a moment, her lips parted under the demand of his tongue.

Breathing heavily, he released her and stood up. Removing his clothes, he returned to the bed and lifted the nightgown over her head. He threw it to the floor and lay down beside her.

"It's time we finished this," he muttered pulling her against him.

Tess forced herself to relax as his hands explored her body. His lips were warm on her neck and breasts. An unsettled feeling began in the pit of her stomach. She gritted her teeth. He moved over her, wedging his leg between her thighs. Bile rose in her throat. She could feel the heat of him, hard and insistent, against her. Nausea swept through her. She could hold it back no longer. Pressing a hand against her mouth, she pushed him away.

Confused, he lifted his head. Correctly assessing the look on her face, he stood up and quickly reached for the basin, handing it to her just in time. He held her hair back and spoke in soothing tones as she retched, again and again, into the bowl.

When it was clear there was nothing left to come up, he wiped her face with a cool cloth and gently tucked the blanket around her exhausted form. Stretching out beside her, he tossed and turned in frustrated silence until at last, exhaustion overtook him and he slept.

Twenty-two

The scene repeated itself the following morning and again, later in the afternoon. Tess managed to consume a normal amount of food at meals, only to lose everything she ate shortly after. Raised from infancy in a family of women, she immediately realized the horrifying nature of her condition. With a sense of inevitability she counted off the months on her fingers. There could be no doubt. She was three months gone with child.

She was distracted by the drum roll below, its sharp staccato rhythm signaling an alarm to all members of the crew.

"What's happened?" asked Tess, clutching the sleeve of a seaman who tried to rush by.

He tipped his cap. "An enemy sail on the horizon," he replied before hurrying on. "It looks British."

"But we've safe passage," whispered Tess.

The captain suddenly appeared beside her and smiled. "I never could resist a wealthy cargo. It might be better if you waited in the hold. Unless British marksmanship has improved, you'll probably be safe, but I wouldn't chance it."

She thought of the dark hold and the stench of the bilge. Shaking her head she said, "I couldn't. Please, don't insist."

He gave her a sharp look but didn't argue.

"Be careful," he warned before shouting, "break out her colors, Mr. Cole."

Men poured from the hatches at the first beat of the drum. The ship had been a whirling beehive of disciplined activity for several minutes. Now, all they had left to do was wait.

The British ship, a clumsy frigate, was very close. The Union Jack and the royal ensign fluttered side by side. Tess could hear a loud cheering. She watched Daniel, his face hard with determination, strap on a sword.

Rushing to his side, she shouted above the voices. "What are you doing?"

"She means to close," he answered. "Waverly needs every man."

"Waverly chased the frigate down. He's risking men's lives for profit." She could feel the deck shudder and leap as the guns discharged. "This isn't your battle."

"The hell it isn't!" Fury contorted Daniel's face. "I spent three months on one of those ships and I've the scars to prove it. I was starved and beaten in the worst pesthole known to man. This is my fight more than anyone here."

"What if something happens to you?" Her voice was so low it looked as if she mouthed the words.

Leaning close to her ear, he spoke deliberately. "Then, you'll have every reason to return to your English duke."

Her face paled as if she'd been struck. Without a backward glance, she turned and walked into the companionway.

"Keep at it, lads," Waverly shouted as a splinter of mast missed his head by inches. The answering roar of the American guns thundered against the frigate's hull.

The ships were so close that Tess could see the agonized features on the faces of the dying men. Even from her position in the safety of the companionway, she knew that the marksmanship of those on the enemy ship was not nearly as accurate as that of the men on the Baltimore schooner.

American seamen were boarding the British vessel. A sail fell, sweeping the men on the frigate across the deck and into the ocean. British seamen fell to their deaths, stilled by the nightmarish precision of American bullets. Crashing to the deck, the mainmast gave way, imprisoning two men as it fell. With a roar, the sloop raked the helpless frigate with a final barrage of bullets.

Tess turned away, sickened by the cries of the dying men. So, this was war. No wonder Nathanial Harrington had argued so forcefully against it.

"Will you lower your colors, sir?" The question, so politely phrased by Waverly to the British captain, struck Tess as laughable. There was one seaman left on the British quarterdeck to relay the message. He stood at the helm, rigid and unmoving, unable to believe the slaughter before his eyes. Only twelve men in all were unhurt. One of them, Tess saw with unbelieving eyes, was James Devereaux.

The battle had lasted less than half an hour. Battered beyond recognition, the British ship, a wreckage of men and sails and rigging, lay on its side in a quiet sea. Most of her crew lay dead or wounded.

Tess watched in numbed silence as the prisoners were ordered below. Only then, did she remember Daniel. He stood in the waist staring at the prisoners as they disappeared below deck. He turned accusing eyes on Tess.

"Is it a coincidence that Langley happens to be sailing across the Atlantic at the same time you are?" Jealousy ate at his insides. "Why do you look so surprised?" he demanded. "Did you think I wouldn't recognize him?"

She didn't pretend to misunderstand. The injustice of his accusation infuriated her.

"Yes," she answered, "It is a coincidence, and yes, I knew you would recognize him." Her eyes were dark with anger. "He isn't a man one would easily forget."

He blanched. She turned away quickly before he could see the tears in her eyes. Making her way below deck, she listened for voices. They came from the dining room. Pushing open the door, she came face-to-face with the duke of Langley.

His shirt was torn and bloody, the cravat missing entirely, and his fawn buckskins were stained. She was sure he had never, in his entire life, been so dirty. But the lean, hard-muscled body was unmarked, and the blue eyes looked at her with an expression that made her want to smile for the first time since Daniel Bradford had come back into her life. She felt like laughing and crying at the same time. No stranger, looking at that straight back and arrogant face, would ever take him for less than he was.

"You've the devil of a nerve," Waverly said, addressing the duke. "Prisoners are usually chained in the hold."

Devereaux's voice was deadly quiet. "I wouldn't do that if I were you, Captain."

The silence was deafening. Tess watched in horror as the captain surveyed his prisoner.

Devereaux, bracing himself against a table, appeared completely relaxed. As usual his very presence made everyone else in the room appear insignificant.

"You must know how the situation stands," Waverly said stiffly. "I cannot turn back now."

"I understand that." The duke's clipped voice allowed no quarter. "I don't mind sailing with you to Annapolis. There, I'll find a return ship."

The two men continued to stare at one another. Tess's palms were damp. She wiped them on her skirt.

All at once the captain laughed. "The hell with you, then. Do as you will. I'll arrange for a prisoner exchange when we reach Annapolis."

Devereaux bowed. "My thanks, Captain." He gave his full attention to Tess. "May I have a word with you?" he asked gently.

Thomas Waverly frowned. "What business do you have with Mrs. Bradford?"

A muscle leaped along the hard line of Devereaux's cheek. "That is none of your concern."

"Now see here," Waverly's face flushed with anger. "Mrs. Bradford is a passenger on my ship."

Tess broke in, her face bright with embarrassment. "It's quite all right, Captain," she explained hurriedly. "The duke and I knew each other in London. Please leave us alone."

"I don't allow interference in the running of my ship," Waverly announced staring pointedly at the duke. "It would be best to remember that."

"I'm only concerned with reaching Spain," Devereaux answered. "If anyone complains of harassment, you'll hear of it."

Unconvinced, Waverly led his first mate and the frigate's prisoners out the door.

All at once, the room was very quiet. Tess felt alone and strangely uncomfortable. Desperately, she searched for something to say. Nothing came to mind.

Devereaux broke the silence. "I'm sorry for this, Tess."

Blood rushed to her cheeks and she lifted her head to look directly at him. "What did you wish to say to me, m'lord?"

He searched her face, drinking in the quiet loveliness he thought he would never see again.

"How are you?" he began.

"Well," she lied.

"You don't look well," he said bluntly.

For one terrible moment, she thought she would weep. Turning away before he could see her weakness, she brushed her eyes with her sleeve.

His hand, steady and warm, closed over her arm. "Tess, look at me," he commanded.

She looked at him defiantly, daring him to mention her tear-bright eyes and trembling chin.

The warmth of his smile startled her. "We know too much of each other to hide our feelings. What troubles you, my love?"

"Don't call me that," she blurted out. "I'm not your love."

His hand tightened on her arm. He swore softly and she shrank from the expression in his eyes. Slowly, the angry blue flames subsided. "Whatever happens, never deny that," he said, in control of himself once again.

For a long time, the world stood still. She looked at his strong harsh face. The warmth of his touch reassured her. With a sigh she went into his welcoming arms. He held her as he had when Lizzie was hurt. The coldness and pain of the last two weeks left her aching body and she closed her eyes.

They stayed together, the dark head bent over the light one

for a long time. Tess heard voices outside the cabin and the world rushed back. She pulled away and looked up at him.

"Thank you, James," she said. "I must go now."

His expression revealed nothing. Without speaking, he nodded and released her.

She left the room and walked slowly to the cabin she shared with Daniel. Once again, the nausea came upon her with full force, and she leaned her head against the door. It opened unexpectedly and she lost her balance.

Daniel caught her in his arms. He looked at her pale face and the beads of perspiration on her lip. Acting quickly, he carried her to the bed and reached for the basin.

When it was over, she lay spent with exhaustion against the cushions. Daniel sat on a chair by the bed and watched her. Her slight body shook from the violent ordeal and the blue shadows under her eyes gave her a bruised, almost fragile appearance.

"You've never suffered from seasickness before," he said, a thoughtful look on his face.

Tess opened her eyes. Pulling herself to a sitting position, she reached for a glass of water. The taste in her mouth repelled her. Swallowing a long draught, she placed the glass on the table and looked directly at the stranger she had once promised to love and honor forever.

"I'm not seasick, Daniel," she answered. Her eyes were level on his face. There was no easy way to tell him. "I'm going to have a child."

For the rest of her life, Tess would remember the way he looked at that moment. He despised her. She could see it in the tight set of his jaw and the bitter hatred deepening his eyes to a brilliant gold.

"I see," was all he said, but she heard a thousand recriminations in the brief words, as if he'd shouted them for everyone to hear.

After a long moment he asked, "Are you sure? After all, you're hardly experienced at these things. Perhaps it's influenza, after all."

Color flamed across her cheeks. She lifted her head and met his hopeful glance. "I'm sure," she replied.

"You can't really know until you've seen a doctor," he persisted.

"Daniel," Tess lost her patience. "I lived with James Devereaux for three months. It was a marriage in every sense of the word."

The ticking of the wall clock was the only sound in the tense silence.

"Does he know?" Daniel asked.

"No."

"Then we won't tell him." He walked to the door, sure of his purpose. Reaching out to push it open, he turned back to her. "The child will be raised as my own. No one need know it isn't a Bradford."

"You can't possibly mean that," she whispered, her outraged eyes on his face.

"Do we have an alternative?"

Her throat felt very dry. She swallowed. "My father and sisters will know of my marriage to Langley. I'm sure they've told someone in Annapolis."

"On the contrary." He gave her a thin-lipped smile. "Few Americans would be overjoyed by their daughters marrying Englishmen, no matter how wealthy or powerful. Your father has most likely kept the news within the family."

"What about Caroline, Langley's sister?"

He opened the door. "I'll handle Caroline."

"Daniel," she jumped up from the bed and ran to clutch his arm. "You can't mean this. The child is a Devereaux. How can you even consider such a deception?"

"You should have thought of that before you climbed into another man's bed," he answered, slamming the door behind him.

She listened to the sound of his angry footsteps until, at last, they died away.

"I thought you were dead," she whispered to the empty walls. "You were supposed to be dead."

Twenty-three

All schooners built in Nathanial Harrington's shipyards were built to withstand an ocean of water rolling across their decks. Thomas Waverly's ship was no exception. The crew gave up trying to outrun the storm, reefed the sails and tied down the masts, their voices raised in an occasional shout of laughter. Tess looked at the sinister skies, and angry dark waves and was afraid.

Suddenly it was upon them and there was no longer any time for fear. Gentle swells became rolling mountains, pushing the small schooner backwards and sideways off its course. Ocean spray covered the ship as it lay on its side in the grey waves, losing everything not securely tied down. Every available hand was needed to take in the sails and save their precious supplies.

Hanging on the hatch, Tess was fascinated by the enormous ocean rolling past her eyes. White lightning and roaring thunder urged the massive tons of water to slam against the thin hull of the deck, spinning the tiny ship like a twig caught in the eddying current of a mighty river.

Unbelievably, she heard the sound of her name through the wind. Turning, she saw James Devereaux, his hair wet with rain and plastered to his head, making his way toward her across the slanting deck. His eyes were wild and exultant as if he were very pleased with the ship and the storm and the very sight of her standing alone near the hatch, the excitement in her expression matching his own.

Tess was not surprised to see him. She knew he and the captain had come to an unusual understanding and that he had the run of the ship.

"I see you couldn't stay below," he said. Holding on to the railing, he made his way to her side. "Are you seasick?"

She shook her head. Suddenly, a crashing wave knocked her sprawling across the deck. Every timber creaked and groaned. The very hull itself seemed to break apart and through it all, the eerie keening of the wind whistled through the masts.

Tess clutched the railing and stared into the churning waters of the angry Atlantic. A thundering mountain swept over the bow, knocking her aside once again. Beyond fear, she closed her eyes and waited for the ocean to claim her.

A strong arm clasped her around the waist, pulling her to the safety of the companionway. Tess lifted her head to the dark, rain-wet face of the duke of Langley. She had never seen him so unrestrained, so completely devoid of his natural reserve.

"Another minute and you would have been washed overboard," he said, holding her tightly against him. "Why haven't you gone below?"

She stared at him, her lips numb. The mute appeal in her eyes was answer enough. With a muffled oath, he took her hand and pulled her after him, down the ladder to the lower deck.

Moments later, she was standing on her feet in a small, well-appointed cabin, allowing Devereaux to remove her sodden cloak and gown.

"Please," she whispered, clutching at his hands, "don't do this."

He looked up from the button he was unfastening. "Don't be absurd. Surely, you know me better than to think I would ravish a thin, pale-faced woman who can't stand the sight of me."

A ghost of a smile crossed her lips as he picked her up and carried her to the bed. Propping his head against the cushions, he pulled her tightly against him. The heaving waves seemed less violent somehow, and the warmth of his body penetrated the thick blanket, sedating her into a restful doze.

"James," she said sleepily.

"Yes."

"I thought you preferred slim women."

"I do." He smiled into her hair. "But, not emaciated ones."

"Perhaps I am rather pale," she admitted.

"More so than I like to see." He held his breath waiting for her to continue.

The steady sound of her breathing told him their conversation was at an end.

Much later, in the early hours of dawn, a weary Thomas Waverly opened the door of his cabin and stepped inside. His eyes widened as he stared at the duke holding Daniel Bradford's wife in his arms. The warning look on Devereaux's face stopped the question in his throat. With a thoughtful look, he backed out of the cabin and quietly closed the door.

He hadn't missed the sight of Tess's arms wound tightly around her protector's neck or the tiny smile on her sleeping face. So, that was the way of it. He whistled softly under his breath. He didn't envy young Mr. Bradford. It was an unfair competition. The duke of Langley was no ordinary man. Waverly frowned in sympathy. The boy from Maryland didn't stand a chance, and the tragedy was, he was intelligent enough to realize it.

Grey light filtered through the porthole and settled on Tess's face. She stirred and opened her eyes. For a moment she forgot where she was. A comforting warmth surrounded her. Suddenly, she remembered. James was holding her against him. Sometime during the night he must have put her to bed and climbed under the blankets beside her. With exploring fingers she reached behind her. Her palm met the solid wall of his bare chest.

Instantly, she was wide awake. Her heart slammed against her ribs. She could no more prevent the descent of her hand than she could stop the storm-lashed sea from heaving past the windows. Gently, so as not to wake him, her fingers moved in a circular motion down to his tightly muscled stomach and across the lean, flat hipbone. She felt him shudder as her arms moved around his waist and her nails lightly raked his thighs.

Tess closed her eyes and breathed in the familiar, clean scent of him. With a sigh of regret, she tried to pull away. Arms, like bands of steel, held her against him. She looked up. Her breath caught in her throat. The scorching flames in his eyes held her spellbound, as his lips took hers in a searing kiss.

For the count of a heartbeat she stiffened in protest and tried to pull away. He released her mouth. The hand that was on her neck moved to her back, turned her around and pulled her hard against him, seeking her mouth. As his kiss deepened, her lips parted, her body relaxed and melted into his. His kiss became gentle, slower and more deliberate. She moaned, a low desperate sound in the back of her throat and moved her arms to encircle his neck.

"Tess," he muttered hoarsely. She was bent back in his arms, and his lips moved to the exposed line of her throat. "I've missed you so."

She did not protest when he slipped off her shift and bent his head to her breast. The rough edge of his tongue laved the ripe peak and when his lips closed over her, she cried out at the shooting stab of desire coursing through her. Cupping her other breast, he kissed and caressed the full mounds until they stood fully erect, like twin peaks in the dim light of the cabin. The tension deep inside her was almost an ache. Her eyes were dilated, her mouth swollen from his kisses and slightly parted, the tip of her tongue barely visible against her upper lip.

James could feel the dampness of her skin against his thighs. Raising himself on his hands, he looked down at her. Her face was flushed, her breathing ragged. She stared back at him, her eyes like lake water, cool and shining and fathomless.

The blood pounded in his ears. He could feel the heat of his arousal demanding that he take her now, at once. Gritting his teeth, he concentrated, straining to prolong the moment.

Her hand closed over the turgid length of him and he lost control. Waiting no longer, he plunged into her tight warmth.

"Tess," he murmured over and over, moving against her, holding himself back, until at last, he felt her shuddering climax. Lifting her against him, he drove deeply, allowing the full force of his passion to explode inside her. Winding his fingers in her hair, he pulled her head back and kissed her.

"You're mine," he muttered against her lips. "Nothing will take you from me. Not Daniel Bradford, not this ridiculous war, or the entire American government." His arms tightened possessively around her. "Do you understand me, Tess? I'll come back for you. You must believe that."

Her eyes widened in dismay. "Nothing has changed, James," she said quietly. "You're an American prisoner of war and I'm married to Daniel."

His eyes were a brilliant, intense blue. "The marriage was in name only. It can be annulled."

"What of the pain and humiliation I've caused him? Can that be annulled as well?"

"Christ, Tess." His hands were hard on her shoulders. "What about our pain? How can you live with a man you don't love?"

"I've loved Daniel Bradford all my life," she protested. "Not in the way it is with us, but it is love all the same. Don't you see, I can't shame him this way? How can you even think it of me?"

The controlled rage in his voice terrified her. "Apparently, I mistook you. Only a whore would respond the way you did to me, and then return to another man's bed."

She whitened as if she'd been struck, her eyes huge and despairing in her face. Making no attempt to defend herself, she watched him leave the bed and pull on his clothing.

Without looking at her, he opened the door and walked out of the cabin.

The schooner reached Annapolis on a foggy morning in late May. The seaport town was shrouded in a blanket of grey mist and the enclosed harbor where they docked was filled with ivory-colored sails and tall masts. Although she couldn't yet see them from her position by the railing, Tess knew, beyond the fog would be quiet streets lined with magnolia and boxwood trees, and brick houses, graceful and weathered with age. The sky was overcast and gloomy, but already, vendors shouted greetings to friends and hawked their wares to early morning shoppers.

Tess thought wistfully of other visits to Annapolis, when she'd been on fire with the excitement of a day away from her chores and Harrington House, when her only thought was to purchase a new bonnet or acquire a novel from the lending library.

Now, the brilliant colors of the wharf held no appeal for her. Neither did the baskets of fish and shanks of smoked ham, despite the fact that she'd been without fresh meat and vegetables for weeks.

Her only thought was of home. She missed her father and sisters with an ache that was almost physical. She longed for the comfort of Clara's scolding tongue and rib-crushing embrace, and to be wrapped in the cocoon of childhood where her problems would miraculously be taken over by those far more equipped to handle them than she.

A hand on her shoulder startled her. She looked up into the serious face of Captain Waverly.

"You're home at last," he said. "Does it seem different to you?"

Tess shook her head. "No."

He looked down at her as if to say something and then stared straight ahead once again. The silence stretched out between them.

"I'll say good-bye now, captain." Tess held out her hand.

There was sympathy and more than a little kindness in the dark eyes that looked down at her.

"There is someone else you should bid farewell to, lass," he said gently. "Surely, you owe His Lordship that."

She gave him a direct, curious glance. "I thought you meant to imprison him?"

He smiled at her. "Did you?!"

"Why didn't you keep him in the hold with the others?" she asked.

"His mission was to report to Wellington, not to make war on America," Waverly answered. "Besides, I enjoy his conversation. I think you do as well."

Tess stared at him in disbelief.

Waverly grinned. "I'm not so bigoted that I can't recognize a good man when I see one."

She smiled, the first he had seen since she boarded his schooner in Portsmouth. Thomas Waverly caught his breath. Tess Bradford, with her mournful eyes and serious face, was uncommonly lovely. But when she smiled, he understood for the first time the murderous look on Langley's face as he watched her enter the cabin she shared with her husband.

"I don't think he would want to see me," Tess replied. "We aren't exactly on the best of terms."

"You're mistaken, but I think I'll allow him his own apologies." He tipped his hat. "God speed, lass."

She turned to wish him well, but the words wouldn't come. James Devereaux crossed the deck to stand beside her. His face was remote, the blue eyes shuttered. Tess was reminded of the first time she had seen him in the American minister's residence. The first thing she had noticed was his height and the arrogant pride stamped on his handsome features. Never had he appeared so unapproachable. Her eyes were dry, her pain too deep for tears.

"Please don't hate me, James," she whispered. "I couldn't bear it."

He turned swiftly, capturing her hands in his own. "I could never hate you, Tess."

Swallowing the lump in her throat, she tried once again, to explain. "If it were only a question of following my heart, the choice would be simple." She clutched at his hands. "If only we had met before."

His smile was bitter. "Before what, Tess? Before the war or before Daniel? It's more complicated than that. Perhaps it would have been the same between us, but I doubt it. It isn't Teresa

Harrington of Annapolis that I fell in love with. It is a woman with the spirit and courage to cross an ocean alone to rescue her husband. Women like that don't exist in my world." He caressed her cheek. "Don't look like that. Choices are never simple."

"What are you going to do?" The pain in her eyes tore at his heart.

"My foolish love," he chided her. "When will you learn to trust me?"

"Don't harm Daniel," she pleaded. "I couldn't go through that again."

Savage jealously wrenched his heart. Did she know what she did to him with her misplaced loyalty? The thought of the risk he took in allowing her to return with Bradford nearly undid him. He knew Tess well enough to believe no intimacy had been exchanged between her and the angry young man who was her husband. But time and forgiveness could change that. The image of her slim body locked in a lover's embrace with another man was a torture too heinous to contemplate. He refused to consider it. Besides, there was nothing he could change at the moment. Wellington couldn't wait and Tess needed the solace of her father and sisters.

He searched her face, committing to memory her delicate, high-boned cheeks, the smoky eyes, small straight nose and determined chin. She stood quietly under his gaze, holding herself with that unusual dignity he had noticed the first time he saw her. How could he let her go?

Swearing under his breath, he damned the captain, her husband, and the curious crowd gathering on the busy waterfront. Pulling her into his arms he bent his head and kissed her with the desperate need of a man swallowing his last available breath of air.

Tess's cry drowned in her throat. Sliding her arms around his waist, she responded to his angry, seeking mouth with a wanton abandon. Melting against him, the world slipped away. Time ceased to exist. She knew nothing but the feel of his lips, his tongue, and the bittersweet fire blazing between them.

"James." A voice shouting from the dock penetrated the fog of their passion. A slim, dark-haired woman laughed and waved her hand in welcome. Two small boys clung to her skirts and stared curiously up at them.

He groaned. "It's Caroline," he said, unnecessarily.

Tess recognized the familiar face immediately. Georgiana's oldest sister had the Devereaux looks and charm. For years, Caroline's home had been as familiar to her as Harrington House. She looked, with dread, at the smiling face of Caroline Devereaux Curtis. It was too soon for her to have heard the news of Daniel's return from the dead. As far as she knew, Tess was her sister-in-law. The sight of James embracing his wife on the deck was unusual, but not inappropriate under the circumstances.

"Don't be alarmed," he reassured her. "I'll explain everything. You need not see her at all if that is your wish."

Tess shook her head. "You don't understand. Annapolis is not London. Caroline is a dear friend to my family. It isn't possible for us to ignore one another." She straightened her shoulders and held out her hand. "Good-bye, James. I'll never forget you."

The words were final, their message unmistakable.

"Have faith, my heart." The blue eyes were filled with tenderness. "You were born to be my duchess."

The tears that for so long had refused to come, blinded her now. "Oh, James," she sobbed, "you won't want me when you know what I've done."

He frowned and would have reached for her, but she pulled away quickly, and ran toward the quarterdeck.

At that moment, Bradford's head appeared at the top of the ladder. Devereaux watched them speak. Tess nodded and followed the younger man down the ladder.

A white line of worry deepened around Devereaux's lips. Her words haunted him. What the devil had she done now?

Twenty-four

Tess didn't recognize anyone on the dock. She hadn't expected to. There had been no time to notify her family that she was returning home. She thought of Adam Bradford and hoped the shock of seeing his son alive, wouldn't cause a relapse in his precarious health.

She stared at the thin, tired face of her husband seated across from her in the carriage. His eyes were closed. Perhaps they could work it out between them. After all, they shared a common history. Surely, such a bond would overcome anything.

Daniel opened his eyes and stared at her. She shrank back, in dismay. The rage in their amber depths was terrifying. Dear God, how could she live with such hate?

"I'm taking you home to your father," he said coldly. "You will stay there until I come for you."

Tess nodded, working to keep her face expressionless, unaware of the staggering relief reflected in her eyes.

Daniel smiled bitterly. If he hadn't wanted to see his father first, and break the news gently, he would have demanded that she come with him. He hungered for revenge. Tess and the duke would suffer as he had.

It was early afternoon when they reached the familiar drive leading to the steps of Harrington House. Tess closed her eyes and breathed in the smell of honeysuckle and gardenia. The droning of the bees lulled her into a false sense of well-being so that when Clara stepped out on the veranda, she was able to greet her with a genuine smile.

Leaping from the carriage she threw herself at the plump, apple-cheeked woman, and after a startled moment, was gathered into a floury embrace. Clara smelled of yeast and molasses and peaches, the comforting smells of spring and home and the Chesapeake.

To her horror, tears flooded her eyes and poured down her cheeks, wetting the broadcloth-covered shoulder of the older woman.

"There, there, child," she crooned comfortingly. "What a surprise. Why didn't you tell us you were coming, and where is your husband?"

The tears flowed even harder accompanied now by racking sobs. Clara's mouth dropped open when she saw the solitary figure inside the carriage reach out to close the door.

Clutching Tess to her ample bosom, she stared as the travel coach turned back up the lane toward Bradford House.

Keeping one arm around Tess, she half-carried, half-dragged her up the stairs to the room she had once shared with her younger sister, Abigail. Easing her on to the bed, she filled a basin with water and wrung out a towel. Laying it on Tess's forehead, she spoke softly, the slow comforting drawl of the tidewater evident in her speech.

"Rest, love. I can tell you've had a time of it. Don't think of it now. There's time enough to figure out what to do. Your father will know. He's at the shipyard now, but he'll be home soon." She brushed back the silky hair, her lips tightening at the thin hollow cheeks.

Although she loved all of Nathanial Harrington's daughters, Tess was Clara's favorite. She had come to work for the family when the late Mrs. Harrington had given birth for the last time. Everyone had made much of Abigail, the baby, and small blond Tess had been forgotten. Only Clara had seen how lonely and neglected the child felt. Reaching out to the girl with the warmth and affection typical of her nature, they had formed a bond between them, unmatched by her love for any of the other Harrington sisters.

Her eyes deepened with anger as they rested on the thin, white face lying on the pillow. Tess's bones protruded, mercilessly clear, through her transparent skin, and her figure was so slight it was painful to see. With fierce resolve, she tightened her hold on Tess's hand. Whatever she had gone through would not happen again.

By the time Nathanial Harrington returned home, he had heard the news of Daniel's remarkable resurrection from the dead. His footsteps were heavy as he walked across the veranda and into the kitchen.

Clara and Abigail worked together in companionable silence, preparing the evening meal. The older woman knew, by the look on his face, there was no need for explanations. Raising a finger to her lips, she glanced at Abigail.

"Where is she?" Harrington asked.

"Upstairs," answered Clara. "The poor child has had quite a time of it. She's dreadfully thin."

His fist came down on the table, rattling the neatly stacked cups. "I told her not to go," he exploded. "The damned British! How could they have made such a mistake?"

"Papa?" Abigail's shocked face stared up at him.

"Try and remember the child," Clara admonished him.

Nathanial Harrington ran callused fingers through his thick, greying hair. "She'll know soon enough, anyway. The story is all over Annapolis." He looked down at his youngest daughter and his eyes softened. "Your sister has gotten herself into quite a mess, Abby. Do you understand any of it?"

Abigail considered the matter. "I know that Daniel was supposed to be dead and that Tess married an English duke. Now, Daniel has come back." She tilted her head to one side. "I can't see that any of it is Tess's fault, Papa. It seems to me that she should stay married to whichever one makes her happier." Her forehead puckered thoughtfully. "I hope she takes Daniel because I've missed her dreadfully."

Nathanial Harrington's voice, even when gentled to the point of tenderness, was loud enough to rattle the windowpanes. When it was raised in anger, it was deafening. "It isn't as simple as that," he roared. "Where do you come up with such notions?"

The child stared back at him in stubborn defiance. "Tess is sick. We won't let you bully her. Will we, Clara?"

"Indeed we won't," the housekeeper said, a martial light in her eye.

"What do you mean Tess is sick?" The blustery voice softened. He was suddenly all concern. "If those blasted limeys have done anything to my daughter, there will be hell to pay."

"Watch your language," Clara warned him. "Tess is waiting to see you. There is nothing wrong with her that a week in bed and three full meals a day won't cure." She put one hand on her hip and wagged her finger at him. "I don't think we can blame the British for her condition. From the way I see it, she and Daniel aren't on the best of terms."

With a thoughtful look on his face, Harrington climbed the stairs to face his daughter. Wishing, for the thousandth time, that the late Mrs. Harrington were there to take this burden from his shoulders, he took a deep breath and opened the door to Tess's room.

The sight of her, sitting up in bed staring out the window, shocked him into silence. His carefully prepared speech was forgotten. She looked terribly like her mother in the last days of her illness. Pain twisted his heart.

"Hello, Papa," she said, formally.

The purple shadows around her eyes gave her a bruised, defeated look. Could this be the same young woman, who seven short months ago, was the acclaimed beauty of the county?"

"I've made quite a mull of things, haven't I?" she said.

His throat worked. Saying nothing, he strode to her side and sitting on the bed, took her in his arms.

"Don't worry, child. Nothing is so bad that we can't find a solution."

"Oh, Papa," the tears began to flow. "Are you angry with me?"

His arms tightened around her. He cleared his throat and held her away from him. "I am angry, but not at you. I know you better than you know yourself, lass. No one in the world could convince me you would intentionally do anything improper."

She wiped the tears from under her eyes with her hand. "I'm married to two men at the same time. I can't think of anything more improper than that."

"Nor can I," he agreed, a humorous glint lighting the penetrating grey of his eyes.

"It isn't funny, Papa. Daniel hates me."

"Nonsense," Nathanial Harrington protested. "The boy is in pain. He's had a terrible shock. He'll get over it. In time, the whole incident will be forgotten." He patted her hand. "You'll have to convince him that Devereaux meant little to you, that you were so besotted with grief that nothing mattered any more. You're a clever girl. You'll figure it out."

"It isn't that simple."

"Why not?" The hopeless look in her eyes frightened him. He had a dreadful premonition that he wasn't going to like her answer.

Tess wet her lips and tried to explain. "Daniel has seen James," she said.

He waited, patiently, for her to continue.

She rubbed her temples. "How can I make you see?" she said helplessly. "James isn't an ordinary man. He's very tall and dark and commands immediate attention. He has a presence, Papa, like no one else I've ever known. He's reasonable and terrifying and wonderful, all at the same time."

"Anything else?" asked her father.

"He's dreadfully handsome," she confessed, her voice very low.

He lifted her chin so that her eyes met his. "What you are trying to tell me is that you're in love with the man and Daniel knows it."

"Yes," replied Tess, pulling away and looking down at her hands. Taking a restoring breath, she said. "There is something else you should know, Papa."

"Well, out with it?" he demanded. "I may as well have it all."

She looked directly at him, no longer ashamed. "I'm carrying James Devereaux's child."

He stared at her for a long time. The bushy eyebrows meeting over his nose gave him a stern, almost forbidding expression.

"I see," he said, at last. "That does complicate the issue."

She nodded. "A life with Daniel is no longer possible."

"Does he know about the child?"

"Yes," she said. "I was sick on the ship. He would have known soon enough, anyway."

"Is there the slightest possibility the child could be his?"

She blushed. "No."

Nathanial rose and walked to the window. He looked out toward the bay. Grey-brown water lapped gently at the shoreline, calming the violence of his emotions. He was a large man, comfortable with his home, his family and his station in life. The times suited him. From next to nothing, he had wrested a fortune from the verdant soil of the eastern forests. He was known for his sharp wit, uncompromising honesty, and the powerful influence he wielded throughout the tidewater. He had married a woman of rare beauty and even rarer intelligence. She had given him six daughters and never, until this moment, had he doubted his ability to protect them with the strength of his love and the power of his reputation.

He turned to look at his fifth and loveliest daughter. Impotent rage reddened his face. He clenched his fists. She would not suffer for another's mistake. He would not allow it.

"It's a miserable state of affairs when a mere girl must suffer for the errors of a few feather-headed politicians," he remarked, gruffly. "If Daniel wishes to annul your marriage, so be it. This is your home. We will welcome your child as we have every new addition to our family. I'll not have you worried any longer." He smiled. "Clara is making sweet potato pie. She would be highly insulted if you didn't come down to dinner."

"I'll be down, Papa," Tess replied. "Thank you."

He paused on his way out the door. "This duke of Langley. How did he take the news?"

Her cheeks flushed a deep rose. "I didn't tell him," she whispered.

Nathanial Harrington frowned at his daughter. "Does he love you, lass?"

A smile crossed her lips. "He did," she answered. "I don't know how he'll feel when he finds out I've kept this from him."

"It sounds as if he intends to come after you."

Tess felt a pain deep within her. She turned her eyes away from him. "He said he would. Now he is on his way to join Wellington. It may be years before he returns. He'll not forgive me for raising his child as an American."

"Perhaps it won't come to that," her father suggested.

"Perhaps not." She chewed the inside of her lip. "I'd rather not speak of him, if you don't mind." Her voice shook. "It's hard enough to bear."

Harrington nodded. Tess was not the same person who traveled to England seven months ago. He needed time to adjust to this stranger who was his daughter. He wasn't sure how he felt about the child she carried. Abby was almost grown. Just as peace had descended upon Harrington House, its quiet would again be interrupted by the squalling of a newborn infant.

He sighed. Life had taken an unpredictable turn and for Tess's sake, he would have to make the best of it. There was something else he must attend to for her sake.

Seating himself at the desk in his study, he opened a drawer and pulled out a piece of writing paper. Dipping his quill into a bottle of black ink, he wrote: "Dear Lady Devereaux, . . ."

The pen moved swiftly across the page. His message complete, he signed the letter and then, read it over again. Satisfied, he folded the paper and sealed it. Leonie Devereaux would know she had yet another grandchild living in America.

Twenty-five

Rain poured down relentlessly on the plain north of Ciudad Rodrigo. Trenches overflowed and mud ran down the hillsides, thick and clinging, the color of yellow slime. Men waded waist-deep in water, their voices low and cautious around their field-marshal. Anyone with eyes in his head could see that Wellington was furious.

Frustrated at every turn by a lack of supplies and by gentlemen officers who had purchased their commissions without ever seeing a battlefield, he had outwitted them all. The victories of Badajos, Ciudad Rodrigo, and Vittoria were behind him. Salamanca and the siege of Burgos lay ahead, and now the weather wouldn't cooperate.

He slammed his fist down on a table, cursing fluently. His army made camp in the hills around the fortress, building rude huts so pathetically constructed they would need rebuilding tomorrow. The rain and cold seeping through the inadequate structures demoralized the men as nothing else had in the whole of this long, dreary campaign.

"Damn Bathurst," he swore. "Does the man think I have nothing to do but plan battle strategy for the colonies?" He gestured toward the seemingly impregnable fort perched on the top of the hill. "We're short on officers and ammunition and we don't even have the proper siege guns. Yet, I'm expected to perform a miracle." He looked down his crooked nose. "The incredible thing is, it will happen, Devereaux. Despite the deplorable conditions, these men will do it. What's the matter with the soldiers in America? Are they all rosy-cheeked mama's boys?"

James grinned and braced himself against the flimsy wall. There was only one chair in the room.

"Not at all," he answered. "They just haven't the heart for it. There are no clear-cut objectives in America, sir. No castles to storm, no cities of any worth to capture, no reinforcements just across the bay. Even if we claimed victory, what would we really have? How could we hold it? The men aren't stupid. They understand these things."

"I suppose they do." Wellington looked at his troops. Under their ragged clothes and relaxed slouches beat the hearts of the finest army in the world. Their lean, sun-burned faces told of four years of blazing heat and bitter rains, of discomfort and danger, of poor rations and low pay, of dirty, vermin-infested lodgings and long, monotonous marches across the flat, arid plains of the Spanish peninsula.

They fought like demons for nothing more than a belief in themselves and their faith in a general who lived no better than they did. If Bonaparte was defeated, the laurels would rest on their shoulders alone.

"What do you advise, Major?" Wellington asked, looking up at the tall, dark man standing before him.

Devereaux laughed, an infectious, merry sound that lifted the general's spirits.

"I'm a civilian, m'lord. You have a habit of forgetting that."

"You sold out to plague me, James. How could you do it? You were worth a company of the dandies they've sent me."

"If you recall, I had little choice."

Wellington stroked his chin, recalling the circumstances. At last he nodded. "At any rate, you're here now, and I intend to make good use of you."

"Well," the clipped voice explained, "the way I see it, you need field officers. Morale is low among the men. Someone should take a platoon and make an attempt to breach the outer defenses of the city."

The general stared at the lean, weathered face of the duke of Langley. He didn't look like a duke at the moment. He looked like an Indian. His skin was dark with the hard, brittle look of tanned leather, stretched tightly across gaunt cheekbones. There wasn't an ounce of spare flesh evident anywhere on the toned body relaxing against the doorjamb.

"Who do you suggest I ask to perform this miracle?" he asked.

Devereaux grinned. "I'll do it."

Wellington shook his head. "I can't risk it, James. You won your spurs at Badajos. A man only has one life. You came to deliver Castlereagh's dispatches six months ago. When are you going home?"

James leaned forward, his palms flat on the table, his eyes a brilliant, piercing blue. "Who else do you have?"

"No one. But it won't be you."

Two days later, Langley took a platoon of men and stormed the outer walls. The French, led by a brilliant commander, were waiting for them. The night was dark and dry, the moon hardly visible behind the clouds. Marching was difficult, for no one could see more than a few paces ahead.

The storming parties were still creeping up the long slope, under cover of darkness, when a flash of light illuminated the sky. They had been seen from the fort. They had no choice but to fire. A cannonball shot out from the ramparts. A high-pitched scream pierced the air.

Men hung from the ladders, their limbs blown away by the barrage of bullets. In minutes, the stench of burning flesh and human hair was overpowering. The night was thick with the smell of gunpowder, the roar of bursting shells and the sharp crack of firing muskets. The troops, blinded by smoke, charged ahead and were mowed down, almost to the last man.

Langley, frustrated beyond measure, stood up, shouting for reinforcements to evacuate the wounded. His tall form, outlined against the city wall, was an easy target for the French marksman directly above him. The soldier lifted his musket to his shoulder, taking careful aim. There was a loud crack. James felt a searing pain in his left shoulder. Then darkness came over him and he felt no more.

Twenty-four hours later, Wellington looked down at the still face lying on the blood-soaked pallet. Even the deep bronze of Devereaux's skin could not hide the deathly pallor. He had lost an enormous amount of blood.

"No matter what it takes," he ordered, "keep him alive."

At the same moment that Devereaux had been attempting his ill-fated storming of the walled city of Ciudad Rodrigo, Tess went into labor. The pain was beyond belief. Earlier that morning, her water had broken and by nightfall she was a writhing mass of agony. Digging her nails into the bleeding flesh of her palms, she refused to cry out, refused to allow the man standing outside the room to hear her suffering.

Constance, her older sister, and Clara were there.

"You must help us, Tess," Constance pleaded, sponging the sweat-drenched brow. "The child won't be born without you." Her voice was filled with desperation. Tess had lost a great deal of blood.

Tess turned her face to the wall, silent tears rolling down her cheeks. Suddenly a pressure, greater than anything she'd ever felt before, racked her body. She held her breath and pushed.

The baby's healthy cry drew a sigh of relief from Clara.

"It's a boy," she whispered as she wiped the child clean. "A handsome boy, with eyes as blue as the summer sky."

Tess sat up, and held out her arms for her child. Moving the blanket aside, she stared down at the infant. He was unmistakably a Devereaux. There could be no doubt as to his paternity. The tiny bit of down on his small head was ebony black, and his eyes were a light, piercing blue. Although the small nose and chin were unformed, Tess could already see that they would soon take on the lean, slightly hawkish cast of the arrogant Devereauxs of Langley. It was almost as if she had had no part in his parentage.

Her laugh was closer to a sob. "He's so beautiful," she

breathed, watching in fascination as the baby yawned, black eye-lashes brushing his cheeks.

Constance smiled and leaned over the small bundle. "Indeed he is." She placed her finger in his palm and was rewarded by an immediate clenching of the tiny, claw-like fingers. "He's also very strong." She looked at her sister. "Daniel is waiting outside. Shall I tell him to come in."

Tess's lovely face hardened. "Not yet." She placed the infant to her breast. "I want to feed the baby first."

Constance nodded. "I'll go and tell him the news." She turned and whispered to Clara. "Wash her face and brush her hair. It will give her time before she has to face him."

Clara nodded and moved briskly toward the dresser. Confident that Tess was in good hands, Constance slipped out the door to the parlor where her father and Daniel Bradford waited.

Ever since Tess had moved back to Bradford House, six months before, at the request of Adam Bradford, Daniel and Nathanial Harrington had shared a tenuous truce. It was a temporary facade, agreed upon to placate an old man. Adam Bradford had been near death. He knew nothing of Tess's adventures in England. He hadn't left his room for months and could see visitors rarely. He died shortly after his daughter-in-law's return. And still, Tess showed no signs of returning to Nathanial Harrington's house.

Constance noticed that the two men sat in silence on opposite sides of the room. She sighed. On what should be an occasion of great happiness, she would have to tread lightly so as not to ignite the smoldering anger between them.

Her father had never been one to hide his feelings. He couldn't forgive Daniel's treatment of his daughter. He wanted Tess and his grandchild home, at Harrington House. Daniel, on the other hand, stubbornly insisted she remain with him. Holding all the Harringtons to blame for what he considered to be a severe defect in his wife's character, he could barely speak to the older man with civility.

"Papa," Constance's soft voice interrupted the strained silence. "It's a boy."

"How is Tess?" Her father's haggard face gave testimony to his long hours of worry. Childbirth was never easy, but for a small woman like Tess, it could be fatal.

"She's tired, but well." Constance hesitated and walked over to stand before her sister's husband. "You'll be able to see her soon." She spoke firmly. "Tess needs you, Daniel. She's had a difficult time. Don't make it worse for her."

Nathanial Harrington held his breath and waited. He could read nothing in the wooden expression of the man he had once heartily approved of as a husband for his daughter. The room was suddenly very hot. He waited, in tense silence, as if Tess's entire future would be told in Daniel Bradford's reply.

"Please," Constance whispered, placing her hand on his sleeve. "This is Tess we're speaking of. You've been friends since before she could walk."

Was there a flicker in the golden eyes? She couldn't be sure. Suddenly he smiled. "When can I see her?"

Constance breathed a sigh of relief. "Now, if you like." Reaching for his hand, she led him down the hall. Knocking on Tess's door, she opened it without waiting for a response.

"Clara," she called out, peering around the door. "Daniel is here to see Tess. Come into the kitchen and I'll make some tea."

Daniel watched Clara and Constance leave and then turned to look at Tess. There was an odd expression on his face. The picture of Tess holding a baby in her arms was difficult to reconcile. He had never thought of her as a mother. She was different from most women, more vital, less restrained, intelligent, not, he thought, the least bit maternal. In marrying his closest friend and confidante, Daniel thought his happiness was secure.

Tess was undeniably beautiful, perhaps the most beautiful girl he had ever known, but she was little more than a child. He desired her, as a healthy young animal is drawn to another, but not once had he taken it a step further. He had never considered children. Now, here she was, mothering another man's child, looking as content as if she had always held a baby close to her heart.

"Are you well?" he asked, moving closer to the bed.

She tightened her arms protectively around the child. "Yes."

The infant, protesting the tightness of his mother's grip, began to cry. Startled, Tess stared down at him.

Daniel sat down on the bed and looked, for the first time, at the tiny, red face of James Devereaux's son.

"He's very small," he volunteered.

"Constance said he was a good-sized baby."

"What will you call him?"

"Justin," she replied.

"He looks nothing like you."

"No," Tess agreed, her voice low.

The baby chewed on his fist and whimpered.

Daniel held out his arms. "May I hold him?"

Tess hesitated and bit her lip. Slowly, she handed the blanketed bundle to Daniel.

"He certainly isn't a Harrington," said Daniel, thinking of the silver-and-rose coloring of the Harrington girls.

"No, he isn't a Harrington." Tess's eyes, a wide clear grey, were filled with resolve. "He's a Devereaux."

Something flashed in his eyes and then disappeared. "Are you going back to him?"

"No." Tess shook her head. "I'm going home."

"You've decided then? There is no changing your mind?"

She lifted her hand in a quick, frustrated gesture. "We don't have a marriage, Daniel. Too much has happened." She looked down at her fingers, thin and long, the nails pale and delicately rounded. "I know about Anne Matthews. Did you think such a thing could be kept a secret?"

His cheeks darkened. Handing her the baby, he walked to the window and stared out at the stark November landscape.

"The widow Matthews and I have done nothing to be ashamed of." He dropped his eyes, unable to meet her steady, reproachful gaze. "Do you think to judge me, after what you've done?" he demanded.

"The circumstances are not the same," she said simply.

He whirled around, his expression defiant. "I suppose James Devereaux would have been faithful were he in my place?"

Tess closed her eyes, remembering a firm-lipped mouth and blue eyes, warming to a heart-shattering tenderness. She heard the low, amused voice muffled against her throat and saw, as clearly as if she stood before her, the predatory gaze of a red-haired beauty. Jealousy seared through her. Her heart slammed against her ribs. She took deep, calming breaths until she could speak again.

"I can't be sure," she admitted. "But I know this. I would wish the woman dead." The rage died from her eyes, leaving only sympathy. "I don't wish that for Anne. I want you to be happy."

"I see." He swallowed and turned away. "There is something you should know."

Tess waited.

"In Dartmoor Prison, I took a man's life. He was dying of lung inflammation. The prison was overcrowded and he was one of several scheduled for release. I didn't think he would last the night, but it wouldn't have mattered. I covered his face with my jacket knowing he was too weak to remove it. In the morning he was dead. When a guard asked his name, I gave him mine and took his." Taking a deep breath, he turned back to Tess prepared for the horror he was certain would show in her eyes. "Devereaux didn't lie to you, Tess. He truly believed I was dead."

Her face was unreadable.

"Do you despise me?" he asked, looking down at her with an expression she couldn't identify.

All at once it came to her. It was the look he wore as a child when his pet hound was mauled under an angry stallion's hooves.

Placing the baby beside her, Tess held out her arms. He stumbled into them. "Oh, Daniel," she murmured, cradling his head on her chest. "It will all be over soon. Perhaps, someday, we can even be friends again."

He clutched her, bruising the flesh of her arms. Harsh, wrenching sobs shook his body. She held him to her, soothing him with her voice and the cool comfort of her arms, until the storm had spent itself. Finally, he raised his head.

"There is no one else in the world I would allow to see that humiliation," he confessed.

She smiled, saying nothing.

"What will I do without you, Tess?"

"You've been without me for a long time," she replied, keeping her voice gentle. "You must go on with your life. Perhaps Anne Matthews can help you."

He had a sudden vision of Anne, a rosy-cheeked woman with lush curves. He looked at his wife, delicate and fine-boned, her hair pale as moonlight, drawn back from her brow. The ache in his chest was so great it threatened to eat out his heart. He was surprised at the normal sound of his voice.

"Shall I start annulment proceedings?"

"Yes, please," she replied.

He rose to leave.

"Daniel," her voice stopped him.

"Yes?" Hope rose in his heart.

"Send my father in."

Nodding, Daniel closed the door behind him.

Twenty-six

Leonie Devereaux watched with grateful relief as her son handed over the reins of his horse to the groom. Two short months ago he had been so weakened by loss of blood that he couldn't lift his head from the pillow. He was still thinner than he should be but the unhealthy pallor of his skin had since been replaced by a healthy bronze.

Her eyes followed him as he crossed the wide, pristine lawn, past the garden and the toolshed before disappearing into the house. Soon he would stand before her, his shoulders filling the doorway, the lean masculine strength of him out of place in her dainty, flower-filled sitting room. Litton would deliver her message and then, she must face him. It was past time. Leonie knew she should have done it months ago, but she had been afraid.

When Nathanial Harrington's letter came, James was with Wellington. She had decided to wait until he returned. When he did not, she felt it was not a thing to explain in a letter. Then he was wounded and she feared the shock would hinder his recovery. Now, there was no longer a reason to delay.

Georgiana entered the room and joined her at the window.

"What are you looking at?" she asked.

"I was enjoying the picture of James on a horse again," her mother replied.

Georgiana frowned. "Have you noticed something different about him?"

"What do you mean?"

Georgiana hesitated. "I don't know. I can't explain it, really. He's always pleasant and courteous, but he's not really the same."

Leonie knew exactly what she meant although she had no intention of admitting it to her daughter. James had resumed his duties at Langley and on the surface he appeared unchanged. But there was a shadowed strain around his eyes and a grim set to his mouth. He never laughed, even with Lizzie, and he would spend hours silently staring at the same page of whatever he happened to be reading. It made his mother very uneasy, especially considering the secret she harbored.

"Did you want something, Georgiana?" she asked.

"I'm going to call on Lady Caldwell. Would you like to come with me?"

"No, thank you, dear," Leonie answered. "There is something I must discuss with James."

Georgiana looked at her curiously. The expression on her mother's face did not encourage the question hovering on the edge of her tongue. She smiled. "I'll be home before dark."

Leonie nodded, waiting for her to leave. When the sound of her footsteps had disappeared, she walked to the desk. Opening a small drawer on the side, she pulled out two letters.

"You wanted to see me, Mother?"

The quiet voice startled her. She turned around quickly, her smile nervous.

"Yes, James." She motioned toward the flowered sofa. "Please sit down."

Crossing the room at a leisurely pace, he seated himself, fixing his gaze upon her.

Leonie looked down at his upturned face. Sunlight from the window fell on the thick, black hair, the same silky darkness she had brushed back from his brow in childhood. The sharp, lean angle of his chin and jaw had long since lost its youthful softness. She longed to press her cheek against his and make everything all right as she had done so very long ago. Obeying an unusually maternal instinct, she walked to the couch and bent over to kiss him.

His eyes narrowed. "What was that for?"

"Can't a mother kiss her own son, on occasion?" she asked, offended.

"Of course." His smile did not reach his eyes. "But I believe there is more to it than that."

She caught her bottom lip between her teeth. "There is," she admitted. "I'm sorry for the delay in telling you, but at the time I felt it was best." She handed him the letters. "Please forgive me, James. I didn't intend to keep it from you for so very long."

He took the letters from her extended hand. With a sense of *déjà vu,* he recognized the bold scrawl of Nathanial Harrington. Unfolding the thin sheets, he began to read.

The silence was oppressive. Leonie could tell nothing from the dark, implacable face beside her. Finally, he looked up. She shrank from the white-hot rage coloring his eyes a deep, angry blue.

"Damn her to bloody hell!"

The ominous voice chilled her bones. Leonie understood anger. She could deal with frustration and shouting. It was this quiet, dangerous fury that terrified her. She looked into the ice of her son's eyes. Swallowing, she attempted to defend Tess.

"The child was born in November. Perhaps she didn't know."

The white line around his mouth deepened. "She knew."

He stood and walked to the door.

Leonie did not question his logic. "What are you going to do?"

He turned, tight-lipped fury still evident on his face. "First I shall visit my solicitor," the clipped voice replied. "Then I leave for America to bring home my son."

"Without his mother?"

His eyes blazed at her from across the room. Without answering, he was gone.

"You can't be serious?" Tess's eyes were huge and disbelieving.

The solicitor smiled regretfully. "I'm afraid it's true. Because f the nature of the," he paused delicately, "circumstances, your narriage to the duke takes precedence over your marriage to Mr. Bradford."

"Do you mean I am still the duchess of Langley?"

"I'm afraid so." Mr. Key would have gone to great lengths to e able to remove the look of dismay from the face of the lovely oung woman who sat in his office.

When Daniel Bradford came to him, explaining his situation nd requesting that his marriage be annulled, Key had sympaized with him. The young man was in obvious pain and it was lear that none of the events leading up to their meeting had been f his doing. That was before he had met Tess.

No one looking into those clear eyes could doubt her character r her sincerity. She had also been a victim of circumstance, and ecause society's rules judged a woman more harshly than a man, he would be the one to suffer most of all. The agonized expresion on her face when she learned she was still married to the nglishman smote Mr. Key to the heart. For one rash moment e considered offering to take her burdens on to his own shoulers. Reason claimed him before he made a fool of himself.

Tess stood. "Thank you, Mr. Key," she said. "I appreciate your me."

"Not at all." He smiled and held out his hand. "I'm sorry you ad to come such a long way. I don't understand why Mr. Bradord didn't seek out someone in Annapolis."

She flushed and pulled her hand away. "Daniel thought it vould cause less of a scandal. We know everyone in Annapolis."

"I see." He smiled gently. "I'm glad to have made your acuaintance, Your Grace."

"Please," her voice was harsh, "don't call me that." She miled, taking the sting from her words. "You may call me Tess."

Francis Key smiled a shy smile. For the first time she realized ow young he was.

"I'd like that." He hesitated. "I'll be in Annapolis at the end f the month. May I call on you?"

"Of course," she assured him. "My father and I will loo
forward to your visit. Good day, Mr. Key."

Francis stared at the door for a long time after she left.

Devereaux turned down the long avenue leading to Harringto
House. Holding the reins tightly, he pulled in the high-strur
bay and stared at the impressive home. His mouth turned dow
in a self-deprecating grin. If only his mother could see this. Sh
would have second thoughts about American provincials.

It was late afternoon in August and unbearably hot. The coo
ness of the shaded veranda beckoned Devereaux. A figure ap
peared on the porch. James walked his horse up th
magnolia-lined lane to greet the man he knew must be Tess
father. Swinging his leg over the pommel, he dismounted.

Holding out his hand to Nathanial Harrington, he said, "Goo
afternoon. I'm Langley."

Harrington ignored the outstretched hand. For an endless mo
ment, he stared into James Devereaux's dark face. For the fir
time he understood why Tess refused to consider marriage t
Daniel. What he saw in the brilliant blue eyes satisfied him. H
reached out to clasp the extended hand.

"What took you so long?" he asked bluntly.

Devereaux's eyes glinted. "I beg your pardon?"

"I wrote you over a year ago," the gruff voice persisted. "Wh
are you here after such a length of time?"

James was amused. With such a father, it was no wonder tha
Tess was out of the common way.

"I was in Spain until November and never received your le
ter," he answered. "Then I was wounded. I came as soon as
knew."

Nathanial wasn't convinced. "Why did you allow her to leav
in the first place?"

Devereaux could feel a muscle leap along his jaw. "Shouldn
I be explaining this to Tess?" There was a hint of ice beneath th
polite words.

"I'll not have my daughter hurt any more."

A red fog clouded Devereaux's brain. Politeness was forgotten. "Your daughter kept me from my own son!"

"Who told her Daniel Bradford was dead?" Harrington countered.

Devereaux's rage died away. "Please, Mr. Harrington," he said, "I've come a long way. May I see my wife and child?"

Nathanial threw a piercing glance at the man before him. "So, you know."

James nodded. "As soon as I read the letters, I saw my solicitor. Our marriage is legally binding." His gaze met Harrington's without flinching. "I've come for my son. Nothing, short of death, will stop me."

"What about his mother?"

Devereaux's hands clenched into fists. "That depends on Tess."

"Do you love my daughter?" the gruff voice demanded.

James stared into the probing eyes. Damn, the man was perceptive. So much for British reserve.

"Yes," he replied quietly. It was a relief to admit it to someone. "I've loved her from the first moment I saw her."

They faced one another. The chirping of the cicadas was the only sound in the stillness. Finally, Nathanial stepped aside.

"Come in, lad," he said. "You must be thirsty after your long ride. Tess is visiting her sister in Washington, but the boy is here." He ushered James into the parlor. "Sit down. I've a great deal to tell you."

Twenty-seven

Even the red Virginia soil looked thirsty. Devereaux would have liked to move faster, but out of consideration for his horse and the aging Nathanial Harrington, he suffered the pace in irritated silence. The longing to see Tess was now so strong it was a painful ache in the pit of his stomach.

To James, accustomed to the cool green of the English countryside, the heat was suffocating, so relentless and all-consuming that it became a personal challenge to remain in his saddle and plod ever forward. The weather alone would defeat the British, he thought ruefully. Wellington's battle-toughened soldiers would shrivel and die in the face of this dripping hot wetness.

As they entered the outskirts of Washington they found entire families fleeing the city. Carts overflowing with children, household belongings, food and farm animals crowded the dusty, nearly impassable roads.

After speaking to one of the refugees, Nathanial learned that General Winder, Commander of the Washington regiments, was riding the length of Virginia and Maryland mustering soldiers to protect the capital. Legions of British soldiers had disembarked at the Patuxent River and were marching toward the city.

Harrington's face was grim. "Apparently Major General Robert Ross is to command troops who are veterans of Wellington," he said. "Do you know anything about him?"

"He's one of Wellington's most brilliant brigadiers," answered Devereaux.

Harrington nodded. "So I've heard. Cochrane has replaced

Warren and, for a long time now, we have dealt with the scourge of the Chesapeake, Admiral Cockburn."

James pulled up his horse and faced Tess's father. "I'm sorry to tell you this sir, but both men are harsh officers with bitter grudges against Americans. They will sack Washington. I would feel much better if we were there with Tess and her sister."

"Surely, they won't bother with Washington," Harrington protested. "Except for the federal buildings, it has less than eight thousand people. It is a capital half-finished."

"That won't matter," replied Devereaux, urging his horse forward. "Taking its capital city demoralizes a country. If we hurry, we can be there by nightfall."

Putting the spurs to his horse, Nathanial hurried to catch up.

Tess watched from behind the shuttered windows of her sister's brick house in the capital. Pale, terrified citizens packed their belongings on travel coaches and wagons, mules and horses, anything they could get their hands on, and fled toward Virginia. Rumor had it that Washington was defenseless, having no regular troops of its own and none could be mustered in Maryland and Virginia.

Unable to keep up the pretense of optimism any longer, Tess had left the bedroom where her sister, Kate, had just given birth. Despair plagued her. Despair and anger. The British had a force of over forty thousand. Madison and his generals, faced with the might of the royal forces, had ordered their battalions to retreat. It was humiliating to know that James had been right. Now that Bonaparte was defeated, the British could turn their might on America. Thousands of battle-trained soldiers were making their way up the Potomac toward Washington. The ill-trained American forces would be cut to ribbons.

Tess thought of her sister's newborn daughter, a small bundle of life and hope in the midst of this terror. She prayed they would survive this night. Closing the shutters she checked to see if the doors were bolted before climbing the stairs to her sister's bedchamber. Mother and child were asleep. There was nothing to do now but wait and hope.

Back in the drawing room, Tess stared at the elegant wheat colored furnishings and silken hangings. She whispered a quick prayer for her brother-in-law. Kate's husband was with the Virginia militia. They hadn't heard from him since yesterday morning. He'd warned Tess to take Kate and his children to the safety of his mother's home in Norfolk if the news was bad. Tess had sent the children ahead with the servants, but Kate's time had run out. Her labor pains had begun late last night and the child was born at the exact moment the first British troops entered Washington.

Suddenly Tess realized the noise was gone. The silence was eerie and terrifying. She stood up and again peeked through the shutter. Were they the only ones left in the entire city? Staring down the empty street, she noticed a movement then a bright crimson color. Her fists clenched. A fierce hatred welled up within her. British troops marched forward, looking neither right nor left, their precise movements and red coats strangely out of place in the small peaceful town of Washington.

Hours later the city was alive with British troops. The sky was stained a brilliant red as they torched the Capitol, the Arsenal, the Treasury and the War Office. The President's House and the Naval Yards went up in flames and the bridge over the Potomac was a charred cinder. The enemy ordered everyone to stay inside, promising that no private property would be confiscated if Americans followed orders.

"Do you think they mean what they say?" Kate, still in her nightgown, her hair a golden tangle over her shoulders, clung to the railing at the bottom of the stairs.

"What are you doing?" Tess rushed to her sister's side, forgetting briefly the drama in the streets. "You're not well. Why aren't you in bed?"

"I heard shouting outside." She sat down on the step. "I hoped it would be news of John."

Tess's throat ached with the effort to hold back tears. Her voice was husky when she spoke. "John won't thank me when he returns to find you ill with fever." She slipped her arm around her sister's waist. "Let me help you upstairs."

Laying her head on Tess's shoulder, Kate allowed herself to be half-carried to her bed.

"It's so hot," she whispered, closing her eyes. "I'm sorry, Tess."

"For what?" Tess tucked the sheet around her sister's slight form.

"If it wasn't for me, you wouldn't be here."

"Hush," Tess placed a finger to her lips. "Soldiers are everywhere, Katie. If I were home, it would be no different. Sleep now. The baby will be hungry soon. It should be cooler in the morning. I smell a storm coming on."

The night passed and most of the next day. By late afternoon the sky darkened and the sweltering heat was replaced by a brisk wind. It was a furious, glorious storm. Torrents of lashing rain and roaring winds swept through the city. Lightning flashed, striking trees and toppling signs with humbling ferocity.

Tess, determined to not succumb to panic, ventured into the kitchen, to prepare dinner.

Suddenly there was a loud pounding on the door. Her mouth went dry. With trembling hands, she removed her apron and walked to the door. Taking a deep breath, she flung it open.

There on the threshold, rain dripping from his greatcoat, stood Nathanial Harrington.

"Papa," she shrieked, throwing herself into his arms. "Oh, Papa, thank God it's you."

His arms tightened around her for a brief moment and then he put her from him. "There is someone who has traveled a great distance to see you. Won't you bid him welcome?"

Tess stood on her tiptoes to look over her father's shoulder. Her eyes widened in shock. Impeccably dressed, blue eyes unscrutable as ever, James Devereaux stared back at her. She noticed that he didn't smile. Her heart thudding against her ribs, she turned away.

"Kate had her baby," she said, her voice sounding not at all like herself. "It's a girl."

Nathanial frowned. "How is she?"

"Mother and daughter are both fine, although Kate is terribly worried about John." Tess looked at her father. "Is there anything you can do, Papa?"

"I'll make inquiries in the morning," he answered. "Now, I want to see my daughter. See that we get some food. It's been a miserable ride." Without another word he strode purposely up the stairs.

She looked down at her hands, searching for words, the tension thick inside the room. "Why are you here, m'lord?" she asked at last. His eyes were bluer than she remembered, and very direct. The tiny flames in their depths was the only sign that she had angered him.

"I think you know the answer to that."

James had never used that tone with her before. A cold sense of dread enveloped her, slowing her thoughts. "I don't understand."

"I think you do." He spoke deliberately wanting her to feel the pain she had caused him. "When I leave it will be with my son."

She gasped. He noticed with grim satisfaction, the sudden greyness of her skin and the way her hands balled into fists at her side.

"How did you know?" she whispered.

"Your father was good enough to write. It seems that he had enough honor to realize I might have some interest in the matter."

She winced at the cold, angry words. They bit into her consciousness like a whiplash against tender flesh. "Don't," she begged, lifting beseeching eyes to his face. "I am so dreadfully sorry, James. There isn't anything I wouldn't do to go back and change what I did."

Taken aback by her unexpected apology, he frowned. For days he had rehearsed exactly what he would say to her. First, he would shame her into admitting the immorality of keeping his son from him. Then, when she was suitably chastened, he would demand the child. She would beg to come with him and he would reluctantly agree. Later, when they were far away from Washington and Annapolis, he would rekindle what they once had together.

"Damn it, Tess," his voice was a mixture of anger and exasperation. "How could you keep such a thing from me? You knew aboard Waverly's ship. I know you did."

Her eyes, revealing as mirrored glass, denied nothing. "Daniel was so terribly unhappy," she explained. "You wouldn't have let me go and I couldn't hurt him more than I already had."

A slow, jealous burn began deep in his chest. With concentrated effort he controlled himself. "It is of no consequence any longer," he said. "We shall go back to Harrington House for the child and soon as transportation can be arranged, leave for England."

Tess's smile was tinged with regret. He was still so arrogant, so very much the duke of Langley. He would never understand what this night had meant for her and all Americans. James was strong and assured and incredibly handsome, but he was an Englishman and therefore an enemy.

"I'm not going with you, James," she said softly. "Surely, after seeing this, you realize how impossible it would be."

To her surprise, he did not attempt to argue with her. He looked grim and unapproachable standing there in Katherine's dainty parlor, a man not easily turned from his purpose.

"Very well," the crisp voice agreed. "I sympathize with your feelings, even if I don't understand them." He leaned against the mantel, his boot propped against the grate. "Stay here if you wish, in the name of your misplaced loyalty, but understand this. My son is a Devereaux. No law on earth, not even an American law, would deny a father his only son. The child comes with me."

"You wouldn't!"

Her horrified gasp squeezed his heart, but he showed no mercy. "You may stay or go as you please," he repeated, his face like stone. "but the child comes with me."

"You would take a babe not even a year old away from his mother?" she demanded, hoping to shame him.

James looked down at the hand clutching his sleeve. He met her gaze with his own deliberate, unforgiving stare.

"That is a strange question to be asking of me, Lady Devereaux," he said coldly. Removing her hand from his arm, he stepped back. "I find I've no longer any interest in food. Tell me which room is to be mine for the night. I'll expect your answer in the morning."

Twenty-eight

Nathanial Harrington wasn't comfortable with the unusual calm that hung over the city, but he was more uneasy with his daughter's brooding silence. Despite his efforts at conversation, she stoically picked her way through the excellent meal, answering him in the briefest of monosyllables.

When Devereaux first presented himself at Harrington House, Nathanial had experienced a surge of relief. This man loved his daughter. That, Harrington was sure of. One look at the fire in those flashing blue eyes convinced him that the angry young Englishman was also worthy of her. Tess would be well cared for in the capable hands of the duke of Langley. He frowned, determined to ferret out the reason for her troubled expression.

"What's bothering you, lass?"

She smiled, the wounded expression in her eyes disappearing for a moment. "Nothing, Papa," she answered.

"Nonsense!" Nathanial's bracing voice brushed away her reply. "Tell me it's none of my business, but tell me the truth!"

The bread she had reached for moments before was a mass of crumbs on her plate. Bewildered, she glanced down at the inedible mess, and then looked back to her father.

"Very well," she said, her voice expressionless, "it's none of your business."

"I believe I know what it is anyway." Nathanial speared a morsel of hen with his fork. "You never could keep anything from me."

"Well then," Tess snapped, at the end of her patience, "if you know what it is, we need not discuss it."

Her father put down his fork and looked at her, sternly. "I'm beginning to believe you are more of a fool than most women."

"Please, Papa," Tess protested, "I can't talk about this now."

"You will listen to me, Tess." Harrington's blustery voice silenced her. "It appears I must explain a few unpleasant truths to you. You are not entirely innocent here, my girl."

"I know," she agreed desperately, anything to stop the logical words from pouring from his throat.

"Take your head from the sand, lass. You knew we were at war when you married him." He leaned his elbows on the table, his thick, working-class hands knotted into fists. "It's not like you to be dishonest with yourself." He reached over and lifted her chin, forcing her to look at him. "Would you have wanted him if he were any different than he is? Would you have loved him?"

"I hate him. I hate all the British," she said fiercely.

Nathanial Harrington sighed and dropped his hand. "No more than I. But this will be over one day. The decision you make will affect the rest of your life. Think on it. That is all I ask." He pushed his chair away from the table and stood, a giant looming above her.

"Papa," she said, a strange look on her face. "Do you want me to go back with him?"

Harrington's face gentled. He reached out a calloused hand to touch his daughter's cheek. "I want you to follow your heart, lass. You've got good red American blood in your veins. Don't forget that. He's an English duke and a prideful one as well. But for all that, he's a sensible man and he has the good sense to love you."

"What if he doesn't want me anymore?" she whispered.

"Don't be an idiot. A man doesn't travel across an ocean, in the middle of a war, for a woman he doesn't want."

"He came for Justin," she reminded him.

"Justin is at Harrington House. Devereaux is here with you." He stretched his arms over his head. "I'm off to bed, now." He stooped to kiss her cheek. "It's a lonely life without a mate, Tess. Remember that."

After reassuring herself that Kate and the baby were sleeping, Tess opened the door to her bedchamber with a grateful sigh. She was tired, with a weariness of spirit that seeped past her aching muscles into the very marrow of her bones. Slipping into her nightgown, she pulled the pins from her hair. Without bothering to brush it out, she turned down the lamp and sank back into the pillows.

Several hours later, sleep still eluded her. She tossed and turned on her hot pillow, disturbing images flashing through her consciousness. James, as she had first seen him in London, handsome and arrogant, his blue eyes warm with appreciation as he bent over her hand. Again, in the library at Langley, when he first kissed her, his mouth and hands awakening a response she'd never known a human body was capable of. The desperate fear on his face when Lizzie was hurt, and the compassion and strength in his arms when she had learned of Daniel's death.

Her cheeks burned when she recalled her shameless flight down the stairs and into his arms after their long months of separation and the brilliant light in his eyes when she agreed to marry him. She remembered the blinding passion as they came together after weeks of coldness when he'd battled his own demons and found that despite their differences, she was the only woman in the world for him.

Tess sat up in bed. How could she have overlooked the most important thing of all? They shared something much more significant than memories. Justin Devereaux, the future duke of Langley, lay in his cradle at Harrington House. She thought of the downy head nestled against her heart and the sweet baby scent of him. A fierce surge of protectiveness welled up inside her. There was nothing she wouldn't do for her child.

Quelling the small voice inside her that deplored using a baby as an excuse for her own desires, she pushed back the covers and climbed out of bed. There was no need for a candle. Bright moonlight streamed through the windows and lit the long hallway.

Ghostlike, in a long white gown, her pale hair hanging unbound to her waist, she moved on silent feet to the door of the room where James Devereaux slept. Taking a deep breath, she turned the knob and pushed. Without a sound, the door swung open and she stepped inside.

Quick as a cat, Devereaux shot out of bed, the pistol in his hand leveled at the door. When he saw who it was, he lowered his arm.

"Are you mad?" he asked, a grim expression on his face. "You could have been killed."

"I didn't expect you to sleep with a loaded pistol by your side," she retorted.

"I'm an Englishman in an enemy nation. It isn't wise to be unprepared."

"Did you expect an assault in my sister's house?" Tess demanded, indignantly.

A lock of Indian black hair fell across his forehead. Impatiently, he flung back his head. "What are you doing here, Tess?" He sounded annoyed, as if dealing with a troublesome child who must be appeased.

Her voice failing her, she could only stare at him with troubled eyes. The rise and fall of his bare chest distracted her. He was still lean and muscled, but the skin on his shoulder, once smoothly bronzed, was puckered and drawn into a jagged scar.

He followed the direction of her eyes. "A souvenir from Burgos," he said. "Does it bother you?"

"Of course it bothers me," she answered, "but not in the way you mean. I had no idea you were wounded."

He shrugged. "I learned my lesson. Napoleon is no longer a threat and I am too old for heroics."

"I would hardly call you old, m'lord," she teased, hoping to coax a smile from him.

He did not oblige her. "You never answered my question. Why are you here?"

Tess swallowed. She should have known he would be difficult. Tess had tried to forget him and move forward with all the resolve she could gather. A year ago, in her anger and humiliation, with an ocean between them it seemed possible, but now, confronted with the reality of his presence, it was another thing altogether.

The silence was agonizing, the space between them infinitely larger than the floor she must cross to reach his side. If she hesitated much longer, he would walk out of her life tomorrow and she would have nothing but memories for the rest of her days.

She remembered the look in Emily Castlereagh's eyes when she spoke of her husband. She thought of the fear on her sister's face as each hour passed with still no word of her husband. Again, she heard her father's words, *"It's a lonely life without a mate."*

Lifting her chin, Tess took one step toward him and stopped. "England is a great distance away," she said. "I hope you know that a woman and a nine-month-old child will be a tiresome burden."

"I'm not unfamiliar with burdens," he replied, his voice cool.

She crossed the room to stand before him. The clock on the dresser ticked. Her heart pounded with the same agonizing rhythm. Why didn't he touch her?

"Tess?" She shivered at the low, intimate way he said her name. "Why are you here?"

"Because you give me no choice."

"Liar," he countered.

The word angered her. "Why do you think I'm here?"

"Because you love me." His face was shadowed, his expression impossible to read.

She stared back at him. The coldness in his eyes disappeared into warm laughter and something else far more disturbing.

"There is that, of course." Her lips turned up in a tentative smile.

"Then say it," he challenged. Keeping his eyes on her face, he willed her to speak the words he had longed to hear for such an endless length of celibate nights.

"I'm here because I love you," she admitted at last. "Despite your nationality, and your damn Langley arrogance, I can't seem to find any happiness in the world without you." Her confidence restored, she smiled a radiant smile and walked into his arms.

James took her face in his hands, brushing away the fine strands of hair. She was so soft, so delicate.

Tess felt the tears well under her eyelids. Hungry with need, she wound her arms around his neck. He lifted her to the bed.

"My love," he murmured against her throat. "Christ, Tess. I thought I'd lost you."

With one sure motion he pushed the gown away from her shoulders and hips and covered her body with his own. Seeking her mouth, he kissed her with the passion fanned by months of pent-up desire.

The touch of his hands burned her skin. In her veins, the blood leaped to life. He entered her immediately. Arching beneath him, she gripped his shoulders. His arms held her tightly, easing only when she cried out and relaxed against him.

Moments later, his hands and the heat of his mouth on her breast awakened the aching tension all over again. Pulling his head down to take more of her into his mouth, she moved to his rhythm. He was slick and hard inside her, like wet steel. She moaned her pleasure and wound her legs around him.

His harsh intake of breath startled her. Confused, she opened her eyes and looked at him. The veins in his neck stood out like thick cords. His jaw was clenched, eyes narrowed. She could feel the pounding of his heart against her ribs.

"James," she whispered, reaching up to touch his cheek.

He groaned. Thrusting deeply, he emptied himself inside her, the shattering climax draining him completely. He lay, damp and heavy, on top of her.

Moments later, he rolled over, pulling her with him and swore fluently. "I'm sorry, Tess. I feel like a schoolboy, but it's been such a long time. I couldn't wait."

A hope, like a tiny flame, grew inside her mind, refusing to be extinguished. Tess propped herself on one elbow and looked down on him in the moonlight. She had promised herself she wouldn't ask him this question, but now she found she had to know.

"Has there been anyone else, James?" Her eyes were smoky grey.

Reaching up to stroke her chin, he smiled. When he spoke, the tenderness in his voice touched her as nothing ever had before.

"I told you once before, that for me, marriage means only you. Nothing has happened to change my opinion."

Flinging her arms around him, she hugged him fiercely. "I don't deserve you," she whispered, "but I'm very glad you came back for me."

"Did you really think I would allow anyone to take you away from me?" His voice was amused. "You are my wife, Tess, and the mother of my child."

"What if I hadn't wanted to return?" her words were muffled against his shoulder.

"That was a point of concern," he admitted, "but I would have carried you off anyway, until you came to your senses."

Tess lifted her head. "You are dreadfully arrogant."

The rest of her sentence was stopped by his mouth on her lips. Sliding his hand down the length of her body, he looked down at her and grinned. Suddenly he seemed much younger.

"Shall we try once more? I guarantee I'll give a better accounting of myself."

Looking at him through her lashes, Tess ran her finger lightly down his chest.

"All right," she agreed, "although you should understand that I'm not complaining of your past performances, Lord Devereaux."

"Very gracious of you, Lady Devereaux." He would have said more, but his wife stopped him in a most effective manner.

Epilogue

"We're home, Tess." Devereaux touched his wife's knee briefly in order to wake her. Handing over his son, he pushed open the door of the carriage and stepped down, turning to take the child from her arms and help her to the ground.

Again, there were liveried footmen waiting to greet them. Litton, his stern face creased in a beaming smile, hurried down the steps to welcome home the duke and his duchess.

A tall young lady with shining black hair rushed down the stairs and threw herself in Tess's arms. "Oh, Tess," she cried.

"Lizzie?" Tess laughed, hugging her tightly. "Is it really you?"

"I've missed you so," the child sobbed. Pulling away with a trembling smile she colored in embarrassment. "I didn't believe you would come back," she confessed, wiping away the tears.

Tess brushed back the dark hair, noticing the changes the past two years had wrought. The child she had found on the banks of the trout stream would not have been embarrassed by tears. Lizzie was a young lady, and every bit as lovely as Tess had known she would become.

She looked into the blue eyes on a level with her own. "I've come back to stay, Lizzie," she promised. "Langley is my home." With a proud smile, she nodded toward the baby in her husband's arms. "Would you like to meet your nephew?"

"A boy at last," Lizzie breathed in awe. "However did you manage it?"

"I had a bit of help," Tess replied, her eyes bright with laughter. "I didn't think your mother would have forgiven me if Justin had been a girl."

Lizzie laughed. "Georgiana said the very same thing. She's married, you know, to William Fitzpatrick. Did James tell you?"

Tess nodded. "I'm very happy for them. William was a very dear friend to me when I was in London. Judith is also engaged, I hear."

"Yes, she's in London with Lady Castlereagh." Lizzie turned toward the stairs. "Here's Mama, at last."

Leonie, slim and regal as ever, stood at the entrance to Langley. Tess held her breath as the elegantly dressed woman descended the stairs and stood before her son. Their eyes met and held in silent communion. James nodded and placed the child in her outstretched arms.

Tess felt the tears burn her eyelids as Leonie stared, in wonder, at her grandson's face.

Justin Devereaux, future duke of Langley, laughed up at her, showing two perfect white teeth. Waving his chubby arms, he grasped the locket around her neck and promptly placed it in his mouth.

Leonie laughed through her tears. "He's the very image of James when he was a child, except for his eyes." She tilted her head, considering the matter. "Your father had eyes this very shade of grey," she pronounced. "I'm sure that's who he takes after."

James opened his mouth to point out the color of Tess's eyes, when he felt the gentle touch of her hand on his arm. Staring into the crystal clear depths, he did not immediately recognize what her silent plea asked of him. He did, however, understand her impatient tug on his arm and promptly bent his head to hear her whispered request.

He looked down and smiled, a look of understanding on his face. Once again, he nodded. His mother's observation was allowed to stand, unchallenged.

Satisfied, Tess turned to her mother-in-law who was buttoning her grandson's jacket.

"What can you be thinking of, Tess, to allow him to go about so. The child will catch his death if you aren't careful. Babies are delicate. Come inside this instant." She moved to the stairs. "I've arranged for a nurse, with your permission of course. She should be here in the morning."

Tess exchanged an amused glance with her husband, but wisely remained silent.

Pressing kisses on the baby's cheeks and forehead, Leonie didn't notice the gradual reddening of his round cheeks. His body stiffened. Small fists pushed against her. She tightened her hold. At the top of the stairs, his loud bellow startled her.

"Good gracious," she exclaimed, turning to Tess who had followed her. "Whatever is the matter with him?"

"I expect he's been cooped up in the carriage too long," she replied. "He's just begun to walk and probably needs to feel the ground under his feet."

"His manners need attention," Leonie stated firmly. "Mark my words, Tess. If you don't start now, he'll be asserting his independence long before you're ready to let him go." She glanced at James who had just entered the hall. "Believe me, I know."

James took his son from Leonie's arms and set him on the marbled floor. After a few shaky steps, the baby gained confidence and toddled toward the stairs. Dropping down to his knees, he climbed to the first step.

Swooping down upon the child, James lifted him to his shoulder. Justin laughed and waved his arms as his father carried him up the winding staircase.

"Not yet, young man, "Devereaux said, "that accomplishment will have to wait awhile." They disappeared around the second landing but the firm voice could still be heard for several seconds. "Come with me," he said to the child. "I'll show you Langley."

Tess turned to speak to her mother-in-law and was shocked at the tears streaming down the older woman's cheeks."

"What on earth?" she began.

Leonie searched for a handkerchief in the pocket of her gown. Wiping her cheeks, she laughed self-consciously.

"It's nothing," she said. "I don't believe I've ever been so happy." She looked directly at Tess, her fine eyes a piercing blue. "All of it is because of you."

"I beg your pardon?" Tess wrinkled her brow.

"My son is smiling and I have a grandson." She looked at the beautiful face before her. Her voice was unusually humble. "Because of you, Langley has an heir. There will be children's voices here again." She reached out her hands to clasp Tess's. "I have everything I've ever wanted. How can I thank you?"

Tess reached out across the last remaining barrier between them and folded her mother-in-law into her arms.

"You just did," she replied. "Much more beautifully than I could ever have imagined."

DANGEROUS GAMES   (0-7860-0270-0, $4.99)
by Amanda Scott

When Nicholas Barrington, eldest son of the Earl of Ul-combe, first met Melissa Seacort, the desperation he sensed beneath her well-bred beauty haunted him. He didn't realize how desperate Melissa really was . . . until he found her again at a Newmarket gambling club—being auctioned off by her father to the highest bidder. So, Nick bought himself a wife. With a villain hot on their heels, and a fortune and their lives at stake, they would gamble everything on the most dangerous game of all: love.

A TOUCH OF PARADISE   (0-7860-0271-9, $4.99)
by Alexa Smart

As a confidence man and scam runner in 1880s America, Malcolm Northrup has amassed a fortune. Now, posing as the eminent Sir John Abbot—scholar, and possible discoverer of the lost continent of Atlantis—he's taking his act on the road with a lecture tour, seeking funds for a scientific experiment he has no intention of making. But scholar Halia Davenport is determined to accompany Malcolm on his "expedition" . . . even if she must kidnap him!

PUT SOME FANTASY IN YOUR LIFE—
FANTASTIC ROMANCES FROM PINNACLE

IME STORM   (728, $4.99)

y Rosalyn Alsobrook

Modern-day Pennsylvanian physician JoAnn Griffin only believed what he could feel with her five senses. But when, during a freak storm, a inding flash of lightning sent her back in time to 1889, JoAnn realized he had somehow crossed the threshold into another century and was ow gazing into the smoldering eyes of a startlingly handsome stranger. oAnn had stumbled through a rip in time . . . and into a love affair so atense, it carried her to a point of no return!

EA TREASURE   (790, $4.50)

y Johanna Hailey

When Michael, a dashing sea captain, is rescued from drowning by a eautiful sea siren—he does not know yet that she's actually a mermaid. ut her breathtaking beauty stirred irresistible yearnings in Michael. nd soon fate would drive them across the treacherous Caribbean, toss- ag them on surging tides of passion that transcended two worlds!

INCE UPON FOREVER   (883, $4.99)

y Becky Lee Weyrich

A moonstone necklace and a mysterious diary written over a century go were Clair Summerland's only clue to her true identity. Two men ved her—one, a dashing civil war hero . . . the other, a daring jet pilot. Now Clair must risk her past and future for a passion that spans two vorlds—and a love that is stronger than time itself.

HADOWS IN TIME   (892, $4.50)

y Cherlyn Jac

Driving through the sultry New Orleans night, one moment Tori's car pins out of control; the next she is in a horse-drawn carriage with the andsomest man she has ever seen—who calls her wife—but whose yes blaze with fury. Sent back in time one hundred years, Tori is falling a love with the man she is apparently trying to kill. Now she must race gainst time to change the tragic past and claim her future with the man he will love through all eternity!

Available wherever paperbacks are sold, or order direct from the Publisher. Send cover price plus 50¢ per copy for mailing and andling to Penguin USA, P.O. Box 999, c/o Dept. 17109, Bergenfield, NJ 07621. Residents of New York and Tennessee must include sales tax. DO NOT SEND CASH.

**If you liked this book, be sure to look for others
in the *Denise Little Presents* line:**

*Available wherever paperbacks are sold, or order direct from the
Publisher. Send cover price plus 50¢ per copy for mailing and
handling to Penguin USA, P.O. Box 999, c/o Dept. 17109,
Bergenfield, NJ 07621. Residents of New York and Tennessee
must include sales tax. DO NOT SEND CASH.*